Liar's Moon

KATE SWEENEY

LIAR'S MOON
© 2010 BY KATE SWEENEY

ISBN 13: 978-1-935216-19-3

First Printing: 2010

This Trade Paperback Is Published By
Intaglio Publications
Walker, LA USA
WWW.INTAGLIOPUB.COM

_ _
_ _

CREDITS
EXECUTIVE EDITOR: TARA YOUNG
COVER DESIGN BY SHERI

Acknowledgments

As always, I'd like to thank the usual suspects: Jule, Denise, and Maureen for their beta prowess and honesty.

And, Tara, if the editing process can be enjoyable, it's because of you.

And finally, to Sheri Payton, who knew moving to Louisiana would be the best thing for me and Intaglio. And she was right, as usual, which is annoying.

The Lover's moon is high and bright
Guides love and truth throughout the night
The Liar's moon with mists of grey
Schemes to drive the truth away

Anonymous

Prologue

Grayson MacCarthaigh glanced around the grassy area behind St. Brigid's Monastery. Wiping the soft rain from her face, she looked down at the headstone and smiled. "Damned Irish weather, Ma," she whispered and lightly touched the cold, wet stone.

She had buried her mother months earlier and remembered how Corky Kerrigan and Neala Rourke stood in respectful silence under an umbrella along with the nuns as the parish priest said kind words about Maeve Grayson MacCarthaigh.

Now Grayson knelt, mindless of the wet grass, and laid the purple sprigs of heather on the damp soil. She bent down and whispered, "You are the best of everything God made, Ma. Take care of Vic and the little Maeve. I'll see you all someday."

She swallowed the emotions that caught in her throat and stood. She felt a hand on her shoulder and turned to Corky, whose green eyes rimmed with tears. "I miss Maeve so much, Gray." His voice cracked with emotion.

Grayson nodded and patted his hand. "No use standing in the rain."

Corky smiled. "You've been out of Ireland too long. This isn't rain." He held out his palm. "It's just a soft day."

Grayson smiled affectionately. "It's rain, Corky."

In silence, they made their way around the monastery on the dirt path. The same path Grayson had walked a hundred times in her youth; she would be bored to death as her mother and the other women in the village had their discussions about life, God, and the ancient ones.

"Have you seen Neala?" Grayson asked.

Corky shrugged. "She's at the museum. Trying to explain what's happened."

"That won't be easy." Grayson took a deep breath and let it out slowly. They stopped in the courtyard of the monastery. "How is she going to explain the loss of an archaeological find?"

"I know. Telling the officials at the National Museum in Dublin that a nearly two thousand-year-old Celtic wizard took the stone to call upon the ancient druids of Ireland somehow doesn't seem—"

"Rational?" Grayson interjected. "How can anyone believe this?"

Corky leaned against the stone wall of the monastery, running his fingers through his unruly red hair. "At least the police in Dublin seem satisfied on the cause of Maeve's death."

Grayson let out a sarcastic snort. "Attacked by a wolf—"

"Well, it's partly true," Corky said softly. "Phelan Tynan is a shape-shifting—"

"Fucking asshole."

"And a wolf. So the inspector seemed to buy it. Especially since you mentioned a rabid dog instead of a wolf."

"Inspector Gaffney did not buy it, rabid dog or not. She'll be back. If she's any detective, she will."

"But I did have Emmett intervene."

"I hope your government friend can keep her off our backs. Inspector Gaffney knows we're lying about Ma's death." The rain had stopped, and Grayson lifted her head to the cloudy sky. She closed her eyes and took another deep breath. "I'm not sure about this goddess and immortal stuff," she admitted in a quiet voice.

"I know, but there's no turning back now. Neala said she'd check in later in the day. Until then, let's get back and see if the prophecy leads us to anything new." He looked at Grayson and smiled. "And you have to hone the powers you have."

Grayson looked down at the crescent-shaped birthmark on her left palm. Because of this birthmark—or birthright, as Corky liked to call it—Grayson's life was forever changed. She was the true descendant, the one who was destined to protect the powers of the Tuatha De Danann, the ancient Irish race of the goddess Danu. It was still all too bizarre for Grayson to comprehend. Her logical world back in Chicago was gone, and being a detective with the Chicago Police Department seemed light years away. In such a short time, a matter of months, her mother had died, her life changed, and now she was some sort of immortal. She looked down at the three rings on her left ring finger. Smiling sadly, she caressed the rings—her wedding ring, Vic's wedding ring, and Maeve's.

Vic, she thought. How she missed her wife still. The visions of her diving in front of Grayson and the other policemen, taking the spray of bullets for her, and dying because of it were still too vivid.

Two women in Grayson's life who she loved, both taken in a violent manner—both dying for her. She felt the tears sting her eyes once again and quickly cleared her throat. She looked up to see Corky watching her, a sad smile tugging at the corner of his mouth.

"It's all too fantastic to believe, but it's all too true," he said in his soft Irish brogue.

Grayson rubbed her face in an irritated gesture. "I know. I know."

Corky looked past the monastery walls and out to the green rolling hills. "You know what I'm wonderin'?"

"I'm so afraid to ask."

Corky laughed. "It's quiet here. Almost too quiet. I wonder what Phelan is planning."

Grayson felt a cold shiver run up her spine that had nothing to do with the damp Irish morning. In all this, she had forgotten Phelan Tynan was still on the loose. After what happened a few months before, how in the world could that be?

"I don't know, but you're right, it's too quiet. He has to be up to something."

For a moment, Grayson looked into Corky's green eyes, filled with uncertainty. The poor guy looked scared, Grayson thought. "C'mon. Let's go read that book of yours. Maybe it'll shed some light."

As they walked into the monastery, Grayson gave her surroundings a cautious glance. Whether it was her newfound power or just her old police instincts, Grayson knew Phelan Tynan was indeed up to something.

Chapter 1

"Of course there must be lightning and thunder," Phelan said as he peered through the tainted window of the limousine. "What a desolate place."

Beside him, Ian laughed and quickly stopped when he received the glare from Phelan. His dark eyes bore into Ian, who immediately swallowed convulsively. "I could have left you back in Ireland, Ian. When we arrive at this hellhole, I want you to keep your mouth shut and give the appearance of some intelligence."

Ian nodded. "Yes, Mr. Tynan. I was just thinking—"

Phelan looked up as if pleading for help. "What did I just say?" Phelan raised his hand. "Never mind. What were you thinking?" When Ian didn't answer right away, Phelan glanced at him. Seeing the confused look, he laughed. "I'm serious, dear boy. You can tell me your thoughts." He looked out the window once again. "Just don't get used to it."

"Yes, sir. I was just thinking this could be an advantageous meeting between you and this Nicholae fellow."

Phelan never looked back at his employee when he spoke. "I'm sure this meeting will prove beneficial for us both." He continued staring out at the rainy night. "It must."

He raised an eyebrow when the stretch limo pulled onto the circular gravel drive and stopped in front of a mansion. Phelan hit the button that rolled down his window; he narrowed his eyes as a feeling of dread tore through him. "This place is evil," he whispered with a grin. "I like it."

Even in the darkness, Phelan could see Ian's pale complexion. "Do get out and open the door, Ian." For a moment, Ian didn't move while he stared at the foreboding building. "Before the boogeyman gets you."

Ian chuckled nervously and exited the limo. He opened the umbrella over Phelan's head as he walked up the stone staircase.

Perched on either side of the front door, two torches flickered with the wind and rain. "These Romanians are so dramatic."

Off in the distance, the baying of a wolf mingled with the wind. Phelan laughed openly. "Oh, please. Dracula must be right around the corner. Have these idiots stay in ancient Ireland. My father would have them screaming for their mothers within a week."

Phelan saw the pure fright on Ian's face as he tried to laugh along. "Ring the bell, Ian."

In a moment, a young woman answered. Phelan regarded the pale-faced woman with dark eyes. She gave him and Ian a cautious look. "I'm here to see Nicholae. I'm Phelan Tynan. He's expecting me."

The woman stepped back to allow Phelan to enter the dark foyer. The dampness immediately hit him like a wall. It was dark and dreary; once again, flickering torches placed on the walls cast the only illumination. It reminded him of the Irish castles from centuries ago.

"If you'll wait in this room," she said and opened two double doors. "I'll tell my lord you are here."

"Yes, you do that." Phelan continued to take in the surroundings. "My lord, what rubbish."

"Must be the library," Ian whispered behind him as the woman left.

Phelan glared at him. "What gave it away? All the books?" He walked over to the roaring fireplace to warm his hands. "Get me a drink."

Ian quickly found the bar. "Do ya think they'll mind?" he asked as he held up the whiskey decanter.

"Do you think I care?" Phelan asked absently.

Ian prepared the whiskey and handed it to Phelan but did not look him in the eye. Phelan had trained Ian well.

When the doors opened, Phelan looked up to see an elderly

gentleman standing in the doorway. With his long white hair pulled back, Phelan saw the similarity between them. Though Phelan's hair was also long, it was coal black, but worn in similar fashion. In this style, it allowed Phelan a perfect view of his face. He expected this man to be ancient, but he did not expect the pure evil emanating from his body. His dark eyes were like glass and his skin the color of alabaster, so transparent Phelan could see the veins running throughout his weathered face and neck.

Behind him was a gorgeous woman. Her flaxen hair fell around her shoulders in thick waves. She was dressed in black, a stark contrast to her white skin and ruby lips. Phelan realized he had been frowning when he looked into her eyes—they seemed to register nothing, like doll's eyes. There was something odd or off about her, but make no mistake, Phelan thought, she is beautiful.

"Mr. Tynan?" the old man asked as he walked into the room. The blond woman followed.

"Yes. I assume you're Nicholae."

"Yes." Nicholae said. Phelan held out his hand, which the woman took with a grin. "And this is Leigh."

Phelan saw her razor sharp canine teeth. He glanced at Ian, who looked as though he was about to faint. "This," Phelan said almost apologetically, "is my assistant, Ian Hennessy."

He raised an eyebrow when Leigh sauntered up to poor Ian and grinned while she held out her hand. "How delightful," Leigh said in a sultry voice.

Ian took her hand. "My pleasure."

"Yes, it is, darling."

Phelan laughed and gently pushed Ian aside; he stumbled over the ottoman and out of the way. Phelan stood in front of Leigh. "Phelan Tynan," he said with a sweeping bow and looked up, "at your service."

Leigh cocked her head in amusement and laughed, as well. "We shall see."

"Are you all through?" Nicholae asked with an air of impatience. "Can we get down to business?"

Leigh pouted and walked away from Phelan; she sat on the edge of the desk and picked up a book.

"Ian," Phelan said without taking his eyes off Leigh, "go sit someplace out of the way. The adults have to talk."

Ian nodded and quickly sat in a far corner. Phelan heard the snicker from Leigh.

"Now tell me just how you think you can help me, Mr. Tynan," Nicholae said.

Phelan heard the impatience in his voice and set the whiskey tumbler down.

Nicholae glared. "Help yourself."

"We have a common purpose."

"Which is?"

"I have someone I need destroyed, and I believe you have someone equally annoying," Phelan said absently while examining his fingernails.

Leigh's head shot up; she closed the book. "Sebastian."

Phelan thought he heard regret in her voice. "Yes, I understand she's a thorn in your vampire side."

Nicholae said nothing as he watched Phelan.

"Who is it that you need destroyed?" Leigh asked.

"Grayson MacCarthaigh." Phelan locked gazes with Leigh.

"Who is he and what is he doing that annoys you?"

"*She* has something that rightfully belongs to me," Phelan said. "The annoying part? She's breathing."

Leigh laughed and clapped her hands. "Oh, I adore this man. Nicholae feels the same about Sebastian. Now how can you help us and why should we be comrades?"

"Yes, good question." Nicholae stood next to Leigh and folded his arms across his chest.

"I believe Sebastian is seeking the assistance of an Irish historian I know," Phelan said. "And I know a great deal. Living for centuries has its rewards. Don't you agree, Nick?"

Nicholae glared at him. Leigh hid her grin as her eyes grew wide with amusement and what Phelan thought might be fear.

As much as this ancient vampire did not intimidate Phelan, he was just that captivated by Leigh and her beauty. He watched her as she gave Nicholae a side glance, as if waiting for the storm. When Phelan saw his dark eyes turn blood red, it impressed him.

When his fangs dropped dramatically, Phelan raised an eyebrow. He then clapped his hands in bored fashion.

Leigh now looked on in astonishment and slightly moved away from Nicholae. "I believe I shall sit with young Ian," she said and scooted out of the way.

"Do not test me, mortal," Nicholae said with a snarl.

"I am more than mortal, ancient one," Phelan said evenly. "I have existed as you have for many, many centuries—"

"Practically eons," Leigh interjected while she looked down at Ian. "Hello, darling."

"I know what you are," Phelan continued. "And I know your time is waning. I also know you want this Sebastian destroyed. She soon may be in league with Grayson. This cannot happen."

"Who is this Grayson MacCarthaigh?" Nicholae continued to breathe heavily. With his fangs still dangerously protruding, he said, "And what will happen should they meet?"

"They've already met," Phelan said with more impatience than he wanted to show; the thought of Grayson and that vampire had the anger welling inside him. He continued lightly, "I fear they may become bosom buddies in the near future. I cannot impress how dangerous that could be."

"How can you stop this?"

Phelan shrugged and glanced back at Ian, who had the look of a deer caught in the headlights while Leigh, sitting on the arm of the couch, ran her fingers through his black hair. Her fangs gently nibbled at his ear as she whispered to him. Phelan grinned inwardly and wondered if poor Ian would survive the night. "Please do not kill Ian, my dear."

Leigh looked up. "Is he your minion?" When Phelan nodded, Leigh pouted. "Nicholae, I need one."

Phelan laughed and turned his attention back to Nicholae, who glared at Leigh. "Leigh, pay attention."

In bored fashion, Leigh grudgingly left Ian and once again stood by Nicholae.

"Now, Mr. Tynan, again, how can you stop this possible alliance between Grayson and Sebastian?"

"Not to worry, Nick. But I will ask you for the time being to stay away from Ireland and let me handle this."

Leigh pouted again, but Nicholae raised his hand. "I don't know why I should trust you, Tynan. However, I will give you this time to see if you're able to assist me."

Phelan grinned and bowed. "Very gracious of you. This is the start of a good partnership."

Leigh offered a wicked laugh. "I dare say you could be right."

"Now I gave you something to assist you. I need it back," Phelan said.

Nicholae nodded to Leigh, who walked around the desk and opened the drawer. Phelan watched as she produced the ancient athame wrapped in the linen cloth. Leigh handed it to Phelan with a grin. "Thank you. It brought me back from the dead again."

"My pleasure." Phelan examined the silver dagger. "It's my hope to finish this with Grayson, once and for all."

"And take Sebastian with her," Nicholae said, still guarded.

Leigh leaned against the desk and swiped the blond wave from her face. "A mighty undertaking for one mortal or...immortal?"

Phelan bowed slightly. "Very perceptive, Leigh. May I call you Leigh?"

Leigh grinned and nodded. "Darling, I insist."

Nicholae interrupted their banter. "I'm trusting you—"

"You don't trust me any more than I trust you," Phelan countered. "We are unlikely comrades you and I."

"Don't forget me," Leigh added.

Phelan smiled. "How can one forget you?" He turned his attention back to Nicholae. "I have waited until the right time. The time is now. I have someone in place as we speak." Phelan grinned, then laughed. "Let the games begin."

Chapter 2

Emily Conroy stood behind the counter, folding the new material that just arrived from Dublin. She hoped these would sell quickly since the tourist season started in a month or so. Maybe then she could afford to take a vacation when the busy season was over. The gentle ringing of the bell above the door brought her back to reality.

There stood a striking woman. With long brown hair, same color eyes, and olive skin, the woman looked Italian or perhaps Greek. And she looked completely lost as she glanced around the shop.

"May I help ya?" Emily asked softly.

The woman smiled and walked up to the counter. "Yes. I must have the attire befitting this time."

"Attire befitting...?" Emily asked and chuckled. It was then she noticed this woman's wardrobe.

"Yes, I feel these clothes are out of date."

"Well, yes, a bit," Emily said. The woman looked as though she stepped out of the nineteenth century.

"I was hasty in my selection." The woman walked around and picked up an Aran sweater. "Is this common?"

Emily raised an eyebrow and wondered where this woman came from. She had never seen her before, and Emily knew everyone in the village. "Yes, ma'am, it tis." She watched as the woman picked up a pair of wool slacks; they were very expensive. The woman held them up to her waist and nodded. "I will need footwear."

"Foot—?" Emily stopped. She turned and picked up a pair

of sturdy shoes, not very fashionable, and presented them to the woman. "How about these? I think they might be your size."

The woman studied her selection and nodded. Emily gave her a wary look. "Are you visiting Dungarin?"

"Yes."

"Do ya know anyone in the village?" Emily prodded as she added on the calculator.

"Yes. Do you know Grayson MacCarthaigh?"

Emily stopped and looked up. "You're a friend of Grayson's? Well, why didn't ya say so?" She stuck out her hand and the woman took it. "What's your name, love?"

"Elinora," she said with a smile.

"That's a lovely name. Now do ya want me to deliver these to Grayson's? Or will ya want to wear them now?"

"Now would be best, I believe." Elinora looked down at her drab clothes.

"I see. Sure enough. There's a changing room right through there."

Elinora took the clothes, and Emily watched as Elinora closed the door behind her. When Emily looked back, she saw three women standing in the window beckoning Emily. She quickly walked out of the shop.

"Who is that, Emily?"

"Well, Mary, she's a friend of Grayson's," Emily said.

"Grayson?" another woman asked.

Emily nodded and looked back through the shop window. "Yes, Therese. She gorgeous but a bit odd."

An elderly woman, who listened, peered through the window. "Where is she from?"

Emily shrugged. "I don't know. She just walked into my shop. I hear the suspicious tone, Rose. What are ya thinkin'?"

Rose Barry continued to look in the window. "I'm thinkin' this woman is more than just Grayson's friend. Coming out of nowhere seems odd to me."

"You're just overprotective of Grayson, Mrs. Barry, because you knew her mother, Maeve."

All four women blessed themselves quickly. Rose Barry took

a deep breath. "I am protective of Grayson, and I did know her mother and her grandmother."

"Enough of your Irish superstitions now," Emily said lightly. "I've got to get back. Now go away with ya. I don't want you staring at the poor woman."

Mary and Therese agreed and walked away. Mrs. Barry pulled her shawl about her head and continued to look in the shop window. "Take great care here. We don't know a thing about this woman. It's as if she dropped right from the sky."

Emily rolled her eyes and kissed the old woman's head. "Go on now, Rose." She laughed as she walked back into her shop, just as Elinora walked out of the dressing room.

"Well, ya look grand," Emily said, then finished with the grand total. "Now how did ya want to pay for this?"

Elinora raised an eyebrow. "I hadn't thought of that. You see, I had to leave and come here quickly to see Grayson."

Emily once again gave her a wary glance. "Well, I'll tell ya what. Why don't I hold this until you see Grayson?"

"That would be best, thank you," Elinora said. She then regarded Emily with a smile. "You have been very kind."

"Thank you. But if you're a friend of Grayson's, you're probably a kind woman yourself."

Elinora cocked her head in disbelief but merely nodded. "I am sure we will meet again." She walked out without another word.

Emily quickly walked to the door and watched her walk down the cobblestone street and out of sight. "What an odd woman."

As Elinora walked out of town, she realized she was being watched. She stopped, noticing an elderly woman standing in the doorway at the edge of town. When she neared, Elinora stopped by the woman. "Good day, Mrs. Barry."

With her back stiffening, Rose said, "Good day yourself, miss. I understand you're a friend of Grayson MacCarthaigh."

"Yes, but she will be surprised to see me."

"Not expecting you, I suppose?"

"No, she is not."

"Hmm. A letter might have been a good idea or a phone call."

Elinora laughed. "Not where I come from. It was nice to meet you, Mrs. Barry."

As she started down the street again, Rose reached out and held her arm. "How did you know my name?"

Elinora looked at the hand on her arm; Rose slowly took it away. "You are a good friend to Grayson. You knew her mother, Maeve, and Deirdre, her grandmother. Being Grayson's friend, why would I not know of you?" When Rose did not answer, Elinora continued, "We will meet again." She then walked down the street and continued out of town.

A half mile or so outside of Dungarin, the white thatched cottage came into view. From the description she had been given, Elinora immediately knew it was Grayson's home. Three generations were born in this cottage, she was told. Each generation, each woman had the "knowing."

Elinora stopped about fifty yards away from the cottage. It had the appearance of being deserted, but it was in pristine condition, and she knew Grayson lived here now when not at St. Brigid's Monastery. So far, all the information was correct.

As she started up the dirt road, she saw no movement, no signs of life. By the time she stood at the front door and knocked, she knew no one would answer. She opened the door and walked in. Instantly, she felt a peaceful, calm feeling waft through her.

"This will not be easy," she whispered.

She glanced around the room, noticing there was nothing out of the ordinary. However, she knew Grayson MacCarthaigh was anything but ordinary. An immortal, Elinora thought as she walked through the cottage. Two bedrooms, one small bathroom, one small kitchen. An immortal living in such a small space, she thought. That such power would be given to a mortal seemed very dangerous. Perhaps her information was incorrect. She picked up a book from the table and leafed through it; she set it down and looked through another. Elinora had a sense or feel of Grayson as she walked from room to room. Finally, she sat in the chair by the empty fireplace and put her head back.

It was a long journey for her, and soon she drifted off with the vision of Grayson MacCarthaigh and the thought of what she was expected to do.

Chapter 3

"Corky, I can't look at another ritual. There's just so much my brain can absorb." Grayson ran her hand over her face in a tired fashion. She pushed the sleeves of the fisherman's sweater up to her elbows and looked at Corky, who was not paying attention. Grayson smiled as she watched him.

With his red head buried in the old book, Corky leafed through the parchment pages. "There are things you have to know, Grayson. We still haven't figured out the powers the immortals bestowed on you. And the villagers are looking at you like some sort of goddess."

Grayson grumbled and folded her arms across her chest. "I don't want to be immortal." She breathed a heavy sigh. "Though I know there's nothing I can do about it now."

"The old ones in the village understand. The younger ones, well, it's just as well they think it's all a myth and you're just part of a noble Irish bloodline. It's possible the younger generation might be looking for someone to lead them." He continued to read from the old book. "We can't bring attention to you anyway until all of this stuff with Phelan dies down."

He looked up then. "Your mother was well loved. It's best if no one in the village finds out what happened to Maeve. And we have to keep in mind the old ones remember your grandmother, Deirdre. All the stories that had faded are now being retold because of your return to Ireland. It's as if you've awakened something in this village."

Grayson snorted. "Like the prodigal daughter?"

"No, Gray, more like the new hierarchy. First it was your

grandmother, then Maeve, and now you. And I'm sure there were many, many more before all of you."

"I just wish I knew what I was supposed to do." Grayson impatiently paced back and forth. "I mean, shit, Corky, in Chicago, I knew my job. I was a cop, and I knew the rules. They were defined, and I had order and now..." She stopped and ran her hands over her face in an irritated, almost helpless gesture. "I feel useless. At least Neala has a job."

Corky peered at Grayson over his wire-rimmed glasses. "We do have a job."

Grayson sighed and sat down, stretching her long legs out in front of her as she slunk farther in the high-back chair. She looked around the library of the monastery as she tried to get comfortable. "Remind me to talk to the sisters about this medieval furniture. I'll talk to Sister Michael."

Corky laughed. "St. Brigid herself sat in that very chair. I doubt the nuns of this abbey will be changing the furniture anytime soon."

"I suppose," Grayson said. "I'm hungry."

He shook his head and laughed. "Let's try it again."

Grayson groaned and grudgingly walked over to him. She looked down into his green eyes, filled with wonder and amazement. She looked at her left palm and ran her fingers over the crescent-shaped birthmark. "I still don't know why I'm the chosen one," she whispered. "I wish my mother didn't have to die to prove it." When she looked back at Corky, his eyes now filled with sadness.

"I loved Maeve. She was part of the prophecy and she understood her role. You were destined. So was Maeve. She loved you."

Grayson smiled and placed her left hand on his shoulder. "Close your eyes."

Corky took a deep breath and did as Grayson asked. The tingling sensation started in her palm again as the visions started. She felt Corky's body trembling and could feel the blood race through his veins. She saw Corky as a young boy, playing in a field with a dark-haired girl. She saw him as a young adult, sitting at a desk with an older man standing behind him with his hand on Corky's shoulder. Visions flew through her mind, so fast she could not keep up. Finally, she pulled her hand away from Corky's shoulder and staggered back.

Corky trembled, slumped forward, and opened his eyes. Grayson rubbed and scratched the birthmark on her left palm as she leaned against the desk. "What did ya see?" Corky asked with excitement.

"Who's the dark-haired girl you used to play with in the field?"

Corky's eye grew wide. "You saw Caitlin?" He sat back and shook his head. "I haven't thought of her in years. I wonder why you saw her."

"I have no idea. I don't have any control of the visions I see when I place my hand on someone. They just come." She laughed and pushed at his shoulder. "Maybe you're thinking about her more than you know."

He laughed nervously and adjusted his glasses.

"Who was she?" Grayson asked.

"A friend I grew up with. She and I dated for a long while. But," he said with a shrug.

Grayson regarded Corky with a fond smile. "Did you love her?"

Corky stared out the window and nodded.

"What happened?"

"She grew tired of this." He placed his hand on the old book. "I suppose I was obsessed with Irish history and its legends and myths. I felt at an early age they were more than legends, more than myths." He looked at Grayson and laughed. "And I was proved right. I know your prophecy was more than an Irish story. And look at what's happened in such a short time."

"And look what you've missed," Grayson gently prodded. "Do you know where she is?"

"We separated after we graduated from Trinity College. She was a journalist, started with a local paper, now works for the *Irish Times*. At least I believe she does." He laughed and scratched his head. "I have no idea why ya saw Caitlin Delaney."

"I don't know, either," Grayson admitted. "But so far, all these things are connected."

Corky's head shot up; his face turned as red as his hair. "You don't think I'll be seeing her again?"

"You're asking me?" Grayson threw her arms up. "I have no idea what the hell is going on with this immortal thing."

"Well, let's get off this topic. What else did you see?"

"An older man standing behind you while you labored over a book like this one." Grayson pointed to the heavy old book.

"My God," Corky said. "That was my father. I was only sixteen when he gave me this book. He told me it was time I started in the family business. I thought the Kerrigan business was Irish history."

"It's much more than that," Grayson said. She ran her fingers over the leather-bound book. "So much more. I still can't believe I'm in that book."

Corky nodded. "I know. It was amazing how we figured out that prophecy and what happened to you under the residual moon that night." He fondly ran his hand over the book. "There is so much history, so much myth and legend in here. It will take a lifetime to decipher." He looked up at Grayson. "Can you still read my mind, as well?"

Grayson nodded. "At times. I supposed if I hone this..." She stopped and tapped her fingertip on her temple, "...gift, I would be able to control it. It comes and goes." She walked over to the fireplace and stared at the glowing bars of peat. "I-I didn't tell you this..."

"What?" He turned around to face her. Grayson continued to gaze at the fire. Corky waited.

"Remember a few weeks ago when we met Sebastian?" She looked back at Corky, who nodded. "I could read her mind. It was quick, nothing major. But...but I think I could control that. We exchanged just a couple thoughts, but it was like a conversation."

"That's wonderful," Corky exclaimed. "You know what this means? If you concentrate and practice, I'll wager you will perfect your gifts. And that can only prove to help you. Because, though he's been quiet, we still have Phelan Tynan to contend with." He swiveled in his chair and looked out the window.

Grayson walked to the big window where Corky stood and

looked out at the foggy morning. The memories of the previous months ripped through her mind—Phelan Tynan killing her mother and how they buried her on the sacred soil of this abbey. Watching him morph into a wolf, then back again, only to disappear out of sight. She knew he would never rest until he got what he wanted.

She looked at her left palm again. And what Phelan Tynan wanted was Grayson destroyed. For some reason, she was destined to be the true descendant, the one who would bring the glory back to Ireland—to be the keeper of all the power and keep it out of Phelan Tynan's hands. When the ancient ones gave her these "gifts," her life as a Chicago detective was gone for good. This was her life now, whether she wanted it or not. When Danu, the goddess of them all, took Grayson's hand, she set all this in motion with her words, "you are human and goddess, mortal and immortal." Grayson had spent sleepless nights since worrying, wondering why it was she they chose. It was her destiny, she thought. We all have a destiny.

"I wish I could read your mind right now."

Corky's voice broke her from her thoughts; she turned to him with sad eyes. "No, Cork," she looked out the window once again, "you really don't."

"Okay, then try to move something," Corky said with enthusiasm.

Grayson have him a disturbed look. "What?"

"Ya know. Move something like..." He looked around and put his pen on the edge of the desk. "Move it. With your mind."

Grayson shook her head. "This is so stupid." She took a deep breath and concentrated on the pen. After a few minutes, it didn't budge. "This is not working."

Corky scratched his head, then snapped his fingers. "Use your left hand. Your hand has to come in contact with me to read my mind, maybe you have to show your hand. Try it."

"Christ." She raised her hand in the direction of the pen. The tingling sensation started in her fingers and shot up her arm. "Oh, shit," she whispered.

In the next instant, not only the pen, but the stapler, as well, flew off the table and past Grayson, hitting the wall behind her before bouncing out the open window. Grayson winced when she heard the stapler break against the stone walk below.

Corky was stunned. "I hope it didn't hit anyone."

They both ran to the window. "Bugger," Corky whispered when Sister Michael picked up the mangled stapler and broken pen. She looked up, searching the windows until she saw Corky.

"I'm sorry, Sister," he called out.

She held up her hand and walked away.

Grayson stared at her palm. "I'll be damned."

Regaining his senses, Corky let out a war whoop and clapped his hands. He quickly looked around and picked up a thick book. "See if you can bring it to you." He placed the book on the edge of the desk.

"Corky..."

"Oh, just try. How will you ever know what powers you have until you try them? Now just concentrate." He stood back and eagerly waited for Grayson.

Grayson shook out her hands and flexed her neck back and forth.

"Ya look like a prize fighter," Corky said with a laugh. "Sorry, concentrate."

Grayson flexed her left hand a few times, as if testing it, then raised her hand, exposing her palm to the book. When Grayson cleared her mind, the tingling sensation started again; her heart raced, and with that, the book, as the pen, flew across the room, but out of Grayson's reach. It sailed over her head.

The high-pitched screech they heard would stay with them for the rest of the day. Grayson whirled around just in time to see the book hit Sister Michael square in the chest; it bounced off the flailing nun, hitting the floor with a resounding thud. With a clang, the broken stapler hit the floor.

"Oh, damn," Grayson mumbled frantically.

Corky stood perfectly still, his green eyes wide and his complexion ashen.

Sister Michael adjusted her veil and picked up the book. After examining it, she said, "At least you didn't toss Saint Thomas

Aquinas out the window. There's hope for both of you."

"We, uh…" Grayson had no idea how to explain.

"Do not attempt to try." Sister Michael set the book back on the desk, along with the stapler parts. "I'll have them place an order for more durable office supplies."

She dusted off her hands and turned back to Grayson, who looked down into the serious blue eyes. "There's someone I want you to meet."

Grayson raised an eyebrow but said nothing as Sister Michael continued. "We have a new abbess. She should arrive shortly. "

Corky exchanged glances with Grayson.

"So soon?" Grayson asked.

The old nun nodded. "I've written the bishop, and with some smooth talking, I convinced him not to reassign the younger nuns, to keep them and me. Although he knows full well he cannot close this monastery. I convinced him we needed a new abbess. Her name is Sister Gabriel. She's coming from a cloistered convent in the Aran Islands. This will be a good place for her."

"How did the bishop agree to this, Sister?" Corky asked. "I mean, I know he wasn't too fond of Sister Daniel and her views on the church and paganism."

"Too true. However…" Sister Michael walked over to the fireplace; she held up her hand to warm them. Grayson watched her as she stared into the glow from the peat fire.

"However?" Grayson gently prodded. She was slightly surprised to see tears well in Sister Michael's blue eyes.

She smiled slightly. "I convinced him Sister Gabriel was not at all like Sister Daniel and did not share her views."

"And this is true?" Grayson asked.

"You have a suspicious nature. I—"

"Sister Michael?" a young nun softly called from the doorway. "Sister Gabriel is here."

"Please show her in, Sister." Sister Michael looked at Grayson and Corky. "Sister Gabriel has lived all her life in seclusion. She is very old school if you know what I mean. So behave yourselves."

Grayson chuckled; Corky looked slightly offended. Grayson

was completely curious when the door opened. In walked a tall woman. The first thing Grayson noticed was the nun's serious posture. Actually, Grayson thought, her face was void of any real emotion.

Dressed in a very severe nun wardrobe, she seemed comfortable in her starched black habit; she wore the stiff white wimple, surrounding her chest, neck, and head, covered by the black veil. The heavy wooden rosary worn as a belt around her waist and the dark crucifix were a dark contrast to the starch white as it hung around her neck. With the habit reaching the floor, Grayson dismissed her childhood curiosity to see if nuns really had legs, fearing she'd go blind should she actually see them. To Grayson, it looked extremely uncomfortable, yet at the same time, Sister Gabriel looked very content.

"She looks like Ingrid Bergman in that American movie with Bing—" Corky groaned as Grayson gently but firmly elbowed him in the ribs.

Sister Gabriel walked into the room and extended her hand to Sister Michael. Grayson watched the exchange. A vision flashed through Grayson's mind. It was disjointed and fleeting; it was of Sister Gabriel and…

"It's good to see you again, Sister."

Sister Michael smiled. "Let me introduce you." She turned to Grayson and Corky. "This is Sister Gabriel, well, Mother Abbess. This is Grayson MacCarthaigh and Timothy Kerrigan. They knew Sister Daniel."

"Mother Abbess." Grayson gently took her hand with both of hers. The tingling sensation shot up Grayson's left arm. Again, the vision flashed. A young woman, no, Grayson thought, two young women talking…

"Sister Gabriel will be fine, Grayson. No need for formality here," Sister Gabriel said and pulled her hand away. Her voice was soft, like the nuns from Grayson's childhood. It was soothing until the ruler across the knuckles came.

She turned her attention to Corky and smiled slightly. "Mr. Kerrigan."

"Sister, it's a pleasure to meet you," he said with a nervous smile. "And please, call me Corky." When Sister Gabriel raised an eyebrow, Corky glanced around. "E-everyone does. It's a nickname."

"Well deserving, I'm sure," Sister Gabriel said.

Corky laughed nervously, the blush creeping up from his neck. "So where were you stationed?"

Grayson hid her grin as Corky realized what he said. "I mean, where…"

Sister Gabriel smiled. "I lived in a small convent on Innishmore."

"That's the largest of the Aran Islands, isn't it?" Grayson asked. "Why pick a place so remote?"

Sister Gabriel looked into Grayson's eyes. "A choice. I wanted a life of seclusion to devote my life to God. This seemed the best way. To be far from the trappings of the material world."

"I understand Gaelic is the primary language."

"Yes, it tis. Do you speak the Irish?"

"Yes, I do." Grayson then recited a poem she had learned long ago from her grandmother. As she spoke, she knew the words were not only traditional Gaelic, but a more ancient dialect.

Sister Gabriel cocked her head. "That is very impressive. To know and understand Gaelic is quite an undertaking. Your knowledge and understanding of the ancient dialect is amazing. Where did you learn that?"

Grayson saw her glance at Corky's book. She could be wrong, but Grayson had a sense that the old nun was trying to look at it. You'd never believe it, Grayson thought; she glanced at Corky. It's not that she wanted to lie to a nun. "My grandmother," Grayson said, much to Corky's relief.

To Grayson, what was more impressive was this nun, who did not look ancient, but knew the ancient Celt dialect. She wanted to know more of the cloistered Sister Gabriel.

"Sister Gabriel, why don't I show you around the monastery and to your rooms? You must be tired," Sister Michael offered, giving Grayson a scathing glance.

"Thank you," Sister Gabriel said.

Grayson was going to offer her hand once again. However,

the new abbess slipped her hands in the billowing sleeves of her habit and nodded. "It was nice to meet both of you. I'm sure we'll meet again."

Grayson nodded with a smile and watched as her long black habit whisked her out of the room. Sister Michael followed.

Corky let out his breath; Grayson laughed at his meek posture.

"Don't laugh. Nuns scare me." He flounced back in his desk chair.

Grayson was still laughing when Sister Michael re-entered. She walked up to Grayson, who stopped laughing.

"And, you, questioning her like that."

Grayson raised an eyebrow. "What? I just asked..."

"Enough." The old nun held up her hand. "Now if you two insist on hiding in this damp library hovering over that book written by heathens, then at least eat something."

Behind her, Grayson saw a young nun wheel in a cart filled with sandwiches and a pot of tea.

"Sit down," Sister Michael said.

Grayson smiled and obeyed. Corky rubbed his hands together. "Thank you, sisters. And it's not written by heathens."

Sister Michael grunted as the other nun poured the tea. "Sister Daniel, God rest her soul, believed you, I know. But I doubt the new abbess will. Now eat," Sister Michael said, then quickly left the room.

Corky and Grayson exchanged glances. They did not tell the other nuns of the abbey who Sister Daniel really was. I mean, really, Corky thought, as he bit into the sandwich. How do ya tell a bunch of nuns, "Your Mother Superior was really the ancient mother of all of us, the goddess Danu?"

"You don't tell them, Cork," Grayson said as she selected a sandwich and took a healthy bite. She saw Corky's stunned look with the sandwich hanging out of his mouth. "Hey, you're the one who wants me to hone my gifts."

"What do you think of Sister Gabriel?" Grayson asked as she took a healthy drink from the mug of tea.

"I don't know." Corky struck a thoughtful pose, then bit into his sandwich. "She reminds me of the nuns from long ago. So severe, so rigid. Yet..." He stopped and shrugged.

"What?"

"Well, she seemed young, I suppose. Too young to appear so old? I'm sure that sounds crazy." He shrugged and took another healthy bite. "But who can tell under all that starched black and white?"

While Grayson ate, she thought of what Corky just said. It was so hard to affix an age to a nun. She looked to be in her late fifties perhaps. Her Irish skin looked rosy and soft; her eyes were green and shining. Without the habit, Grayson assumed she had graying hair. All at once, she chuckled inwardly, the old Detective Sergeant Grayson MacCarthaigh reared her head, and for an instant, she missed her years on the Chicago police force. She brought herself back to the present when Corky spoke.

"I wonder how nuns choose their names," he said and drank his tea.

"I thought they took their family name."

"Well, if not that, Gabriel is a surprising name for a nun who chose a life of seclusion and being cloistered."

Grayson looked up from her sandwich. "How do you figure?"

"Gabriel was the archangel who announced good news. He was the messenger of God." Corky wiped his mouth on his napkin. "He proclaimed the Annunciation to Mary that she was chosen. How can you do that if you're cloistered and kept away from people?"

"You know your Catholic history, as well."

Corky shrugged. "She still scared me."

Grayson chuckled and finished her tea. Although Sister Gabriel did bring back her parochial school days, there was something about Sister Gabriel that Grayson could not put her finger on. It was the sadness in her eyes perhaps, she thought. With her lunch finished, Grayson stood and stretched. "Well, let's take a break. I'm going to head home. What are you going to do?"

"I'll read a bit more. We can get together tomorrow when Neala arrives from Dublin."

Suddenly, Grayson realized she missed Neala. Usually, she was around. "Good, she needs to be here."

"You miss her, don't you?"

"Yeah." Grayson patted him on the shoulder, and once again, the vision of young Caitlin Delaney flashed through her mind. This time, for some reason, Grayson did not tell Corky.

Chapter 4

Grayson took the mile walk from the abbey to Dungarin on her way back to the cottage. This gave her time for her mind to wander, which was or was not a good thing. Now she remembered her mother, Maeve. She missed her terribly. Everything that had happened in the past six weeks had been completely surreal for Grayson, and she knew it was that way for Corky and Neala.

Finding out she was part of an ancient prophecy and the true descendant was mind-boggling, even though Grayson grew up surrounded by mysticism and druidism. Her mother was proud of her heritage and reveled in being a druidess. Grayson smiled, remembering how her mother believed in the gods and in God, how all things were connected on some level. Nothing was left to chance. When Maeve found out, through Corky's prophecy, that she and Grayson each had their destiny, Maeve immediately accepted it. Grayson, on the other hand, was not so readily convinced; her logical brain would not allow it. But now? After what happened nearly six weeks earlier, Grayson could not deny her destiny. The power of the ancient druids of Ireland was on the verge of getting into the evil and dangerous hands of Phelan Tynan.

The stars aligned, the residual moon foretold the time when Grayson would stop Phelan's bid to procure the "knowing" and use it for his dark purpose. His father, Figol, the ancient wizard and druid, placed Phelan in the real world, and on that autumn night under the residual moon, Phelan nearly carried out his plan with the ritual.

Grayson ran her fingers through her black hair and shook

her head as she stopped by the short rock wall that lined the dirt road and sat down. She looked across the green sloping fields remembering the night.

"It was close, Phelan. You almost did it," she said with a sigh, then smiled sadly. "I only wish I could have destroyed you that night. Now you're out there somewhere. You wolfen shape-shifting, asshole." She picked up a stray rock and angrily threw it into the field. She then laughed and looked to the heavens. "I know, stop swearing. Sorry, Ma."

She stood with a deep sigh and started up the road and into town. Grayson saw Mrs. Barry right off as she stood outside her doorway. "Hi, Mrs. Barry."

"Good day, Grayson," she said. "Have you been at the abbey all this time?"

Grayson nodded. "Yeah, I'm just picking up a few things, then heading home before it starts raining."

Mrs. Barry raised an eyebrow. "You've not been home then?"

Grayson cocked her head. "Not since this morning. Why?"

"An old friend is here to see ya."

"Old friend?" Grayson asked.

"That's what she said."

"She?" Grayson raised an eyebrow and smiled. "It's not Neala Rourke?"

"No. I believe she said her name was Elinora. Dark hair, dark eyes. Looks Greek."

"Have you been to Greece?" A smile tugged at Grayson's mouth.

"Don't sass me, young lady."

Grayson laughed. "Well, I have no idea who that is. She's at my house?"

"I believe so, though I'm not sure."

"Hmm. This is curious." She looked at Mrs. Barry. "Is she attractive?"

The old woman narrowed her eyes. "You're a sinful woman, Grayson MacCarthaigh." She pushed at her shoulder. "Go on with ya. And be careful."

Grayson took her hand and lightly kissed it. "I will, Mrs. Barry. Thanks."

"You're like your father, you blue-eyed devil. Go on…"

Grayson laughed, then leaned in and kissed Mrs. Barry on the cheek. "Thanks. I…" She stopped and ran her fingers through her hair.

Mrs. Barry put her hands on Grayson's shoulders. "I miss your mother, as well, darling."

Grayson took a deep breath to steal away the tears that threatened once again. She nodded, not wanting to take the chance to speak.

"She loved you very much, Grayson. Just as your grandmother loved her, and so on…" Mrs. Barry then stepped back and picked up her shawl. After tossing it around her shoulders, she slipped her arm through Grayson's. "Come, I'll walk with ya."

They walked down the dirt road, away from Dungarin. "How many times have I walked this road on my way to see your mother?" Mrs. Barry said wistfully.

Grayson nodded and looked around the green hills. "I remember you and Ma sitting at our kitchen table." She gave Mrs. Barry a side glance, "gossiping."

"Go on with ya," Mrs. Barry said with an indignant tone. She then chuckled along with Grayson. "Well, maybe a little bit of town gossip. Do ya remember your grandmother and how she used the tea leaves?"

Grayson frowned for an instant. "Yes, I remember."

"Don't be frownin'."

"It was all so long ago." Grayson stopped then and looked at the old woman. "Why bring that up?"

Mrs. Barry leaned back against the stone wall that lined the dirt road. Grayson helped her ease against it and sit down. "You must have moved the cottage, Grayson Fianna. I don't remember the walk bein' this far."

"I must have." Grayson laughed and kicked at the stones on the ground. "Now tell me why you'd bring up the tea leaves."

"I want to read yours."

Grayson hung her head and groaned. "Oh, no."

Mrs. Barry laughed quietly. "You can't get away from your heritage, girl."

"Now you sound like my mother."

"Come with me," Mrs. Barry said. When Grayson didn't follow, she raised an eyebrow in motherly fashion—Grayson followed her back into town and to Mrs. Barry's house.

Mrs. Barry led her down the hall to the kitchen. "Sit ya down."

Grayson sat and watched as her old friend prepared the tea, then set two small plates on the table. She groaned when Mrs. Barry placed the large cup in front of her. "Ya know what we're going to do."

"Do we have to?" Grayson asked, impatiently running her fingers across her brow.

Mrs. Barry smiled. "You look so much like your father. Dermott MacCarthaigh was a handsome devil. Hair as black as coal, but you've your mother's eyes, God rest them both."

Grayson said nothing as Mrs. Barry set the china teapot on the table. She watched the ritual that she remembered from her youth. She could almost picture her mother and her grandmother, Deirdre Grayson, sitting around the kitchen table with Mrs. Barry preparing the tea.

"Look, Mrs.—"

She looked up and grinned. "I think by this time in our lives, you can call me Rose."

Grayson laughed nervously and scratched her neck. "After all these years, I don't think I can."

Rose Barry laughed along as she carried the boiling teapot and the tin of loose tea to the table. "This was my grandmother's finest china."

"I know."

"Handed down to me—"

"Yes, I know."

"Shut up, dear."

Grayson laughed and continued watching the ancient art of reading tea leaves without further interruption. Rose placed the large teacup, which looked almost like a soup bowl, in front of

Grayson, turning it so the handle was on Grayson's left. She then opened the tin and placed the tea in the china teapot without using a spoon; she picked up the leaves by hand.

Grayson watched with affection, remembering as a child how Rose Barry would say, "Never use a metal spoon. It corrupts the reading." She poured the boiling water into the teapot and replaced the top, then placed a linen towel over the teapot.

When she returned from the stove, she sat with a groan. "These old bones."

"You're not that old, Rose," Grayson said, surprised at how easily she said her name. It felt natural, as if she should have been saying it all along. This was an odd feeling; though if she were honest with herself, since she got on the plane with her mother and Neala from Chicago, everything had been odd. In such a short time, her life as she knew it was over. She was no longer a detective using her beloved logic to solve a crime.

With the events of the recent past, Grayson now was a part of Irish mythology; she was the true descendant of the gods and goddesses, bestowed with their ancient powers and destined to protect them and Ireland. Not bad for a detective from Chicago. She stared absently at the teapot under the linen towel. She raised an eyebrow. "What's steeping in that teapot besides tea?"

"We'll find out soon enough." Rose adjusted the linen towel.

"I suppose." Grayson looked into Rose's smiling blue eyes for a moment before looking around the familiar kitchen. "Nothing much has changed."

Rose laughed out loud, nearly scaring Grayson in the process. "Oh, darlin', everything has changed. Can't ya feel it?"

Grayson gave her a wary glance when she heard the near giddiness in Rose's voice. Rose reached over and placed her warm hand on Grayson's forearm. She then turned the arm over to expose Grayson's left palm. Running her fingers lightly over the crescent-shaped scar, she said, "There is a shift in the universe, Grayson Fianna. And this is the cause." She lightly tapped on the scar, then sat back.

Grayson immediately felt her palm itch and mumbled, "I don't want to be the cause."

"Don't pout so." Rose lifted the makeshift tea cozy off the teapot. "Now hold the cup. You remember."

Grayson, still grumbling, lifted the cup by the handle with her left hand and presented it to Rose, who poured a liberal amount of tea. Grayson watched as the leaves, along with the steaming tea, flowed out of the long, china nozzle of the teapot. She then set the teacup down in front of her.

"Let it steep more."

Grayson nodded, watching the expanded leaves swirl and settle into the bottom of the teacup. The idea, Grayson remembered, was to sit around, talk about your life and anything else as you drank the tea. When you were finished, Rose would read the leaves as they lay around the bottom of the cup. Grayson would feel better if she didn't feel like she was drinking from a soup tureen. She felt the urge to relieve her bladder already.

"What I cannot believe," Rose started and sipped her tea, "is that this is all true."

"You and me both," Grayson said and drank the tea. She smiled as the taste instantly brought her back to her childhood when she would sit with her mother and father, drinking hot strong tea and eating warm soda bread or brown bread lathered in butter and jam.

"But it is true."

"I know. It's just so hard to believe Ma's not here sitting with us." Grayson quickly took a drink, hoping Rose didn't hear the catch in her voice.

Rose stared at her cup and whispered, "I know, darlin'."

They sat in silence for a moment before Rose spoke. "She came to me, your mother did."

Grayson looked at her so quickly, she nearly spilled the tea. "What do you mean?"

"The other night. I was sleeping," she said and laughed. "I thought I was anyway. And there she was, sitting on the edge of me bed." She stopped and took a drink. "Take care of Grayson, she said to me."

Grayson's bottom lip quivered as she listened.

"She said she fulfilled her destiny, but she left you all alone."

Grayson held back the sob that threatened to overtake her as she drank the tea.

"Then she said the queerest thing." Rose leaned forward and whispered, "Liar's moon." She narrowed her eyes as if to gauge a reaction from Grayson and waited.

"Liar's moon," Grayson said. "What does that mean?"

"I thought you'd know." Rose sat back, looking dejected. "Maybe the little redhead will know."

Grayson cocked her head, then laughed. "Yes, maybe Corky will know what it means. He'll probably find it in his book of wizardry."

"Don't sass the gods," Rose said, then blessed herself.

"Was that the whole dream?" Grayson drank more tea, which was now lukewarm.

"Yes, that was it. I woke up. And as much as I loved your mother, I was grateful not to see her sitting on me bed. But I wish I knew what she meant by liar's moon."

Rose looked into Grayson's teacup. "All right, now hand it to me."

Grayson obediently handed Rose the cup with her left hand. Rose took the cup and slipped her glasses on the bridge of her nose. Grayson patiently waited as Rose examined the leaves with an occasional grunt.

Finally, Rose sat back and looked at Grayson. "Look at this." She motioned to Grayson, who leaned forward.

"I see tea leaves."

Rose ignored her and pointed to one section. "See the way that leaf is situated, and it's on the left, by the handle. In this position, it's your immediate future."

"Okay," Grayson said. She had no clue what Rose was getting at. "What does it mean?"

"Deception."

Grayson sat back and chuckled. "Well, that's nothing new. For the past few months, that's all—"

"No, that would be your recent past, which is here." Rose pointed to another section of the cup. "See this leaf? The shape indicates loss but renewal." She looked up at Grayson and took off her glasses. "This position is your immediate future, and in it is deception."

Grayson nodded, still not fully understanding, but one thing came to mind. "Liar's moon."

Rose nodded and stood. She walked over to the cabinet above the counter. She pulled down a brown bottle and two small glasses. Grayson raised an eyebrow as Rose poured a small amount of whiskey in both glasses. As she examined them, she added a little more to both. Grayson remained silent as Rose corked the bottle and sat.

"I have a feeling here, Grayson." She sipped from the glass.

Grayson winced as the whiskey warmed her to her toes. "A feeling of what?" she asked when her voice came back.

Rose shook her head. "I'm going to study these leaves. It's an interesting read. And with Maeve coming to my dreams, and you have this friend coming to you."

"Who I don't know."

"Exactly. Deception. With all that has happened, you must take great care, dear. Where did she come from, I wonder."

Grayson stared at the whiskey glass. "I don't know."

"Darlin', I want you to know something."

"Okay, though I'm not sure I want to hear this."

Rose laughed softly. "Ireland is an ancient country."

"This I know."

"No, I don't believe you do."

Grayson looked up when she heard the serious tone. "What are you saying?"

"When I was a young girl, your mother and I were best friends." She laughed and shook her head. "We'd get ourselves in the most unusual trouble. Her mother was a wonderful woman but very eccentric."

"How do you mean?"

"I'm not sure if Maeve told ya, but her mother had what the old folks called the knowing. Do ya know what I'm talking about?"

Grayson nodded. Her mind traveled back to that rock dwelling Sister Daniel took her to. She was inside for only a few minutes, but to Corky and Neala on the outside, it was a full twenty-four hours. In those moments, Maeve and Vic visited her and showed her all the generations of women who lived and died to bring Grayson to this point. All of them had the knowing. Now it didn't surprise her that her grandmother had it, as well.

"What are you thinking?" Rose asked as she lightly touched Grayson's forearm. "You haven't said much about what happened the night Maeve died or why she died. And now with Sister Daniel suddenly transferred, it's all a mystery. Tell me what happened."

Grayson searched her blue eyes. "It appears, Rose, that Grandma passed the knowing down to me or at least some of it. And it seems I'm some true descendant and—"

"Then it's true." Rose sat back in her chair. "Your mother was right. She mentioned it only once. Only once did she tell me of an ancient stone that held all the magical power of the gods and goddesses. They broke into three sections, each piece given to the ones who would protect their section from the dark forces that would use the power of Ireland for their own gains. They would protect it until the exact time when the true descendant would be revealed." She looked at Grayson in awe. "It's you. Mother of God." Rose quickly blessed herself. "It's true."

"My mother gave her life for me. The prophecy that Corky had been working on all his life, like his father before, foretold her destiny and mine." Grayson reached over and took Rose's hands in her own. "You must always be careful. Always. There is a man who murdered Ma. He's still out there. I can't even begin to tell you how evil he is. And he'll stop at nothing to destroy me, and I'm sure anyone else. So please—"

"You're not to worry about me. Now who is this man? What is his name?"

"Phelan Tynan. Right now, he's a millionaire philanthropist. He's given millions to the National Museum in Dublin, which pretty much gave him carte blanche to do whatever he wanted. Remember in the news last year, the archaeological find here at the abbey?"

Rose nodded. "The stone. It was said to be dated over a thousand years." Her eyes grew larger as she whispered, "That stone is *the* stone?"

"Yes, and Phelan procured two of the three sections throughout the centuries, and he took the third stone when the exhibit came back from Chicago to Ireland. He tried his best to reunite the stones and gain the power. But we stopped him, and during the ritual, the stones just…poof."

"Poof?" Rose repeated.

"Yep. I got the gift, and the stones vanished. So Neala's problem now is what to tell the board of directors at the museum. We can't tell the truth. Who the hell would believe it?"

"True enough. I'm having a hard time myself, and I believe all this. Why did he kill your mother?"

Grayson felt the anger rising as it had since Maeve's death. "He thought she was the true descendant."

"Grayson, your mother was attacked by a wolf or a rabid dog. But you say he killed her…"

Grayson scratched her head. "He, um, he's a…" She stopped and winced. "A shape-shifter."

"He's a what?"

Grayson nearly laughed at the completely befuddled look. "You heard me."

"What in God's name is a shape-shifter?"

"Are you telling me you know about the stone, the knowing, and Irish mythology, but you—?"

"Grayson," Rose said in a warning voice.

"He can morph into a wolf."

Rose blinked several times as if to register this information.

"Rose, you look like you're signaling a ship."

"Are you serious?"

"As a heart attack."

"And he's on the loose?" Rose took a healthy sip from the whiskey glass.

"He is. And I'm only telling you all this so you'll understand the seriousness of this mess. Phelan is a wizard. His father was an ancient sorcerer, who wanted the power for himself and his son. He didn't like the idea of it being kept safe. So he defied the druids but didn't get all the sections. Phelan was sent to procure the remaining sections. He's evil."

"I understand," Rose said in a coarse voice. "This is all too fantastic. But true."

"Yes, it is."

They sat in silence; Grayson glanced at Rose, who looked as if she were trying to absorb what Grayson had told her. Finally, Rose spoke. "Now you have someone else to consider. You need to meet this new friend." Rose lifted her glass to Grayson, who did the same. "Sláinte," Rose said and downed the whiskey. "Ah, good stuff."

Grayson did the same and choked. She truly hoped that was not a sign of things to come.

Chapter 5

"What do you think it means, Cork?" Grayson peered over his shoulder. She decided to go back to the monastery and talk to Corky about Rose's dream before going home and meeting her new friend.

"I'm not sure." Corky absently leafed through the almanac. "But I will find out."

Grayson heard the determination in his voice and patted him on the back. "Maybe it's nothing."

Corky looked up at Grayson, his green eyes sparkling over the rim of his glasses. "We both know that's not true."

"I know, but I can dream."

"Aha," Corky exclaimed and sat back.

Grayson once again looked over his shoulder. "What?"

"According to this, there are many types of moons. The basics, you know, waning, waxing, full. But it says here there is also the harvest moon, which naturally occurs after the autumnal equinox. And," he said and laughed while shaking his head, "what has been called liar's moon. It is called such because this full moon is shrouded in haze, as if to give the illusion of hiding the moon or its secrets." He looked up at Grayson. "I love this kinda stuff."

"The moon has secrets?" Grayson scratched her head.

"Metaphorically speaking, the moon does many things and influences much, as we both know. But in this case, I think perhaps it's those of us who have secrets under the liar's moon." He turned back and leafed through the book once again. "The moon has strange and wonderful powers."

Grayson stood by the window and looked out at the green hills. "But what did Ma mean when she said it to Rose?" She turned back to Corky. "And why Rose? Why not come to me or Neala or you?"

Corky let out a laughing snort. "Because I would have pissed myself."

Grayson laughed along at the truth in his statement. "So who's lying about what and why? Then Rose tells me I have a visitor."

Corky looked up then. "Really?"

"Yes. She told Rose she was a friend of mine. From Rose's description, she's tall, dark, and a Greek beauty."

"You mean you haven't seen her yet?"

"Rose thinks she may be at the cottage waiting for me. I just wanted to run this by you first before heading home."

"Seems very curious, Grayson."

"Very. I can't imagine who she is."

Both stopped when they heard a noise by the door. Grayson walked toward it just as Sister Gabriel walked by. "Good evening, Sister."

She stopped and turned back. "Good evening, Grayson. You two are working late."

"We're just going over a few things."

Sister Gabriel nodded, looking into the room. Corky stood and nodded. "Hello, Sister."

"Have a pleasant evening," she said and continued down the hall.

Grayson watched her until she was out of sight. Corky was right behind her, watching, as well.

"With no disrespect meant," Corky said, "she gives me the creeps."

"I hear ya. That's the second time I've heard her in this hall when we've been in here."

"Well, she is Mother Abbess now." Corky walked back to the desk. "Why don't we stop for now? You go see to your Greek beauty and I'll head back home. We'll start again tomorrow." He patted Grayson on the shoulder. "Liar's moon could mean nothing at all, just a dream Rose had."

Grayson laughed as she walked out. "Corky, after all that has happened since we met, do you really believe that?"

"No," Corky said quickly. "But I was hopin'."

As Grayson approached her cottage, she felt a tingling sensation in her left hand. Lately, this was a premonition, for lack of a better word—something odd usually happened. She took in her surroundings and noticed nothing out of the ordinary. She cautiously opened the front door and walked in.

Immediately, she knew something was wrong. Out of habit, she reached for her revolver, which of course was not there. Her mouth went dry as she stepped in and closed the door. She turned on the desk lamp, the room now dimly lit, and looked around. She realized she was alone, but she knew, or felt, some presence. She walked down the hall, checking the two bedrooms and bath, then the kitchen.

"Okay," she said with a sigh of relief.

As she walked back into the living room, Grayson stopped short when she saw a figure standing behind the desk next to the bookcase. Grayson found it hard to shallow as she stood perfectly still, straining to see who or what was lurking in the shadow of the lamp.

"Who are you?" Grayson asked, her voice as steady as her dry mouth would allow. She had that aching pins and needles feeling prickling up and down her left arm.

The figure didn't move, didn't say a word, but ever so slightly walked out of the shadows. It was a woman, that was plain to Grayson, but still she couldn't see her face.

"Answer me," Grayson said more forcefully. The woman now stood by the desk in the corner of the room, shrouded by the soft glow of the lamp. Grayson's heart nearly jumped out of her chest.

Grayson could easily see her now and quickly took in her appearance—tall, long brown hair, olive skin, dark eyes. Dressed in wool slacks and an Irish sweater. The woman was smiling slightly, leaning against the desk.

"I'll only ask you one more time. Who are you?" Grayson asked, never losing eye contact.

"My name is Elinora, Grayson." Before Grayson could ask another question, she put up her hand. "I'm here to help you."

"Help me with what?" Grayson watched as Elinora gracefully walked around the desk. She seemed preoccupied, as if studying her surroundings.

Elinora absently picked up a book and leafed through it. She looked at Grayson and grinned. "With whatever it is you need help with."

There was something about this strange woman that captivated Grayson, and at the same time, she felt she should be on guard.

"You're cautious of me. That's good," Elinora said.

"I'd be cautious of anyone who broke into my home and hid in the shadows like a thief."

It unnerved Grayson when Elinora continued smiling, as if reveling in some private joke. However, Grayson was not in the mood for jokes. Too much sadness surrounded her lately; she felt her anger mounting.

"I have been called many things but never a thief."

"Okay, cut the cute routine. Why are you here and what the fuck do you want? And don't give me the cryptic bullshit."

Elinora raised her eyebrows. "Such vulgarity for an immortal."

Her words surprised Grayson, who now stood by the desk. She wanted to keep her distance from this woman. "If you don't tell me what the hell you're doing in my home—"

Elinora swept her long brown hair from her face. "You'll what? Throw me out?"

"If need be."

She threw her head back and laughed. "I highly doubt that. You don't have that in you—yet." She then crossed her arms in front of her chest. "That's where I come in. And you haven't said a word about how I'm dressed."

That comment took Grayson completely by surprise. She regarded Elinora's dress. To Grayson, it was nothing special. She said so.

"I'm hurt. I wanted to blend in with the mortals."

"Mortals?" Grayson rubbed her forehead. "You're really pissing me off."

Elinora laughed then. "I am sorry. Let's go for a walk."

She walked to the door, stopped, and gave Grayson an inquisitive look. Grayson groaned and opened the door, allowing Elinora to precede her. "Thank you."

"Yeah," Grayson mumbled and followed her outside.

They walked away from Grayson's cottage, down the narrow dirt road in silence. It was really irritating Grayson, who frowned deeply but said nothing as they continued.

"Much has changed in this place over the centuries," Elinora said in a wistful tone. "As you may imagine, I've been around."

"But from what starting point?" Grayson asked; she remembered Rose Barry and the tea leaves and kept her distance.

"Good question." Elinora stopped and faced Grayson. "I have been sent to help you. Help you with your newfound immortality. Though I have never met an immortal who is also a mortal. We believe this is what is holding you back from understanding your powers."

"So I'm getting a crash course on how to be an immortal?"

"I hear an edge to your voice. Don't you like being an immortal?"

"Not particularly," Grayson said.

"Hmm." Elinora reached over and took Grayson's left hand. She examined the crescent-shaped birthmark. "This is the source of your power."

The tone in her voice suggested more of a question than a statement of fact. Grayson couldn't help but feel very cautious and guarded with this woman.

When she placed her palm in Grayson's, Elinora closed her eyes. Grayson watched her warily as Elinora's eyes darted back and forth. It reminded Grayson of REM sleep. Suddenly, her left arm tingled, and she became dizzy; she felt weak as if she had no strength to pull away from Elinora. In the next instance, Elinora shuddered and sucked in gulps of air. When she quickly let go of Grayson's hand, both women staggered back.

Feeling as though she had stuck her finger in an electrical outlet, Grayson flexed her hand in rapid movements. "What the fuck was that?"

"I wanted to see for myself what all the talk was. You impressed them, Grayson MacCarthaigh. And now I can see why. You have lived a full life." She reached over and placed her hand above Grayson's breast. "And this is the source of your strength. It beats honest and true."

Grayson looked into her eyes for a moment.

"I am very sorry for the loss of your woman and your mother. Maeve was much respected, as was your grandmother."

For a moment, Grayson felt sick to her stomach at the thought of Vicky and her mother. However, she quickly recovered. "Thank you. Now what's next?"

"I'm hungry."

Grayson's mouth dropped. "Beg pardon?"

"I'm hungry. I haven't had an iced dessert in centuries." She turned and started up the road back to the cottage. "Chocolate," she said over her shoulder.

Grayson stood there staring as Elinora gracefully walked—nearly marched—away from her. She cocked her head as she watched the shapely hips sway. "An immortal who wants chocolate ice cream." Grayson sighed and followed. "Why not?"

"Emperor Nero was the first to have an iced dessert," Elinora said as she ate her ice cream.

"Really," Grayson said dryly. "And you were there?"

Elinora grinned. "He would have his slaves go to the mountaintops and bring back the ice, then add fruit to it." She stopped and cocked her head. "I suppose it was more like sorbet, but iced nonetheless. He was quite pompous. Did you know he had his mother killed?"

"Fascinating," Grayson said, rubbing her temples.

"I suppose you had to be there."

"And I suppose you were."

"I told you I got around." Elinora wiped the corners of her mouth with the napkin. "You have many friends here."

Grayson drank her tea, looking around the store. A few villagers sitting at other tables watched them with a great deal of curiosity. Grayson saw their cautious glances toward Elinora;

she didn't object to the wary glances, she felt the same doubt. "They've known my family for many years. Some even remember my grandmother."

"Deirdre, yes."

Grayson looked at Elinora while she concentrated on her ice cream. "Where do you come from?" Grayson asked.

Elinora hesitated, not looking at Grayson. "It's not important."

"Humor me."

Elinora looked up then and searched Grayson's face. "You have been given a great gift."

"So I've been told," Grayson said quickly and leaned forward. "Now listen to me, Elinora. In the past six weeks, my entire life changed. I'm suddenly the key to some ancient Irish prophecy." She held up her left hand, showing the crescent scar on her palm to emphasize her point. "And as part of that prophecy, my mother was savagely murdered by some shape-shifting ancient wizard that is still around planning what I don't know. And for all I know, you could know him, as well. I've had to leave America and my job as a detective, which I loved. This gift you so easily talk about may be wondrous to you, but to me, not so much. So start talking and quit with the 'great gift' crap."

Elinora dabbed the corner of her mouth with the napkin as she listened to Grayson. "That was quite a speech and very good ice cream."

Grayson leaned back in her chair, not saying a word.

Elinora continued, "I don't blame your frustration. And as I said, I am sorry for the loss of your mother and your woman. I suppose you are entitled to an explanation. I can only tell you this. You have been chosen and given this great gift and responsibility. Your family had been chosen long ago, knowing you would be the true descendant. The one to keep the power of the Tuatha De Danann safe from the likes of Phelan and his father, Figol."

"I know all this. What are you doing here?" Grayson felt her impatience bubbling to the surface. "And just for the record, Phelan knew all this, as well. I'm still not convinced you don't know him."

"As I said," Elinora continued calmly, which was really irritating Grayson. "I am here to help you understand and embrace the power you have been given." She reached across the table and took Grayson's left hand. "The power is not only here, but in your head and your heart, as well. You are a good, loyal person with a sincere and true heart. You must forget all that has been and be ready to accept all that may be. You must ready yourself, and I am here to see that you are prepared and that you learn how to use the power they saw fit to bestow on you."

"Why should I trust you?"

Elinora shrugged. "I suppose you really have no reason to."

Grayson felt this woman was still being too evasive for her. There was something she did not trust about Elinora; it unnerved her when she couldn't figure it out. The words liar's moon kept creeping up in her mind. For now, she would go along with this goddess or immortal or teacher, whoever Elinora was.

"Now tomorrow we shall start your training."

"Training?"

"Yes. Just as you trained to be a detective, you shall train to be an immortal. Though being human, as well, will be an obstacle."

"How so?"

"Emotions," Elinora said. "It has been my experience they get in the way each and every time."

"And you have none?" Grayson looked into Elinora's eyes and waited.

"No, I do not, which is why I was sent. There is no time for that. So do not attempt anything."

Grayson grinned and leaned forward. "Like what?"

Elinora leaned forward, as well. "We will not be having sexual relations."

Grayson tried to hide her shock. She didn't do it very well by evidence of Elinora's reaction. "I can see that was on your mind."

Was it? Grayson thought. She genuinely laughed, which appeared to catch the immortal off-guard. "Well, I am human. But don't worry, Elinora, your virginity is safe."

Now it was Elinora's turn to laugh. "I am hardly a virgin. But I am virtuous. We will start soon."

"Remember, you are mortal but also immortal," Elinora said as they walked up the path to Grayson's cottage.

"Fine, fine," Grayson said. "Where are you staying? You can stay..." She turned to see she was standing alone by her front door. "...here if you like." She sighed and walked into the cottage and closed the door.

After starting a fire, she went into the kitchen and took the old coffeepot down. She scooped the coffee grounds into the pot and added water. Mindless of what she was doing, she took the metal pot back to the fire and placed it on the bricked section of the fireplace, close to the burning peat bricks.

Grayson stepped back in confusion. "Why did I do that? Why didn't I make the coffee on the stove?"

In the next instant, a vision flashed through her mind: an elderly woman, white hair pulled back, a crucifix hanging around her neck. Bent over the fire, she placed a similar pot on the bricks. The woman stepped back and pulled the shawl around her shoulders.

She looked right at Grayson and seemed frightened. "Who are you?" the old woman asked and blessed herself. She held the cross that hung around her neck. "Who are you?" she insisted.

When this vision spoke, Grayson staggered backward, falling into the chair. She was sweating and breathing rapidly. "What the fuck was that?" she whispered. Did she recognize the old woman? Was it her grandmother? She knew it was not. Who was she?

This was a different vision from the ones she recently had. This woman seemed to see Grayson, as well. And she spoke; neither had yet to happen in these visions. She sat there for some time, the vision mentally draining her. The coffeepot boiling over and hissing on the hot peat bricks brought her back from wherever the hell she was.

She poured a cup of coffee and sat back again. Once again, there were questions unanswered, which Grayson truly hated. She thought of Rose's dream about Maeve and liar's moon. What did that mean? It only corresponded with Rose's tea leaf reading of "deception."

"Lying and deception." Grayson blew at the steaming cup. "Now all I have to do is figure out who or what or why and how. Sister Gabriel? Elinora? Phelan is a given." She sighed and put her feet up on the ottoman in front of her. She took a drink, then set the cup on the table. "Simple."

She must have dozed off; she woke with a start when she heard the rapid knock on the door. "Okay, okay."

It was Corky. "What are you doing here?" Grayson glanced down at the leather-bound book that Corky reverently cradled in his arms. "And I guess whatever it is, it's in there."

Corky laughed as Grayson stepped back; he walked in and shook his head. "Soft night." He took off his glasses and wiped them on his shirt, which Grayson realized was also wet.

Grayson looked out at the torrential downpour and winced at the flash of lightning. "Very soft," she mumbled and shut the door.

"I couldn't wait. I think I've found a wee bit more about our liar's moon."

Grayson smiled at the joyful tone in his voice. He sat at her desk by the fire and opened his beloved book of Irish myths, legends, and prophecies. She marveled at his knowledge and openness to accept the unbelievable so easily; Grayson envied that in him. All this was so foreign to her. Grayson lived in the real world of good guys and bad guys. You catch the bad guys and put them in jail. Not much of a gray area for her; though now, everything was in that "in between"—the hazy unknown that was now her life. With her mother gone, Grayson realized her destiny, but still deep down, she wanted her old life of being a detective, catching the bad guys. She watched Corky with affection as he leafed through his book.

"Did you ever think of doing anything else?" she asked, leaning against the fireplace.

Corky looked up. "Like what?"

Grayson shrugged. "I dunno. Something that doesn't involve druids, vampires, wizards, and shit like that." She was getting irritated. "Ya know, normal, logical."

Corky took off his glasses and turned his chair to face her. "What's wrong?"

"Nothing," Grayson said. "I'm just asking."

"Well, then. The answer is yes. I had thought of doing something other than this." He put his glasses on and continued reading. "But someone is already the pope."

Grayson glared when she saw the smile tug at the corner of his mouth. "Very funny."

"I know this isn't what you thought your life would be like." Once again, he looked at her. "But whether you believe it or not or agree, you've been given a great gift."

Grayson snorted, but she remembered the words spoken to her in that rock dwelling, where she had the vision of her mother, Vic, and all her ancestors, all the women who went on before Grayson who had the knowing. The voice told her she had been given a great gift. At that time, with her mother just murdered by Phelan, Grayson did not feel so thankful for this "gift." And although she had accepted her fate, or destiny, everything had happened so fast, so furious she hadn't had time to breathe.

"I know it's a gift," she conceded and walked over to the window. "I just...I don't know."

"The minute I saw you at my doorstep, I knew you were the one."

"You fainted."

Corky laughed. "Yes, I did. I was astonished. Do you know, while I believe all this," he motioned to the opened book, "I really never truly believed it would come to fruition. Not until I met you and we deciphered that prophecy. I'm sorry, but there really is no turning back."

"I know. Ma didn't die for nothing," she whispered, damning the tears that flooded her eyes. She looked over at Corky; the look on his face broke her heart.

"I loved Maeve," he said, his voice quivering with emotion. He sniffed and looked back at the book. "Now let's get back to this liar's moon. When you left earlier, I must have drifted off to sleep. I had a dream."

Grayson sat on the hearth, pulling her knees up to her chest.

"Oh, no," she mumbled.

"Oh, yes," Corky said.

"My mother?"

"Yes, and also a younger woman, blond. They stood side by side." He looked up at Grayson.

"That must have been Vic."

Corky nodded. "They stood in front of the desk. Vic smiled at me, and Maeve looked around while she was smiling. She looked like she always did." He stopped when his voice trembled. He looked at Grayson with tears in his eyes. "Ya know?"

Grayson fought the same tears and only nodded.

"Then she says to me, 'liar's moon will be in your hands soon, sweetie.' Then I woke up."

"Will be in your hands soon? What does that mean?"

"I don't know. I figure she means in this book. Do you think?"

"Why not? Have you found anything?"

"I've been looking and reading. So far, I see nothing that even hints to it."

Grayson stretched her legs out and groaned. "I'm sure it's the same thing as with the residual moon. Something will probably happen or some event. But what and why?"

"Again, I don't know." Corky sat back and took off his glasses. "Hey, what happened with your Greek beauty? Did she show up?"

Grayson laughed. "Oh, yes."

Corky leaned in grinned. "Who is she? What's her name?"

"Her name is Elinora."

"That's beautiful."

"Yes, it is. And as for who she is?" Grayson shook her head. "She says she was sent here to help me with my newfound immortal-ness."

Corky turned serious. "Sent by who?"

"Whom. Sent by whom."

"Grayson—"

"I suppose from..." Grayson pointed to the ceiling. "Those guys."

"Will you be serious?"

"I am," Grayson said very seriously. "From what she said, they sent her because being a mortal, as well, might hinder me from being all the immortal I can be."

"You're not kiddin'?"

"I am not kidding."

"You sound like you don't believe her."

"Well, let's just say I'm cautious and very leery."

"I don't blame ya. What's she like?" Corky asked, completely enthralled.

"She likes chocolate ice cream." She looked at Corky. "It concerns me that you don't think this is odd."

"Why should it be? Given all that has happened to you, I'd think you'd be more accepting. But I understand your reticence. Really I do. With Phelan still out and about and with this liar's moon business, like I said, I don't blame you." He leafed through his book once again. "Ya see, with me, I've always been around this. It's been part of my life and my family since, well, for generations. I wasn't surprised when that vampire—what was her name, Kendra—came to me and wanted the glamour."

"I remember you telling me. What did Kendra need it for?"

"Remember, she was working in the catacombs in Guys Hospital in London. She wanted a spell that hid her from anyone finding out what she was up to." He laughed then. "Neala was scared to death when I told her about Kendra."

Grayson chuckled. "I'll bet she was scared. This is new to Neala, as well."

Cory nodded. "Poor Neala felt better when I explained that a glamour is a spell of sorts that hides you or what you're doing and showed her the glamour I used from my book." He patted his beloved book and continued, "But the vampire part was another story for her, but not me. Remember when we met Sebastian? I was shocked only because I had read about her in this book. She's a legend in her world, then to come face to face with her."

"You're amazing. I truly admire your steadfast trust in all this and your willingness to accept it so quickly." Grayson smiled then. "I really need you and Neala. You've been through a lot with me in such a short time."

"It was meant to be. I agreed with Maeve, we're all connected on some level for some reason. That's why her coming to me and Rose in our dreams means something. It wasn't just a dream. I wonder if Neala has had a dream like this."

"I don't know. I know she's coming this weekend. When I talked to her, she sounded so tired. I know the people at the museum are worried about the stone. She tried to tell them that Phelan is keeping it for safety purposes because, God forbid, she can't tell them the truth."

"I know. Telling the National Museum in Dublin that an Irish artifact has disappeared into thin air during an ancient ritual, and by the way, speaking of ancient, your primary benefactor, Phelan Tynan, is the son of a wizard from nearly two thousand years ago, but no matter."

Grayson laughed at the absurd but true explanation. "I suppose poor Neala has her hands full."

"Yes, but the museum officials are very forgiving and understanding since Phelan—"

"The shape-shifting asshole."

"—has contributed millions to the cause." He tiredly rubbed his eyes. "So when do I get to meet Elinora?"

"I have no idea. One minute, she's eating ice cream, and the next, I'm talking to myself."

Corky slowly started chuckling. Grayson joined him, and in a moment, both were laughing hysterically.

"And not just any ice cream," Grayson said through her laughter. "Only chocolate if you please."

"No!" Corky said, drying his eyes.

"Oh, yes, Mr. Kerrigan. Chocolate only."

"An ice cream-eating Greek beauty. What next?" Corky asked, still laughing.

In another moment, they stopped and pondered that question.

Chapter 6

Grayson had a fitful night's rest. She woke tired and for some reason irritated. It was possibly due to the tossing and turning.

She met Corky early in the morning. The tired, but anxious feeling still hung around her. Leaning against the desk, she looked out the window and watched as Sister Gabriel sat on the wooden bench in the courtyard of the monastery. While she read, it struck Grayson how peaceful she looked, like the nuns from her youth. "Why would a nun wear that old starchy habit?"

Corky gazed out the window, as well, and shrugged. "I don't know. Some nuns, especially here in Ireland, are very dedicated to their order. If Sister Gabriel has been cloistered all this time, as she said, she really didn't know much of the outside world."

"Yet she's very intelligent and doesn't seem surprised or shocked by anything." Grayson turned to Corky. "If she was cloistered, kept in seclusion, then brought here, I would think there would be a little culture shock."

"I see what you mean," Corky said. "What's your point?"

"I don't know why I keep going back to why."

"Why what?"

"Why would a seventeen-year-old girl want to choose a life cut off from the outside world?"

"A vocation. Maybe this is her calling. This is how she chose to live her life."

"Or hide from it."

Corky looked slightly stunned. "Where would you come up with that?"

Grayson heard his defensive tone. "I'm not accusing, but

there's something here that I find very curious about Sister Gabriel." She sat at the desk Corky vacated. "Since she arrived, have you noticed she's usually around?"

Corky scratched his head. "You know, come to think of it. Every time we're in here reading from this book, she—" He nearly swallowed his tongue when he looked up to see Sister Gabriel walking by the door. "Grayson," he whispered and motioned to the doorway.

Grayson got a glimpse of the black habit flowing past the door. Both were silent for a moment as they heard the wooden rosary beads, which hung from the nun's waist, tap together with each fading step Sister Gabriel took.

"What does she want?" Grayson cautiously walked to the door and peered down the hall; she listened to the eerie silence.

"Looking for the end of the rainbow?"

Grayson nearly jumped out of her skin as she whirled around to see Neala standing there. She laughed as Grayson put a hand to her heart. "Geezus, Neala. Don't do that."

Corky laughed, as well, more, Grayson thought, out of relief than anything else. She turned back into the room and joined in the laughter.

"I can't stay long, so tell me what you two are up to." Neala got a hug from Corky. "Ya look very guilty."

"Grayson is suspicious of Sister Gabriel."

Neala raised her eyebrows and wagged her finger in Grayson's direction. "Grayson MacCarthaigh, shame on you."

"Oh, please. I realize she's a nun, but she's still human." Grayson cocked her head. "Isn't she?"

Suddenly, the three of them laughed and snickered like school children.

"Now tell me why you're suspicious," Neala said.

"I can't put my finger on it. It just seems like she's always around."

"Well, she's new. Perhaps she's just trying to fit in and get acquainted with the monastery," Neala said.

Corky and Grayson nodded, but somehow Grayson was not convinced. She decided to leave it for another day. She looked at

Neala and smiled. "So how are things in Dublin?"

Neala sighed. "Very tense. I'm trying to convince the powers that be that Phelan has the stone for safe keeping. For now, they seem to believe the theory of a letter and stealing the stone. Personally, I think they'd believe anything Phelan told them if he handed them a check."

"For now, that's fine, Neala. It's bad enough that inspector from Dublin asked questions."

Grayson agreed. "As I told Corky, Inspector Gaffney will be back if she's worth anything. So if you can keep the museum officials quiet, that might satisfy her."

"Ya don't sound very positive," Neala said.

"I don't feel very positive."

"Neala, did Grayson tell you about her new visitor?" Corky asked with an innocent smile.

Grayson glared at him and avoided Neala's curious look. "No, what visitor?"

"A Greek beauty."

Neala raised an eyebrow. "Really? A friend? From Greece?"

Corky lifted his eyes upward and pointed to the ceiling. Grayson continued to glare.

"She's an angel?" Neala asked with a grin.

"Only in Grayson's heart." Corky put a hand over his.

Neala stopped grinning. "Interesting."

Grayson quickly explained Elinora and her purpose. Neala listened with a mildly surprised expression. "So she's no angel," Grayson said.

"But beautiful," Neala said, hiding her grin.

Grayson felt the color rush to her face. She could have gladly hit Corky with his book of wizardry at that moment.

"Sadly, I have not met the beautiful Elinora yet," Corky said in full pout.

Neala laughed and kissed Grayson on the cheek. "Well, I want to meet her, as well. Now I can't play with ya anymore. I'm off. I have to get back to the museum. I'll be back over the weekend."

"Maybe during the week, I'll—" Grayson stopped and shrugged. "We'll see you on the weekend."

Neala smiled. "Okay. We'll all go out for dinner."

"Sounds good," Corky said. "Safe trip, Neala."

For a moment, Grayson looked at Neala, who was smiling. "Well, I'd best be going." As she walked out, she said over her shoulder, "By the weekend, maybe you can say what's on your mind, Grayson."

Grayson frowned deeply when Corky snorted with laughter.

"Shut up." Grayson looked at Corky, who had shuffled papers in front of him.

"Don't be sour. Now let's get back to this. I've scanned a few pages here. I'd like ya to read when you can. It's in the ancient dialect I think you know now."

"Fine," Grayson said absently. Her mind was elsewhere; it was on Neala, who was now on her mind more than Grayson wanted to admit.

"I'm leaving it here in this folder. I have to go to Galway. I'll be back later this afternoon." Corky gathered his briefcase and looked at Grayson. "Gray?"

"What?" Grayson said, looking up. "Oh, sure. Go. I'll read it later and see if I can decipher it."

Grayson picked up the folder after Corky left. She then tossed it back on the desk. "I need some air."

"Good morning, Grayson," Sister Gabriel called out to her as Grayson walked through the courtyard. She was still sitting on the bench.

Grayson smiled and walked over to her. "Good morning, Sister."

"Would you like to sit?"

"Sure."

"It's a chilly morning." Sister Gabriel closed her book and looked around the courtyard. "This is peaceful."

"Yes, it is. Was the convent in Innishmore peaceful?"

"Yes, it was. But it was different. More isolated than peaceful. One had plenty of time for contemplation."

"I can imagine. What did you contemplate? If you don't mind my asking." Grayson shifted to face the nun.

Sister Gabriel smiled as if she were thinking of what to

say. "I don't mind at all. I suppose I thought of many things, as anyone would. Your life, your mistakes, what you did right. How to change and how to ask for forgiveness. How to go on and do God's work."

Grayson nodded. That was quite a litany. "It's a big leap from a cloistered life to an abbess of a monastery. What made you want to enter society again?"

"It was time, I suppose. When Sister Michael contacted me, then the bishop, I thought it was God's intervention. Perhaps He was telling me it was time." She looked at Grayson then. "I am sorry about your mother."

"Thank you, Sister."

"There's a reason for everything, child."

Grayson fought the tears once again; she nodded.

"You find comfort in these walls. I know. And though you may not know it now, God is watching out for you. He would never lead you where He couldn't keep you."

Grayson's head shot up. "That's exactly what Sister Daniel said to me when I was a small girl."

Sister Gabriel placed her hand on Grayson's. "And she was right." She stood then. "Now I must talk with Sister Michael. Thank you for the conversation."

"My pleasure, Sister."

She watched the nun walk away thinking there was still something about her she didn't understand. Sister Gabriel was a curious thing to Grayson. From the moment she met the cloistered nun and shook her hand, Grayson had a deep feeling Sister Gabriel was not all she appeared to be. The vision Grayson had when she shook her hand was fleeting at best, but it was distinctive. It was of three women, one a young woman perhaps a teenager and the other two were nuns. They were in some stone building; Grayson remembered the cold feeling she had during the vision and wondered what it meant. She also remembered trying to shake the sister's hand when she left and Sister Gabriel quietly slipping her hands into the sleeves of her habit, avoiding Grayson. Looking down at the palm of her left hand, she wondered why.

Grayson walked back into the office ready to read the folder

Corky had left. When she sat at the desk, the folder was not there. "Shit," she mumbled and searched the papers strewn on the desk left in Corky's wake. "He's a slob."

She heard something outside and stood by the window, overlooking the courtyard. She watched Sister Gabriel now as she walked the courtyard once again, rosary in one hand and a prayer book in the other. Instinctively, Grayson knew this was a ritual for Sister Gabriel; this must have been a daily routine in the convent in Innishmore, and old habits were hard to break. What amazed Grayson was not that she kept her routine, but how long it was. Glancing at her watch, she realized the nun had been walking in a circle around the courtyard for nearly an hour, and more amazing, Grayson had stood there watching her the entire time, mesmerized by the nun.

"That's some dedication," Grayson said as she watched from the window of the office.

In a moment, the bell tolled in the monastery, causing Sister Gabriel to close her book and walk out of the courtyard. It was exactly noon. Grayson would be curious to see if she meditated the same time every day.

With nothing to hold her interest, Grayson turned back into the room and sat at the desk where Corky kept all his writings, notes, and scanned pages he had taken from reading his "bible," as he called it. Grayson looked on the desk, but she still couldn't find the manila folder he had. He had all his notes from this prophecy he had been working on. He had left it on the desk for Grayson to look over the scanned pages from his book of wizardry... She laughed inwardly, knowing Corky hated it when she used that name to describe his book of spells, prophecies, and legends.

"Well," Grayson said as she searched the desktop. "The folder seems to have vanished into thin air. Can't anything be normal anymore?"

Figuring Corky must have taken it with him, Grayson gave up looking for it. For some reason, she looked at the doorway, just in time to see the fleeting image of Sister Gabriel. Grayson quickly went to the door and got a glimpse of a floating black blur rounding the corner. Out of the corner of her eye, she saw another black blur. It was one of the younger nuns. The place is crawling with nuns, she thought.

"Are you looking for someone?"

Grayson let out a yelp and whirled around. "Geezus!"

"Mary and Joseph," Sister Michael said. "I'm sorry I startled you."

"That's okay, Sister, Neala did it to me earlier. Hey, have you seen anyone by Corky's desk? I'm missing a manila folder that he left for me."

"I was gone this morning."

"You weren't here?"

"No, child. I had to see the bishop, and that takes all morning. I've just returned. Why?"

"No reason. So you haven't seen Sister Gabriel?"

"Not as yet. Now why all the questions?" She gave Grayson a scathing look. "I highly doubt any of the sisters are thieves, Grayson."

Grayson felt her face get red hot. "Oh, I didn't mean to imply. I-I..." She stopped and chuckled. "I'm sorry."

Sister Michael grinned. "I forgive you. Three Hail Marys and two Our Fathers should do it."

Grayson laughed along. "Yes, ma'am. Can I ask you something?"

"Certainly."

"How well do you know Sister Gabriel?"

Sister Michael raised an eyebrow. "Walk with me."

"Uh-oh, we have to walk for this?"

Sister Michael laughed as they walked out to the courtyard. Grayson glanced at her. "She seems to have a routine of prayer. I saw her out here earlier."

"Yes. When you live your life alone and away from human contact, a routine of prayer and meditation is a necessity."

"I suppose it would be." Grayson strolled next to the nun.

As they walked out of the courtyard and away from the monastery, Grayson waited for her to continue. "We'll have an early spring," Sister Michael said, looking around the green rolling hills.

"You sound sure of it."

"I am."

"Divine intervention?"

"Farmer's Almanac."

Grayson laughed quietly but said nothing more.

"Sister Gabriel, I believe, had a special calling. I cannot tell you much, except to say she found God early in her life and has been devoted ever since."

Grayson nodded but said nothing; she felt Sister Michael watching her. "You are not convinced?"

"Oh, no, no," Grayson said. "I'm just naturally curious of anyone who would hide themselves, for what—maybe thirty years?"

"To live a life of a cloistered nun or a monk is not hiding. It is their way of serving God."

"I know, Sister, and I'm not judging. There's just something about her." Grayson noticed Sister Michael seem as if she wanted to say something.

"It's getting chilly," she said quietly.

They turned and headed back to the monastery in silence until Grayson couldn't take it anymore. "If there was ever anything you'd like to talk to me about, I'll listen."

"A confession?"

Grayson stopped and looked at her. "If that's what you'd like to label it."

She smiled and continued through the courtyard. "I will keep that in mind, my child."

Grayson nodded and watched her walk away. She scratched her head in an irritable fashion and headed back to the office where she found Corky sitting behind the desk. He looked up and smiled. "Had a nice talk?"

"Yes. Hey, what did you do with that file you were supposed to leave for me?" Grayson asked.

Corky gave her a curious look and held up the file. "I left it for ya."

"No, you didn't. I checked all over and it wasn't there." Grayson stood in front of the desk. "Was it here when you returned?"

"Yes. It was just where I left it."

"Where?"

Corky raised the folder to eye level and dropped it on the desk. "Right there."

"Corky, I'm telling you it was not on this desk. I searched the desk, looked up, and saw Sister Gabriel floating by," she said and got a chuckle from Corky. "And then I walked out into the hall, saw another nun, then Sister Michael scared the crap out of me. We went for a walk. I wanted to ask her about Sister Gabriel, then I came back here to you."

"When I came in about five minutes ago, it was sitting just where I left it. Right on top of my mess so you'd see it. I thought you read through it already. Do you think someone took it?"

"That's exactly what I think. That file was not there and now it is. Whoever it was had it slipped it back here while I was out with Sister Michael and before you came back."

"Who would want to take it?"

"What's in it?" Grayson took the file, leafing through it. "Looks like Gaelic."

"It's an ancient dialect that I'm having a hard time deciphering, and with you now able to read and understand it, I took a picture of the page from my book so you could read it." He scratched his head. "Well, it was useless to them."

Grayson looked up at Corky. "Why?"

"It's an ancient dialect. I doubt any nun here would know it. I don't even know most of it." He saw Grayson smile then. "What are you thinking?"

"Remember when we first met Sister Gabriel, and she understood the poem I recited in the ancient dialect?"

"Why would she care? And why take the folder? I would have let her read it."

"Not if she doesn't want anyone to know she's interested." Grayson thought of Rose and the tea leaves; she thought of liar's moon.

"Grayson, you have to be careful here."

"About what?"

"You must tread lightly. We're here only because of His Eminence's good grace."

Grayson rolled her eyes. "You mean the bishop who wanted Sister Daniel carted off to parts unknown? Who probably thinks Ma was a heathen and not worthy of heaven."

"I agree with you, but if you go off and start accusing nuns, especially the newly appointed Mother Abbess by the bishop—"

Grayson held her hand up. "Okay, I get it. I'll tread lightly."

"Are you thinking Sister Gabriel took the folder, read the pages, and put them back? Again, why?"

Neither said a word for a long moment until Corky looked at Grayson. "Are you thinking what I think you're thinking?"

Grayson watched him curiously. "I don't know. What are you thinking?"

"Who's the only one who wants this book and to understand all that's in it because he probably doesn't know the ancient dialect?"

"And Sister Gabriel knows the ancient dialect."

"And it would be just like Phelan to use a Catholic nun to do his bidding. If that's what we're thinking." Corky gave Grayson a wary glance. "Is that what we're thinking?"

"I am now." Grayson sighed and slumped back into the chair.

Chapter 7

As Grayson started to decipher Corky's notes, she looked up when the door opened.

"There's an Inspector Megan Gaffney here to see you, Grayson," the nun said.

Grayson winced but nodded. "Thank you." She stood when the inspector entered the room. "Inspector Gaffney." Grayson held out her hand to the detective, who took the offering with a thin smile.

"Ms. MacCarthaigh," she said.

Grayson held her hand for a moment longer than necessary. If Inspector Gaffney realized this, she showed no sign. Grayson watched the inspector with interest. She had come from Dublin to question Grayson, Neala, and Corky after Maeve's death. Though she seemed to believe the coroner's findings that Maeve MacCarthaigh was indeed attacked by some animal, perhaps a wolf or rabid dog, Grayson knew Megan Gaffney was no fool and took the coroner's report with skepticism. Grayson knew she'd be back.

And here she was.

"What can I do for you, Inspector?" Grayson asked.

"I know this may be hard for you to talk about, Ms. MacCarthaigh, but I'm curious." She sat in the chair Grayson offered. Grayson sat opposite her on the couch; she waited for the inspector to continue. "I'm aware you were a detective back in America. I suppose I'm wondering if you would believe a wolf attacked and killed your mother."

Grayson raised an eyebrow and sat forward. "Well, you saw

the wounds left on my mother's neck." She felt the anger rising, not from the inspector's questioning, but from the memory of Phelan Tynan and what her mother went through in the final minutes of her life—the life she gave up for Grayson.

"As I said, I'm sorry to bring it up again."

Grayson continued to watch as the inspector ran her fingers through her dark hair. She looked tired; the dark circles under her eyes told Grayson she had not slept. Grayson knew the feeling. How many days did Grayson go without sleep trying to find the murderer back in Chicago, only to find she was involved along with her mother and Neala? She wondered how this policewoman would take it if Grayson came out with the whole truth.

"It's all right, Inspector. I know what you're thinking, and I must admit, I'd think the same." She stopped when she saw the hopeful look and quickly continued, "But you can't deny the facts as they are. Those wounds were not man-made."

Inspector Gaffney looked Grayson in the eyes. Grayson was struck by how deep blue her eyes were and how penetrating. "It's just that we don't have many wolves in Ireland."

"Perhaps one."

"They travel in packs," Inspector Gaffney said, studying Grayson.

"You got me there." Grayson sat back. "I'm not sure what else I can tell you."

"I was reading the paper this morning. Seems Dr. Rourke is in the headlines. Some artifact missing from the National Museum in Dublin."

Grayson hoped her surprise was not evident on her face. Neala tried to keep it out of the paper. "Bummer."

The inspector cocked her head in confusion and Grayson chuckled. "Sorry. I mean that's a shame."

"Yes. It is." Megan Gaffney rose along with Grayson. "Well, thank you for your time, Ms. MacCarthaigh. If you think of anything else, please give me a call." She handed Grayson her card. "I'll see myself out."

Grayson took the card and watched as the inspector walked out of the library. Through the light rain that pelted the window,

Grayson watched further as the inspector walked to her car, pulling the collar of her coat around her neck against the rain.

"Something tells me, Inspector Gaffney, you are not going to leave this alone." Grayson turned back to the desk and concentrated once more on Corky's pages. But she couldn't get Inspector Gaffney out of her mind.

How would Grayson ever be able to explain all this to someone? Would she have to carry this around and avoid the police for the rest of her life? Inwardly, she laughed at the idea of avoiding the police. It would be like avoiding herself, she thought. At some point, this will all come out. Phelan will keep a low profile, but his arrogance won't keep him in the back row for long. Sooner or later, he'll step into the limelight and once again ingratiate himself to those in power. With his wealth, he'll snake his way into the public eye. He'll get himself on a board of directors at some big company, and it will be as if he'll be taunting me. "Come and get me." She could almost hear him laughing.

But it would be true. Grayson knew this would happen—at some point they would be thrown together again. Though Grayson had survived her battle with Phelan and started off on her destiny as the true descendant, she knew she would need to be stronger each time Phelan would come after her. Perhaps this was why they sent Elinora to help her. Grayson looked down at her left palm and traced the crescent-shaped birthmark that bisected her palm. She then smiled when she looked at the three rings on her finger, remembering how they appeared there after the vision of her mother and Vic. She would never take them off. It was a constant reminder of their sacrifice, of how they fulfilled their destiny to help Grayson realize hers.

She angrily ran her fingers through her hair, remembering how Vic died that day, saving her and the other policemen. And how Maeve died at Phelan's hands to fulfill the ancient prophecy. Fuck him, she thought, feeling the growing rage deep inside. She clenched her left fist, looking at the rings, trying to calm the anger within her.

"Too much displaced emotion."

Grayson's eyes flew open to see Elinora sitting in the high-back chair, one leg lazily hanging over the arm of the chair, one arm draped over the back. She looked bored.

"Where have you been?" Grayson asked when her heart rate returned to normal.

"I've been observing you and your townspeople. You are truly loved here whether or not you believe it. Your family is well remembered. Did you know one villager, very old, remembers his father talking with your great-grandmother about his crops and how she helped him save the very farm he is living on today?"

"No, I didn't know that." Grayson sighed and put her head back.

"There is a great deal you must accept. These people have very long memories and are extremely loyal. I must admit, I have never experienced anything like this in all my travels." She smiled then. "And I've had many."

"I'm sure."

Elinora laughed. "I will enjoy our time together, Grayson MacCarthaigh. Now let us begin."

Grayson lifted her head. "Now?"

"And why not?"

"I have no idea. Okay, where to?"

"Right here in this place your mother loved."

Grayson said nothing as Elinora continued. "She loved this monastery, no?"

"Yes, she did. We spent a lot of time here when I was little before we moved to America."

"Yes. And you enjoyed this time with your mother and Sister Daniel and the villagers. Do you remember how they took care of you? Do you remember the festivals of Samhain, the end of the summer, the bonfires?"

Grayson nodded; she watched Elinora's smiling face, lulled by her soft voice.

"Then close your eyes, come with me and remember," Elinora whispered.

Grayson's eyelids fluttered and closed; she put her head back, suddenly feeling as if she were weightless.

"Come with me," Elinora whispered in her ear. "Listen to them."

Grayson saw the bonfire, the villagers standing in a circle

around the fire. She saw Mrs. Barry walk up to her, but Grayson was a small girl now, the way she was all those years ago.

"Grayson Fianna, here, take this now, as your mother did and as her mother before." Mrs. Barry handed Grayson the thin piece of oak from the tree. "Light it now, girl, and keep us safe for the winter."

Grayson turned to see her mother standing there with Sister Daniel. Maeve smiled and winked. "Go on, honey."

She took the piece of wood and held it to the fire. As the end burned, the villagers each came to her and lit their torches from Grayson's. Unsure of what to do, Grayson held the burning wood to each one that approached her. She watched as they took their torches and walked to their homes. Grayson knew they would use the flame to start the peat fires in their cottages.

It was the ritual of Samhain; the beginning of the Celtic New Year and the beginning of the "dark half" of the year. The fire taken from the bonfire would keep them warm and safe during the dark, cold winter months.

The old women touched Grayson's cheek. "God bless you, child," they would whisper to her.

When they had finished and the villagers had gone, Maeve, Sister Daniel, and Grayson walked home and lit the fire in their fireplace. Grayson sat by the fire, mesmerized by the glowing flames. Sister Daniel and her mother were in the kitchen, drinking tea; Grayson could hear her mother's soft lilting voice laughing along with her old friend. Grayson felt safe, loved, and warm. She closed her eyes and felt her mother's arms around her and leaned into her. She felt the warm tears flow down her cheeks. "I love you, Ma."

"I love you, too, sweetie," Maeve whispered and kissed her head.

Grayson wept silently. When she opened her eyes, she was in Elinora's arms, gently rocking back and forth. Grayson sobbed uncontrollably as if she would never stop. She clung to Elinora, the ache in her heart to see her mother once more. But the time was gone, the time she would never have again. She pulled back and quickly wiped the tears from her face.

"Why did you show me that?" she asked almost angrily. "Fuck you for showing me this all over again and remembering." Grayson tried to focus through the tears flooding her eyes. "What are you—the fucking ghost of Christmas past?"

"You must never forget," Elinora said softly. "You will have much to deal with from now on in your immortal life, but you must never forget where you came from and how much you were loved. Your mother wants you to know this. So does your woman, Vic."

"It felt like she was holding me," Grayson whispered. "I felt like I was ten years old again."

"And so you were," Elinora said. "I am sorry if this causes you pain. But you must accept what you are now. You are both woman and goddess, mortal and immortal. You are a child of the Tuatha De Danann, a child of magic. Many have lived and died for this moment to come to fruition. Do you understand?"

Grayson took a deep quivering breath and nodded. "Okay, so now what?"

"Now we eat."

Grayson hung her head, then started to laugh. "Figures I get stuck with a hungry goddess."

"I am no goddess but a mere immortal." She walked up behind Grayson and placed her hands on Grayson's shoulders. "Now let us eat."

Chapter 8

"What is this called?" Elinora asked with a mouthful.

Grayson took a long drink from the pint of Guinness. "Colcannon."

"It is heavenly," Elinora exclaimed, taking another forkful. "Do they always eat this well?"

"Elinora," Grayson said. "It's just mashed potatoes and cabbage. Not lobster."

"Do not be so cross. What are you drinking?"

"Guinness."

"Ale?"

"No, much better. Here." Grayson offered Elinora her glass.

"Thank you," Elinora said happily and took a drink. She licked the foam from her upper lip and grinned. "I have been gone from this isle too long."

Grayson hailed the waitress.

As Elinora feasted on colcannon and Guinness, an elderly gentleman walked up to their table. "Excuse me, I hate to interrupt your meal," he said in a low voice.

Elinora waved her fork in the air. "Not at all, sir. Have you eaten? This is marvelous."

Grayson tried to hide in her pint glass.

"Thank you, no." He looked at Grayson and held out his hand.

Grayson took the weathered, calloused hand in a firm handshake. The old man smiled. "I knew your grandmother. Deirdre was a lovely woman. It's your mother you're named after, they tell me. I think I remember you as a young girl, but that was so long ago, and my mind isn't what it used to be."

"Whose is?" Grayson raised her glass with great sarcasm and received a glare from her immortal friend. She gently cleared her throat. "Sit down, please."

"Oh, no, no. It wouldn't be right. I wanted to pay my respects is all and bid you welcome home."

"What's your name, sir?" Grayson was struck by his sincerity and immediately felt bad for being sarcastic.

"Ah, that's not important to ya."

"Yes, it is," Grayson said. "If you knew my mother and my grandmother, I'd like to know you."

He smiled. "Fair enough. Jerry Roche. My family has been in Ireland for six generations and lived in this village. Can I get anything for ya? Are you going to stay in the cottage? My grandson can give it a good thatching if ever ya need it."

Grayson heard the pride in his voice. "Thank you, Mr. Roche. I'll keep that in mind. I appreciate it."

"Not at all. You're Deirdre's blood. It's only right. Good day to ya." He nodded to Grayson and Elinora, who was still eating.

"A lovely human," Elinora said, drinking her stout.

And with that, Corky walked into the restaurant.

"Another lovely human," Elinora said without looking up. "You are blessed, Grayson."

Grayson wasn't sure what she meant by that as she watched Corky. He saw Grayson and waved as he made his way over to them.

"Grayson, here you are. I just talked to Neala. She's on her way—" He stopped when he saw Elinora and grinned.

Elinora looked up. "Timothy 'Corky' Kerrigan, please join us."

"Thank you," Corky said, never taking his gaze off her as he sat. He immediately ran his fingers through his unruly red hair and straightened his jacket.

Grayson rolled her eyes and hailed the waitress once again. "Three pints, please."

"You must be Elinora," Corky said. "Grayson was right, you are beautiful."

"Thank you. Have you eaten?"

"Uh, no. I haven't." He glanced curiously at Grayson who raised her glass.

"Then you must have something."

"I will, thank you, Elinora," Corky said with a wink.

Grayson kicked him under the table. "You just talked to Neala?"

Corky winced and rubbed his shin. "Oh, bugger. I nearly forgot." He took out his phone and dialed. "Neala, we're at the Dungarin Inn. Yes, at the north end of town. Right, see ya in a bit." He snapped the phone shut and picked up his pint. "She's on her way. She's done with the museum folks for now and wanted to get away for the night."

"Seems a long way for her to travel for the night," Elinora said.

Corky grinned. "Yes, but Neala seems to love the company." He looked at Grayson, who scowled. Corky picked up the menu; he now glanced at Elinora. Grayson couldn't blame him. Elinora was strikingly attractive. Grayson wasn't sure if it was the shining dark hair or her deep brown eyes. Maybe it was the olive skin that looked as smooth as silk, just begging to be caressed. Yes, the immortal was very beautiful.

Elinora leaned in. "We are not having sexual relations," she reminded Grayson.

Corky spat up his Guinness and furiously wiped his sweater with the napkin.

Grayson merely shrugged. When she heard the door creak open, she looked to see Neala and waved her over to the table. Grayson stood and pulled out a chair for her.

"Thanks, Grayson," she said breathlessly and looked at Elinora. "Hello, you must be Elinora. Grayson was right, you are very beautiful."

Elinora raised an eyebrow in Grayson's direction. Grayson shrugged and waved her off. "I know, I know. No sexual relations."

Neala's jaw dropped and Corky leaned over and whispered, "I'll tell ya later."

"And you are Dr. Neala Rourke," Elinora said, watching Neala.

"Yes, I am," Neala said with a smile. She glanced at Grayson when Elinora still watched her.

"And you have traveled across the country to see Grayson just for the evening?" Elinora asked.

A smile tugged at Grayson's mouth when Neala blushed deeply. "Well, it's not all that far." She buried her head in her menu.

"Well, let's eat," Corky said. "I'm starved."

When Corky and Neala ordered the seafood fare of mussels, clams, and whatnot, Elinora looked at Grayson, who hailed the waitress.

"So tell me about yourself, Elinora," Corky said as they ate.

Elinora replied between bites, "There is not much to tell. I am here to assist Grayson so she may be more comfortable with her abilities. You and Neala do not seem as reticent to believe in me as Grayson does."

Corky laughed. "A non-believer. But she'll come around."

"Quit flirting, Corky. You will not be having sexual relations," Grayson said with a smirk.

Corky turned bright red and glared at her.

Elinora nodded. "This is true, Corky. We will not."

"See?" Grayson said and ate her salmon. She glanced at Elinora, who eyed the plate.

"And what of you, Neala?" Elinora asked.

Neala's eyes bugged out of her head. "I-I..." she stammered helplessly, avoiding Grayson's questioning grin as Neala glanced at Elinora's cleavage. "Um..."

"Are you a believer?" Elinora continued between bites.

"Oh," Neala said, seemingly relieved. Grayson laughed quietly and drank her beer. "I suppose so." Neala stopped to take a sip of her wine. "There's too much out there that we can't explain to simply discount as nothing. And since I've met Grayson and Corky, the idea of not believing seems silly now." Neala regarded Elinora for a moment. "And what are you going to teach Grayson?"

"To accept her destiny and learn how to use the powers that the gods bestowed upon her."

"That sounds so simple," Grayson said.

Elinora buttered yet another piece of brown bread and popped it into her mouth. "It will be as simple or complicated as you make it. I have a feeling things will get quite complicated."

Neala and Corky exchanged smiling glances.

Grayson avoided all of them and noticed a small gathering of villagers at the far end of the bar. Each of them looked her way and smiled. She nodded and returned their smile; she hailed the waitress.

Soon, the villagers, with fresh pints, looked as though they might make their way to Grayson's table. Corky noticed and wiped his mouth with his napkin. "I'll take care of it."

Before Grayson could say anything, Corky walked over to the bar and spoke with the men there. He slapped them on the back, and they all laughed. Grayson watched as Corky made his way back to the table and sat down.

"What did you say to them?" Grayson asked.

"I told them who you were and you've come home. You'll probably get a visit from time to time. But they won't bother you right now. Oh, and you owe them another round."

"Between their thirst and this one's appetite," Grayson motioned to Elinora, "I'll go broke."

"I adore humor," Elinora said, still eyeing Grayson's plate. She nodded her thanks when Grayson slid it in front of her.

"Don't you get full?" Corky looked completely enthralled as he rested his chin on the palm of his hand and watched her.

"No, it comes with being immortal. I can eat and not get full, but I still taste the food. I can drink and enjoy the flavor and not get intoxicated." She waved her fork in the air. "It is truly the best of all worlds." She then glanced at Grayson and continued, "Which Grayson needs to embrace."

"You mean Grayson can do that?" Neala asked.

Elinora shook her head as she ate. "No. I mean the best of all worlds she has at her fingertips, and the sooner she believes and accepts this, the better off she will be and more productive and useful."

Grayson grunted. "You make me sound like a pack mule."

Elinora put her fork down and sat back. "You can be quite surly when you want to be."

Corky, once again, spit up his beer. "Sorry."

"There's a great deal we're all learning about each other," Neala said, glancing at Grayson.

Elinora stood. "Well, I must go."

"Where do you go?" Grayson asked. "You must stay somewhere."

"I will be in touch," Elinora said.

"When is all this training supposed to start?"

"When you grow up and begin to believe." Elinora looked down at Corky and Neala. "Thank you for a lovely evening—"

"No ice cream?" Grayson interjected.

"—We will meet again," Elinora said, ignoring Grayson.

Corky stood and took Elinora's hand. "Where are you staying?"

"Corky," Grayson said, swirling her glass. "If the immortal can eat and drink like a Roman goddess, I don't think we have to worry about where she's sleeping. Do you sleep?"

Elinora smiled and walked out of the pub. It did not go unnoticed that the heavy door opened and closed by itself.

"I think you pissed her off," Corky said.

Neala watched Elinora's dramatic exit, then turned back to Grayson. "She's a curious…"

"Immortal?" Grayson offered. She watched Neala, who toyed with her wineglass. Grayson reached over and poured another glass for her. "What's on your mind, Doctor?"

"Oh, nothing really. I just find it curious that she appears out of nowhere and we accept that she's here to help."

"What are you suggesting?" Corky asked.

"I don't know really. With all that has happened and with Phelan on the loose, I'm not sure I'd trust anyone who just appears."

"Maybe Neala's right, Grayson." He stopped and laughed nervously. "I was taken by her beauty, and I admit I haven't given the idea consideration. I mean, really, how does one go about checking the credentials of an immortal? It's clear she's not human."

"Neither is Phelan." Grayson tiredly rubbed her face. "We'll just have to keep our heads about us. She's here for a reason. If what she says is true, then she's here to help me."

"And if it's not?" Neala asked.

Grayson looked at her worried face. "Then we'll just have to see."

"Neala, have you had any strange dreams lately?" Corky asked.

"Nice segue." Neala thought for a moment. "Not really. Why?"

"Because I had a dream about Maeve the other night, and from what Grayson said, so did Rose Barry. In both dreams, Maeve said 'liar's moon,' and I just wondered if she might have come to you in a dream, as well."

"No, not at all." She looked at Grayson. "Has Maeve come to you?"

"No. But two dreams in as many nights is a little too coincidental. There has to be something about it."

"What does it mean?" Neala asked Corky.

"Well, it appears that the liar's moon is a full moon, which has a haze or shroud around it as if it's hiding something. And the fact that Maeve came to our dreams saying that to me means something is about to happen during that time."

"Does it have anything to do with the residual moon, ya know from your prophecy?"

Corky shook his head. "Not that I can tell. Well, not so far anyway."

"There's so much it could be," Grayson said. "But I agree with Corky. For Ma to come to them and say the same thing, something's going on. I wish I could tell when this liar's moon is."

Corky was staring out the window. "I think whatever it is, it'll be soon."

"How do you know this?" Neala asked.

Grayson watched Corky; her left palm instantly itched. She could almost feel the blood running through her veins; she felt light-headed and at the same time keenly aware of her surroundings. Grayson stood and walked over to the window; she felt Corky and Neala at her side.

The moon had risen above the buildings; it was a half-moon, shrouded by a white haze.

"We've got about four days," Corky said. "I wish I knew what was about to happen."

Chapter 9

With Neala on her way back to Dublin and Corky driving back to his home, Grayson for some reason felt lonely. She had offered her other bedroom to Neala instead of the drive to Dublin, but she refused, saying she had a big day ahead of her. What was wrong with that? Grayson thought. It was logical and sound thinking on Neala's part. Grayson fought the nagging idea that she somehow wanted Neala to stay.

Grayson kicked at the stone wall that lined her property. What did she want from Neala? She looked at the crescent birthmark on her palm. What could she offer Neala? She had no idea with her life far too convoluted now to keep a normal thought going.

She looked up at the hazy half moon that hung low in the sky. Grayson gazed over the green sloping hills and watched the moon start its trek.

"Liar's moon," she said. "What are you?" She pulled the heavy corduroy jacket around her. It may have been early spring, but it was still cold in the evening.

She sat back on the wall that lined the narrow dirt road. Was her mother visiting Rose and Corky in their dreams a coincidence? Or did it mean something when Maeve said "liar's moon"? With all that had happened in the past few months, Grayson dismissed nothing as coincidence. After her mother died, Maeve told Grayson she would "be around" from time to time. Was this one of those times?

Grayson let out a thoughtful sigh, wondering what, if anything, liar's moon meant. Once again, she felt that helpless feeling, the same feeling after her mother died. Everything had happened so fast—the murders in Chicago, meeting Neala, then Phelan. Her mother's admission to her part of guarding the ancient mythical stone, which, as it turns out, was not mythological but very real. Just as Phelan, though an ancient wizard and asshole, was real. Oh, yes, Grayson thought with a wry chuckle, let's not forget he's also a shape-shifter.

Someone changing into an animal was something Grayson knew only from the movies—that is until she met Corky. Now she knew one firsthand. And while she was on the subject, Grayson now knew a vampire. "Can we add any more immortals to this equation?"

This had her thinking of Sebastian; she wondered what the mysterious vampire was up to and what happened with the resurrection of Leigh. "I never believed I would be actually involved with a vampire." Grayson shook her head, still trying to wrap her mind around all that had happened.

"Actually, you're not involved with a vampire, per se."

Grayson whirled around to see someone several feet away standing by an oak tree half hidden in the moonlight.

When the figure walked toward her, Grayson put a hand to her heart. "Goddamnit," she exclaimed.

Sebastian raised an eyebrow. "Such language coming from an immortal."

"Oh, shut up. You scared the shit out of me. What are you doing here?"

Sebastian sat on the wall and looked around. She leaned back, stretching her long legs in front of her. Grayson remembered how sexy this vampire was, dressed in a long leather coat. She looked at the long legs, then up to her hazel eyes, sandy-colored short hair, and brooding expression. Sebastian grinned slightly, her canine teeth showing.

Grayson felt the color rush to her face as if Sebastian could read her mind. "A beautiful night."

"Yes, very romantic," Grayson said dryly. "What's going on? When we never heard from you again, I thought you might be dead."

"I am dead."

Grayson blinked several times. "I keep forgetting that. Did you stop Leigh's resurrection?"

"Sadly, I did not."

"Nuts."

"Sadly, she is."

"Did you at least find the—"

Sebastian slipped a book out of her coat and held it up to Grayson.

"I thought you had to find Tatiana's box."

"I did. Its contents took me on a treasure hunt of sorts and led me to this book."

Grayson took it with her left hand. Her heart pounded in her chest; she slammed her eyes shut as visions flew in front of her so fast, she had no idea who or what it was. However, there were flashes of what she had seen when she was in that dwelling after her mother died—visions of robed people standing in a circle around a huge bonfire. One member was wearing something very odd on his head. The vision, like all the others, faded quickly. Grayson was acutely aware of two things: the tingling sensation that shot up her left arm that was paralyzing and someone calling her.

When Sebastian snatched the book from her hand, her eyes flew open; she was breathing like a bull.

Sebastian, holding the book, frowned deeply and watched her with a good deal of curiosity. "Would you like to share what just happened?" She glanced down at the book in her hand.

Grayson pointed to the book with a shaky hand. "Want to tell me what the fuck that is?"

Sebastian hesitated, still carefully watching her. "This is the reason I was late in stopping Leigh's resurrection. In it lies the answer to our beginning and all the power Tatiana possessed, which is now mine."

"Is that all?"

"What happened, Grayson?" Sebastian asked.

Grayson groaned and ran her fingers through her hair. "I saw visions maniacally galloping through my brain."

"Visions of what?"

"I don't know. There were too many and too fast. But there was one part," Grayson said. "I saw a group of people in long dark robes—"

"Standing around a bonfire. One in particular had some sort of a headdress."

"Yes," Grayson said. "Like some Grand Poobah or something. So you've had this vision, too." She looked at the book once again. "What's the answer?"

"I don't know," Sebastian said. "It's written in an ancient Celtic language, hence my reason for being here."

"You need Corky," Grayson said. "Well, let's get back. I'll call him. He'll be thrilled to see you." She glanced at Sebastian and grinned. "He's very odd that way."

Grayson dialed Corky's number while absently glancing at Sebastian. "Would you like some tea, coffee," she said and grinned, "B positive?"

Sebastian glared. "Just make the call."

Grayson laughed as Corky answered. "Hey, Corky, guess who I'm with?"

"I can't imagine," Corky said.

Grayson waited, then Corky exclaimed, "Sebastian!"

"You're so embarrassing."

"Come right over, Grayson."

"It'll take a while to get there. If you didn't live out in no man's land."

"Tell him we'll be there in a moment or two," Sebastian said.

Grayson gave her a dubious look.

"Trust me."

Grayson was really worried now. "We shall be there momentarily, Lord Corky," she said in a haughty English accent.

"How? How?" Corky asked.

Grayson shook her head at the excited tone in his voice. "I have no idea. Just sit tight."

She snapped her cell phone shut while Corky was still asking questions and gave Sebastian a curious look. It took every ounce of her being not to back up as Sebastian inched away from her and opened her leather coat.

Sebastian smiled, showing sharp canines, and beckoned Grayson. "Don't be scared, just put your arms around me."

Grayson glared back. "I'm not scared," she mumbled and walked into her arms. She felt Sebastian's strong arms around her, and she cleared her throat.

"It's the only way for immortals to travel."

Grayson felt the pulling sensation throughout her body; her heart beat so fast she thought it might burst from her chest. In an instant, it stopped and she opened her eyes. Sebastian released her as she looked around. They were standing in front of Corky's home.

"What a fucking rush," she exclaimed.

Sebastian raised an eyebrow but agreed. "I will admit it is one benefit of the undead."

Grayson ran her fingers through her hair and laughed. "Man, what a feeling. My scalp is tingling. It was like being on a roller coaster. How did you know where Corky lived?"

"Your mind is an open book. You need to work on that."

"Well, so is yours."

"Really?"

"Yeah, you ghoul. I—" She stopped when Corky opened the door.

"I thought I heard your voice. Am I interrupting?"

Grayson realized she was still inside Sebastian's coat with Sebastian's arms around her. "I think we've landed."

Sebastian stepped back and closed her coat. Her toothy grin was evident—Grayson bowed slightly.

"How the devil did you get here so quickly?"

"Corky, you've got to try this," Grayson said in giddy fashion.

Sebastian leaned her shoulder against the door and said nothing.

"Try what?" Corky asked eagerly, looking from the exuberant Grayson to the bored Sebastian. "Oh, and please come in."

"Grayson, please try to remember you're an immortal," Sebastian said as she walked in.

Grayson chuckled at the serious tone in the vampire's voice.

"I'll try." Grayson leaned down to Corky and whispered, "But it was cool."

"Bugger. Do ya think she'd…?" He stopped when he looked at Sebastian, who grinned, exposing her fangs. He adjusted his wire-rimmed glasses. "Perhaps not. Now tell me," Corky said. "How did it go with the resurrection? Did it work? Did ya find the box?"

"First, thank you for the invitation, Corky."

Corky smiled. "You're very welcome in my home, Sebastian. Now tell me."

Sebastian shook her head. "I was too late to stop Nicholae from resurrecting Leigh. I had to find the box first."

Corky's eyes lit up. "And did ya find it?"

"I did. As I explained to Grayson, its contents led me to this." Sebastian pulled the book out of the inside pocket of her coat. Corky, almost reverently, took it from her. "It's written in an ancient Celtic language, I'm told."

"Who told you?" Corky examined the book.

"Tatiana," Sebastian said. Corky quickly looked up. "She came to me in a vision."

Grayson heard the sadness in Sebastian's voice and thought for sure she saw it in the vampire's eyes, as well. "You really cared for her."

Sebastian scowled deeply and ignored Grayson's comment. Corky, still enthralled with the book, went on, "Maeve came to Grayson in a vision after she died. How do you open this?"

At the mention of her mother's name, Grayson felt the tears sting her eyes. She took a quick breath and said nothing, but she glanced at Sebastian, who was watching her. Grayson looked into her hazel eyes and felt a low buzzing in her ears.

You did care for Tatiana. It's okay to admit that.

Let it lie, mortal.

But I'm immortal.

Sebastian glared at Grayson, who smiled slightly, almost missing what Corky was saying.

"This looks like metal." He turned the book over in his hands. "How does it open?"

"May I take a look?" Grayson took the book from Corky as she glanced at Sebastian, who was smirking.

"You won't be able to open it," Sebastian assured her.

Grayson heard the challenge and scoffed. "It's only a book."

"But it's encased in metal, Grayson," Corky added as he peered over her shoulder.

It was indeed surrounded by metal, but also there was a clear tube-like border around the book. She yanked and pulled to no avail.

Corky rolled his eyes. "You're so stubborn. Give it to Sebastian. We're wasting time."

Grayson grunted and handed it over. "So much for my immortality."

"It has nothing to do with you." Sebastian took the book and placed her ring in the lock. Grayson peered over her shoulder and watched along with Corky as Sebastian pressed the top of her ring in place. Grayson was amazed when she saw the blood flow through the clear tube and the lock. With a twist of her ring finger, the lock opened.

"Absolutely amazing," Corky said, adjusting his glasses. "I take it only your blood will open it."

Sebastian nodded. "And Tatiana's."

"Very clever," Corky said.

Grayson wasn't so sure. "What's to prevent a vampire who hates your guts to get your blood and this book?"

"Good point." Corky grinned. "Grayson was a detective in America."

Sebastian leaned back against the desk and gently handed the book to Corky, who looked as though he would jump out of his skin. "Let me give you a lesson in vampire hierarchy."

"Vampires 101?" Grayson asked with a grin. "Let me get my notebook."

"Gray, please," Corky pleaded.

"Tatiana was very careful whom she sired. She was ancient, nearly two thousand years old."

"Two thousand?" Grayson repeated in awe.

Sebastian nodded. "She was smart, very smart. She knew a

vampire must keep the bloodline pure if they are to progress in the hierarchy. It's the same with mortals, she told me."

"This is true," Corky said. "The English royalty did it. I mean, imagine what Queen Victoria did with her nine children. It wasn't pure, but she had them married into royalty all over Europe."

"So Tatiana picks you to be the only one she bites."

Sebastian smiled, her fangs protruding. "No, Tatiana did her share of biting and then some. I'm the only one she turned. Only I have Tatiana's blood."

"And alive to talk to about it," Corky said. "Well, as alive as a vampire can be. So how do we decipher this?" He carefully leafed through the pages. "If this is an ancient Celt language, as Tatiana told you, it's beyond me. But perhaps..." Corky stopped and looked at Grayson.

"You can translate this?"

"I don't think I like that incredulous tone, Seb," Grayson said. "It seems I might be able to do something you can't."

Sebastian stared to her. "It would appear so."

"You mean my immortal powers are better than yours?" Grayson smiled innocently.

"In this instance, yes."

"So..."

"Do you really want to test this further?"

Corky took off his glasses and rubbed his eyes. "Ladies, please." He motioned to the letter.

"Okay, Cork," Grayson said.

"Please be careful with it," Corky pleaded.

"Okay, okay. I'll be gentle."

As she perused the letter, her eyes bugged out of her head and her jaw dropped.

"What is it?" Corky asked, his excitement apparent. Sebastian leaned in.

Grayson looked up. "You won the lottery!"

For a moment, Corky seemed confused. Sebastian glared, then grudgingly grinned, producing the razor sharp canines.

"Grayson, that was not funny." Corky tossed his glasses down on the desk. "Would you please be serious?"

"Sorry." Grayson cleared her throat and started again.

It was amazing to Grayson that she could easily translate from this ancient dialect. "It's like a prophecy more than a letter."

Sebastian groaned. "Another puzzle. Why can't it be simple?"

"I hear ya," Grayson said as she read it again. "I want to make sure I'm right here."

"Take your time," Corky said quietly.

Grayson nodded as she read.

"Don't rush it now."

Again, Grayson nodded.

"If ya need us—"

"Corky," Grayson and Sebastian said.

Corky held his hands up in defeat and adjusted his glasses. He and Sebastian waited for Grayson to finish.

Grayson could tell Sebastian was losing patience. "No fanging," Grayson said absently as she read. "Okay, Corky. I'll read it, and you'd better write it down and see if it makes sense."

Corky retrieved the pad of paper, his pen poised to start.

Grayson looked at Sebastian. "Here goes nothing."

In the shadow of the crescent
A mark is cloaked unseen
The traitor's song eclipse the moon
Blackheart betrays the queen.

One emerges from the night,
At the behest of ancient call
A star falls from a distant realm,
Uniting and revealing all.

Midnight calls upon the light
Uniting moon and stars and trees
To see with eyes no longer veiled
Embrace the path of destiny.

When Grayson finished, she looked up. Corky stopped scribbling and leaned back in his chair.

"What does it mean?" Sebastian asked.

"Don't look at me. I'm only the translator. Corky is the master historian." Grayson gently folded the letter, handing it back to Sebastian.

Corky seemed oblivious to Grayson and Sebastian. When Sebastian opened her mouth, Grayson put her hand up to silence her. She put her finger to her lips. Sebastian scowled but said nothing.

Grayson had to admit she was getting as restless as Sebastian, who paced back and forth in front of the fireplace. "Why don't you go get your fangs sharpened or something until Corky's finished? You're buggin' me."

Corky looked up and laughed. "I'm sorry. But this is very curious to me. Sebastian, what did Tatiana tell you about this letter?"

Sebastian thought for moment. "I had asked her what the Celts had to do with us and our world. She told me we were all connected. That our world was not unlike the mortals, and I would see that. That the letter was the key to this."

Corky took off his glasses and nodded. Grayson saw his grin.

"Okay, you whacky historian, what's so funny?" she asked.

"Yes, I'd like to know, as well." Sebastian stood in front of the desk and waited.

"Let's just look at the first part." Corky put on his glasses. "Just listen." He cleared his through and began.

In the shadow of the crescent
A mark is cloaked unseen
The traitor's song eclipse the moon
Blackheart betrays the queen

He looked up at both confounded faces. "Don't you see? The words crescent and moon are in the first stanza. What are the odds of a vampire having ancient Celtic text that just coincidentally has a reference to a crescent moon, which, oh I don't know, just happens to be Grayson's birthmark?"

Grayson flopped into the nearest chair. "Holy shit."

"Indeed," Sebastian said.

Grayson saw Corky's frown as he read. "What now?"

"I'm not sure what 'a mark is cloaked unseen' means, but in the next line, 'the traitor's song eclipse the moon' is curious."

"Traitor? Well, that's obvious. Someone is a traitor," Sebastian offered.

Grayson hid her grin at the hopeful, near human tone in the stoic vampire's voice.

Corky nodded; he then looked up and grinned. "And what is a traitor?"

The hair on the back of Grayson's neck bristled, and she shivered uncontrollably. "A liar."

"Yes. A liar," Corky said.

"Liar's moon," Grayson said.

"What is liar's moon?" Sebastian asked.

"Corky and a dear friend had a similar dream of my mother. In that dream, she said liar's moon but did not elaborate on when or what it was."

"In the almanac, and from what I can find so far in my book, they say a liar's moon is a full moon and has a haze around it simulating deception of sorts. So they say," Corky added.

"So someone is lying." Sebastian walked over to the window and looked out into the night. "And the moon should be full in a matter of days." She turned back into the room. "Am I correct in assuming something dreadful is about to happen?"

"Well." Grayson let out a long sigh. "You know what they say about assuming, but in this instance, I'd say it's a safe bet."

"I still can't get over the fact that this letter from Tatiana has something related to Grayson in it. How in the world could she possibly know?"

"She didn't," Sebastian said. "She told me this book was written long ago. More than two millennia." She looked down at the ring on her finger. "In a vision, she told me never to take this ring off."

Grayson stood next to her and held out her left hand. Sebastian looked at the three wedding rings on Grayson's ring finger. "My mother said the same thing to me in a vision after she died." Grayson looked at Corky. "What's going on, Corky?"

"I wish I knew. But it would appear you two are more connected than you might know. This prophecy is the key. I'm sure of it. I'll wager once I decipher it, it will tell us what you have in common and who our liar is."

"And who could these liars be?" Sebastian asked.

"Well, there are only a couple of new people in our midst." Corky looked at Grayson.

"Sister Gabriel."

"Who is she?" Sebastian asked quickly.

"And Elinora," Corky said.

"Who is she?" Sebastian asked with an edge to her voice.

Grayson was enjoying the helpless tone this vampire exhibited now. But she knew now was not the time to tell Sebastian this. "Well, let's see. Sister Gabriel is the mysterious nun who's been cloistered for over thirty years, locked away in a self-imposed prison for God, and now is the Mother Abbess of the very well-known St. Brigid's Monastery."

"Right after your mother is killed," Sebastian said.

Grayson nodded.

"And who is Elinora?" Sebastian asked.

Grayson and Corky exchanged quick glances. "She's not that easy to explain." Grayson scratched the back of her neck.

"Give it a shot," Sebastian said.

"Well, she appeared the other day. In a nutshell, she says Danu sent her to train me and get me familiar with my newfound immortal powers."

"What's so hard about that?" Sebastian asked. "I've been around for half a millennium. Seeing another immortal is not new."

"One that has a penchant for chocolate ice cream?" Corky asked.

Sebastian raised an eyebrow. "You have me there."

"There is someone else who is new," Grayson said.

"Who?" Corky asked.

Grayson looked at Sebastian, who bowed slightly.

"It would appear you have your hands full, Grayson," Sebastian said. "And what happens when the moon is full?"

"I'm not sure," Grayson said.

Corky looked out the window. "Whatever it is, it will happen soon. The moon is nearly full. I just know the prophecy has something to do with this." He turned back into the room. "Someone is lying, and it has to do with both of you. The answer is in Tatiana's letter."

Grayson looked out at the moon. "What in the hell do we have in common?" She examined the three rings on her finger. When she looked up, Sebastian was toying with the ring Tatiana had given her.

Sebastian locked gazes with Grayson. "What indeed?"

Chapter 10

Grayson felt someone watching her as she sat behind the desk. She had no idea where Sebastian had gone off to the previous night; she only hoped Sebastian would stay out of trouble. That was all Grayson needed—something else to explain to Inspector Gaffney.

Suddenly, her left palm itched, her heart rate quickened, and she felt a buzzing in her ears. These were all indicators regarding her new abilities bestowed on her from the gods. She tried to get acquainted with them and understand them; it was a slow process. Looking up from the book, she saw Sister Gabriel standing in the doorway.

"Hello, Sister. Can I help you?" Grayson scratched her palm.

The nun walked into the room. Grayson saw the frown on her face when she looked at the book on Grayson's desk. This was not the first time Grayson saw the disapproving look. She decided this time not to let it go.

"What's on your mind, Sister?" Grayson asked as Sister Gabriel sat down.

"What is your work here, Grayson? I don't mean to pry, but being the Mother Abbess now, I feel a certain responsibility. Sister Michael has told me a little of what you're doing."

Grayson closed Corky's book and sat back. "I don't know how much she told you."

"Enough to know your mother was killed and Sister Daniel has been transferred. There was also a conversation about that." Sister Gabriel motioned to the leather-bound book in front of Grayson. "Though Sister was vague on what it contains, I heard the disapproving tone in her voice. I suppose I wonder what you're doing and why. And I'm sure it's something the church would not approve of."

"We're not doing anything to hurt the church, Sister."

"I understand Sister Daniel was in league, for lack of a better word, with you and your mother. I'm truly sorry for your loss. I'm told your mother was a remarkable woman as was your grandmother, Deirdre Grayson."

Grayson said nothing as the nun slowly rubbed her hands together as if to warm them. She looked out the window at the rainy morning before she spoke again. "Do you follow their beliefs?"

"Which beliefs?" Grayson studied her as she seemed to search for the right words. Grayson laughed. "Sister, you can say anything. I won't be offended."

"Sister Michael was brief when she explained what happened to your mother and Sister Daniel being transferred."

Grayson remembered Sister Daniel had been very clever to leave the letter for Sister Michael telling her she had been transferred and could not say where. Grayson still had a hard time believing Sister Daniel was also Danu, the goddess of the Tuatha De Danann, the mythical race of Irish. Well, Grayson thought as she scratched her head, they're not entirely mythical.

"Where do you think they sent Sister Daniel?" she asked.

Grayson shrugged. "I don't know. You know the church. You go where they say with no questions."

Sister Gabriel nodded. "It just seems odd."

"Kinda like a cloistered nun being asked to be Mother Abbess of a well-known monastery."

Their gazes locked for a moment; Grayson stared into her eyes, trying to gauge this nun and her intentions.

"What's your point?" she asked softly.

"No point really. You're right, some things seem odd."

"Tell me what's in your book." Sister Gabriel completely changed the topic. "It has Corky hovering over it all night. He won't let it out of his sight."

"Legends, myths, spells, and white magic, I assume."

Sister Gabriel frowned then; Grayson saw her cheek muscle twitch. It was then she knew that Sister Gabriel was hiding something, that perhaps she had some hidden agenda. Her instincts told her not to confront the nun—for now.

"Being a Catholic, I'm sure you don't believe in such things," Grayson said, looking at Corky's book.

"Being a Catholic, I would assume you do not, as well."

Grayson looked up then. "There's more to it than that, I'm afraid."

"What more is there than God?"

Grayson chuckled ruefully. "We were talking about Catholicism. Sometimes, the lines are blurred. Before Christianity, there were gods and goddesses. There were druids and druidesses and those who had very strong religious beliefs that had nothing to do with the man-made laws of Catholicism. I'm not denouncing the church, just realizing there is more out there, for over two thousand years."

Images of Phelan Tynan flashed through her mind: the night, under the residual moon when she almost lost her life and the power that had been entrusted to her.

She looked at Sister Gabriel. "I believe in God, Sister. I also believe there are things in this world and the next that we can't explain. He knows, I'm sure, but when the other world invades this world, I get a little nervous. I'm funny that way."

Sister Gabriel smiled for a moment before growing serious once more. "Whatever you, Corky, and Neala are into, I shall pray very hard that nothing happens to you."

"Thank you, but what do you think we're into that we could be harmed?"

"Look at what happened to your mother," Sister Gabriel said in a deliberate tone. So much so, the hair on the back of Grayson's neck bristled.

"My mother was killed by some rabid dog or wolf."

Sister Gabriel hesitated. "Of course she was. You're right. As I said, I shall pray for all of you to be safe and trust in God."

"I have great faith. It's the religion I have difficulty with."

"Then I shall pray for that, as well."

Grayson chuckled and held her hands up as if in defeat. "Okay, you win. I'm grateful for any prayers you throw my way." She regarded Sister Gabriel for a moment. "You're a curious woman."

"How so?" She smiled but gave Grayson a wary look. "You're still wondering why I left a life of seclusion to come here."

"Yes, I suppose."

For a second, Grayson thought she might confide in her. However, Sister Gabriel rose. "There's nothing curious about it. The bishop summoned me and I obeyed. I suppose it was time to change and serve God in another way. Well, I will leave you to your work." She smiled and walked toward the door. "Whatever that is."

Grayson smiled. "When I find out, I'll let you know."

Before she left, Grayson noticed the disconcerting frown once again. "I hope it won't come to that."

Grayson watched as she walked down the hall. She laughed when Corky poked his head around the corner. "Come to what?" He walked into the room and sat down.

Grayson explained her conversation with Sister Gabriel. Corky listened intently as he cleaned his glasses on his sweater. "What are ya thinking?"

"I don't know. I just keep getting a creepy feeling every time I see her. There has got to be a reason for her coming here other than her reasoning of it being time to serve God in another way."

"Well, really, it does seem logical. Perhaps her life of solitude lost its appeal."

"After thirty years, wouldn't you think she was resigned to it? And why now? With all that's happening." Grayson closed Corky's book. "No. She's here for some reason, I can feel it."

"I can't think why. But you know, since I had that dream of Maeve and she said 'liar's moon,' I'm suspect of everyone. I know that sounds daft."

"Not at all. You had that dream and so did Rose. Neala didn't have it and neither did I. I have no idea what that means."

"If anything," Corky said.

Grayson had to agree. It could mean nothing at all. "None of this makes any sense."

"I disagree." Corky sat behind the desk. He leafed through the old parchment pages. "We found the prophecy that foretold you as the true descendant in this book. Perhaps we will find out what liar's moon means. I don't think it's coincidental, and I think it's all connected. Let's try the letter you translated from Tatiana once again." He took Grayson's translated paper and paced while he read.

Grayson leaned back in the chair and waited patiently.

"All right then," Corky started. "In the shadow of the crescent..." He sat on the windowsill and gazed out the window. "Shadow..."

Grayson noticed his smile then. "Okay, what?"

"In the shadow, perhaps that means after the crescent moon. Which could mean, after the residual moon and all we—well, you—went through."

"Fair enough," Grayson said quietly, not wanting to derail his train of thought.

Corky continued with the prophecy. "A mark is cloaked unseen." He stopped again. "What if this liar has a mark, perhaps like yours." He looked at Grayson, who nodded. "Cloaked unseen... It's hidden. This liar is marked, but hidden."

"Kinda like Damien and the three sixes?" Grayson asked, leaning forward. "Ya know, like the movie..."

"*The Omen*. Yes, perhaps. Though I sincerely hope we're not dealing with Satan. Phelan is bad enough."

"Do you think Tatiana is talking about Phelan?"

"Hmm. Maybe, but until we're certain, let's keep an open mind."

"Okay, continue for now. You're on a roll." Grayson sat back once again.

"Right then. The traitor's song eclipse the moon." Corky took a deep breath while he contemplated the verse. "Traitor's song..."

"Maybe whoever this is, their lying is their song so to speak."

Corky grinned and nodded. "We don't know what their lie is, but it obscures our view of the moon, metaphorically speaking... Liar's moon."

"So we're being duped and we don't know it," Grayson said.

Corky agreed. "Sadly, yes. But if we can decipher this further, we won't be in the dark for too long."

Grayson let out a rueful laugh. "Good luck with that."

Corky laughed along and glanced at the clock on the mantel. "Aren't you supposed to meet Neala for dinner?"

Grayson jumped to her feet. "Damn it." She dashed out the room, but not before turning back to Corky. "Do not decipher anything without me."

Chapter 11

"I'm sorry, Neala," Grayson said breathlessly as she slipped into a chair opposite Neala.

Neala sipped from her glass of wine. "It's all right. I had an impromptu meeting with Inspector Gaffney. I just arrived."

"Shit," Grayson said. "I hoped she was finished with the questions."

"Somehow I don't think she'll go away."

"I don't blame her. When you think about it, it's a fantastic story. Wolves in Ireland."

The server came to their table. Grayson looked at Neala's glass of wine. "I'll have a bottle of whatever she's drinking."

Neala laughed and agreed. The server placed the loaf of brown bread covered by a linen napkin on the table.

Grayson quickly dove in. "I'm starving." She took a piece of the warm bread and lathered it with butter. "Now enough talk of wolves and wizards. Let's be normal. Tell me about your life, Dr. Rourke. Do you have any brothers, sisters?"

The server came with the bottle of wine and took their dinner order of prawns and pasta. Grayson handed the server the menu and waited until he had left. "Okay, so..."

"No, I'm an only child. My mother died when I was young. I don't really remember her."

Grayson frowned. "I'm sorry. I—"

"It's all right. It was long ago. My father moved to England. He lives in Liverpool. I haven't seen him in almost a year. But he's happy and content."

"Do you miss him?" Grayson asked.

"I suppose I do. We aren't very close."

"What does he do for a living?"

"He works in the shipyards."

Grayson saw the faraway look as she drank her wine. "I'm sorry if I intruded."

Neala smiled. "You didn't. I just haven't spoke of them in a while. Now tell me what you and Corky have been up to. I'll be able to come out this weekend."

"Well, Sebastian is here."

Neala nearly dropped her fork. "Seriously? Will she be there this weekend?"

Grayson heard the hopeful tone and frowned. "I guess. Why?"

"Why?" Neala asked with a laugh. She then leaned in and whispered, "A vampire? And from what Corky said, very sexy. And you're asking me why?"

Grayson shrugged and ate her bread. "One vampire is like any other."

Neala raised an eyebrow. "And you've seen so many, Grayson MacCarthaigh?"

Grayson chuckled but said nothing.

"Now tell me what else has been happening."

"Well, Corky's reading his beloved book. And Mrs. Barry read my tea leaves."

"Tea leaves?"

They waited as the server brought their dinner. He poured both another glass of wine before leaving them.

"Wow, that looks great."

Neala placed her napkin in her lap. "I told ya. The best in Dublin."

"Don't tell me you don't know anything about the art of reading tea leaves," Grayson said between mouthfuls.

"Well, yes, but why did she want to read yours and who is she?"

Grayson laughed. "She's a good friend of my mother and grandmother." She shrugged and continued eating. "Guess she had a dream the other night and Ma was in it. In the dream, Ma said something about liar's moon."

"Liar's moon? What does that mean?" Neala asked.

"I have no idea." Grayson sat back. "Corky's trying to find it in his book, but he did find something in the almanac. Apparently, a liar's moon has a haze around it as if it's hiding or shrouding something."

"So what did Mrs. Barry find out?" Neala finished her meal, dabbing the napkin on the corner of her mouth.

Grayson noticed her intense gaze and laughed. "You look so serious. Rose Barry is a wonderful old woman who thinks she can read my future in tea leaves. All she came up with is deception, which could correspond with her dream of my mother and liar's moon. She's being protective, I suppose."

Neala was quiet for a moment as she toyed with her wineglass. "You can't blame her. You've been through a lot of pain, Grayson. I'm amazed at how the villagers love you because of your mother and your family. "

Grayson reached across and took her hand. "You and Corky have been there to help. You'll never know how much that means to me."

Neala looked down at their hands for a moment, then smiled. "I was glad to do it."

"If only I could have gotten that asshole Phelan." Grayson patted her hand and sat back.

"But you saved the stone and the power. You fulfilled your destiny," Neala said.

"Part of it anyway. I have no idea what's going to happen next."

"Life was much simpler before," Neala said thoughtfully.

"That sounds like you have a little more to say."

"Not really. But so much has happened since we've met. Everything is now upside down. Between Phelan, the ancient stone—"

"Which you have to explain."

"Which I have to explain. And your mother dying at Phelan's hand, I'm surprised you haven't chucked it all and gone back to Chicago. I'm amazed, actually. Yet since I've met you, I've seen your inner turmoil and inner strength you possess. I truly believe the ancient ones knew what they were doing when they chose you to be the true descendant—the guardian of the Tuatha De Danann's power and the protector of Ireland."

"I'm not sure about that, but one thing is sure. There's no turning back. I..." Grayson stopped when she saw Inspector Gaffney come into the restaurant with another woman.

They were laughing as they waited to be seated. Grayson caught her eye and Megan Gaffney cocked her head and nodded. Grayson nodded in return; she noticed the inspector's look at Neala. She also saw the scrutiny in her gaze, as if she were committing the scene to memory. Grayson couldn't blame her. That's exactly what she'd do given the same situation and given Grayson was still a detective.

"I suppose she's following you now," Neala said, watching Inspector Gaffney. "She's pretty."

Grayson raised an eyebrow and grinned. "Now, now, Dr. Rourke. Green does not look good on you." She then stopped grinning. "On second thought, it goes very well with your eyes."

She watched Neala as she smiled and drank her coffee. "You really are very pretty. I wish things were different. That we could have gotten to know each other first."

Neala chuckled then. "Well, you and I didn't get off to the best of starts."

Grayson smiled. "This is very true. I wasn't at all sure you weren't a murderer."

"And now you know I'm not..."

Grayson continued to smile when she heard Neala's soft voice. "I'm very happy you're not."

Neala once again drank her coffee. "That's good to know."

"You're a good woman."

Neala looked at her then. "Thank you. And it's getting late. Unless you're spending the night in Dublin, we'd best be leaving."

However, neither made a move to leave. Grayson looked across the table into Neala's eyes.

"What are ya thinking?" Neala asked.

"I'm not sure."

Neala smiled. "It's getting late. You're more than welcome to spend the night. I-I wouldn't mind at all."

"I don't feel like driving across the country."

"With all this still going on, I—"

Grayson reached over and held her hand. "Remember back in Chicago, I said we were destined to share a bed. Let that be enough for now."

Neala nodded and caressed the back of Grayson's hand. "And if you don't cut that out, I'll change my mind."

Grayson stood in Neala's living room and looked around.

"What's the matter?" Neala asked.

"Oh, nothing. It's a nice place. Nice fireplace. It's cozy."

The flat was modestly decorated mostly with Irish artifacts, paintings, and sculptures. The furniture was also somewhat on the antique side but comfortable. To Grayson, it felt like an extension of the museum. It was befitting a curator.

Neala looked around, as well. "It's getting late. I have a spare room if you like." She absently ran her fingers through her hair.

"Thanks, or if you don't want to be alone…"

"I really don't."

Grayson walked up to her and put her arm around her. "Me either."

Neala turned off the lamp and took Grayson by the hand, leading her through the darkness.

The moonlight streamed through the bedroom window. Neala seemed awkward; Grayson couldn't blame her as she watched her rummage through her dresser. "Here, I've got something you can wear."

Grayson took the clothes and headed for the bathroom. "This reminds me of when we were at my mother's back in Chicago."

Neala chuckled. "I know. Go on…"

When Grayson came back, Neala was already in bed. She tried to ignore how her heart pounded in her chest as she watched Neala before crawling into bed. "Okay?"

"Yes," Neala whispered.

Grayson shifted, trying to get comfortable.

"It's an old mattress," Neala said.

Grayson laughed softly. "Did you get this from the museum?"

"Very funny."

"It'll do. Thank you."

Grayson turned on her side to face Neala. "You know so much has happened here. You and I have never had much time to get to know each other."

"We'll have time."

"Would it be all right if I held you?"

"Yes," Neala whispered and sidled closer. She turned away from Grayson, who spooned behind her, wrapping her arm around her waist.

"Good night, Neala."

"Good night."

Grayson lightly kissed her hair. When she felt Neala relax and fall asleep, she too felt the weight of the day and closed her eyes.

The next morning, Grayson woke early; she felt restless for some reason. Dreams from the previous night caused her to have an uneasy sleep. She hated when she couldn't remember her dreams, and the night before was no exception. Neala was in her dream somewhere. She looked over at Neala, who slept peacefully. Perhaps she was the reason for her restlessness.

As she watched Neala in a serene repose, Grayson leaned over and lightly brushed the red hair from her face.

Grayson succumbed to the urge and lightly kissed her cheek.

Neala's eyes fluttered opened, offering Grayson a sleepy smile. "Good morning."

"Morning," Grayson whispered.

"How did you sleep on my ancient mattress?"

Grayson smiled. "Just fine."

Neala rolled away from Grayson and cuddled her pillow. "I'm glad."

Grayson lay on her side and couldn't help but run her fingers across the flimsy material of the tank top Neala wore. Grayson took the opportunity to gaze at her soft, white skin, running her fingers up and down her arm. Before she knew it, her left hand had found its way to the curve of Neala's hip and the waistband of the flannel pajama pants. She smiled when she heard Neala's breath hitch; her body trembled under Grayson's touch. As Grayson smiled, she caressed her hip and once again up her spine, then down to the small of her back.

Neala suddenly rolled over and laughed nervously. "You have wayward hands, Miss MacCarthaigh."

Grayson laughed along. "Sorry." She raised her left hand, examining the palm. "It's this damned birthmark. It has a mind of its own." She was a little surprised when Neala laughed and got out of bed. "I-I meant no disrespect."

"No, no. It's just I have an appointment in an hour, and if we keep this up..." She laughed again and shook her head.

"Another time?"

Neala smiled and leaned down to Grayson, gently touching her cheek. She then placed a brief kiss against her lips. "Definitely," she said. Grayson's grin spread across her face as Neala ruffled her hair, then grabbed her robe. "Now go make coffee."

As Grayson drove back to Corky, she thought of the dreams she had the night before and of the soft kiss from Neala. She smiled as she slowly licked her lips and looked forward to what might lie ahead for them. Grayson wished all that had happened was behind them so she and Neala could really explore any feelings they might have. It was so hard to be normal now, but perhaps she and Neala could find the time together. It was a bright light at the end of this convoluted tunnel in which Grayson found herself.

And speaking of which, Grayson remembered the dream she had the night before. Corky was in her dream as was Neala and for some reason Elinora. During the night, she had a vision of Elinora, telling her to go to the cliffs and wait for her that morning. Grayson figured she meant the cliffs overlooking the Atlantic, a few miles out of town. So she headed out and started to walk the few miles, hoping it would ease her uneasiness—it did not.

Thinking of the immortal, Grayson laughed and scratched the back of her head. She wanted to believe Elinora was here to help her hone her newfound powers, but there was something in the back of her mind that made her uneasy. Perhaps Elinora was the reason for her restlessness. Grayson didn't like the way this immortal got under her skin and into her mind as if she knew what Grayson was thinking, which of course she did. It unnerved and irritated her. If she were honest with herself, she'd admit Elinora captivated her. Her beauty was obvious, but the way she seemed to look right through Grayson unnerved her; it was downright intimidating. And with all this talk and dreams of a liar's moon, Grayson didn't need to feel any more daunted than she already did.

She had walked nearly the entire way to the coast. The morning was overcast and damp, and with the low fog that hovered over the ground, it didn't help her feeling of dread; she shivered and pulled the collar of her jacket up.

You think too much.

When Grayson heard Sebastian's voice in her mind, she looked up to see her standing in the road, the fog swirling around her feet. Grayson thought she looked remarkably sexy in her black leather coat. The ghoul, she thought.

I am not a ghoul. I'm a vampire.

"Where have you been?" Grayson walked up to meet her.

"I've been hanging around," Sebastian said. "And I see we're not alone."

Grayson followed her gaze to see Elinora sitting by the cliff's edge. She looked back at the sexy smirk on her vampire friend.

"Hey," Grayson said to Sebastian. "What are you staring at?"

Sebastian was indeed staring at Elinora, who was sitting in a yoga position and meditating, her eyes closed and her dark hair blowing in the wind. When Sebastian didn't respond, Grayson poked her hard on the arm. What neither vampire nor immortal expected was the force behind the poke. Sebastian reeled backward, completely caught off-guard, as she stumbled over the rock wall.

Grayson was stunned. She watched Sebastian tumble, her long coat flapping in the breeze, then looked down at her index finger. "I'll be damned. I do have it."

In a flash, Sebastian was nose to nose with Grayson, her eyes glaring and her fangs protruding. "Not amusing in the least."

"You vampires are all alike." Grayson tried not to laugh at the flustered posture. "You were staring."

Sebastian took a step back as they glanced at Elinora, who seemed oblivious. Sebastian opened her mouth.

"Oh, yes, you were," Grayson leaned in and whispered.

"I cannot believe they made you an immortal."

"Just keep your fangs to yourself," Grayson said, becoming very serious.

Sebastian grinned, exposing said fangs. "It's not good form for an immortal to show jealousy."

"I am not jealous. I'm in my protective mode."

"Ladies, please," Elinora called out, her eyes still closed. "I'm trying to find my center."

Sebastian raised a devilish eyebrow. "Perhaps I can assist?"

Grayson glared at her rakish pose. "You are one disgusting vampire. Don't make me poke you again."

"You were extremely lucky. It will not happen again."

"Grayson, I am ready," Elinora said, suddenly standing next to them. "I hope you are, as well. There is much to do." She looked at Sebastian. "Are you going to watch, vampire?"

"I thought I'd stay, perhaps I might help."

Grayson ignored her. "Okay, what's first?"

"I must evaluate you physically. You seem to be in fit condition."

Grayson sported a jaunty grin. "I try to keep fit." She ignored Sebastian, who rolled her eyes and sat on the stone wall.

"Very good. Let us begin. Prepare yourself."

What happened next was quite embarrassing for Grayson. One minute she was grinning, the next, she couldn't breathe and was staring at the sky, flat on her back.

"I said prepare yourself," Elinora said, her hands on her hips.

Grayson rolled onto her side and groaned. As she stood,

she dusted off her hands. She tried to breathe but only wheezed painfully.

"Are you all right?" Elinora asked.

Grayson waved her off. "Fine, fine. Let's go."

"This is going to be harder than I imagined. You are far too mortal and not nearly immortal enough."

Grayson glared at her. "Well, pardon me for being human."

"You cannot help it. It is not your fault. But you must use your being differently now, Grayson. Now, again."

It was the same. But at least Grayson got a glimpse of Elinora before she nearly sent her into another dimension.

As she lay on her back, staring at the sky and wheezing, Sebastian's face came into view as she bent over Grayson. "Best two out of three?" she suggested.

"If I could get up," Grayson said in a threatening whisper.

Sebastian offered her hand, which Grayson took.

Elinora shook her head. "This is going to take longer than I expected. Too human," she mumbled.

"I cannot watch the bloodshed." Sebastian started to walk away.

"Where are you going?" Grayson asked, still flexing her back.

"I want to talk to your historian and see if he can shed some light on the book."

As Sebastian walked away, Elinora said, "Good, the vampire was a distraction."

"For whom?" Grayson asked.

Elinora watched Sebastian's exit. She turned to Grayson. "For you. I sense the camaraderie between you but also a competitiveness that is not productive for you. So it is a distraction."

"Hmm. I thought maybe you thought she was attractive."

Elinora sighed. "Emotions again. They will be your downfall."

"Not in the human world, goddess."

"I am not a goddess. If I were, I would not have to be here trying to get a human to act like an immortal. You understand this is a gift, do you not?"

Grayson looked at Elinora. She was certainly attractive. Her brown hair was long and shiny, and her eyes matched that coloring.

"We will not have sexual relations."

Grayson laughed nervously. "I'm only human."

"A major point, unfortunately. I can see I need to take a different tack. Come with me."

Elinora walked back toward the cliff's edge. Grayson followed without a word. She watched as Elinora walked to the edge and closed her eyes. Grayson stood behind her, noticing how her feet were precariously close to the edge. Below was the Atlantic, a sheer drop of six hundred feet or so. When the tourist season starts, this area would be flooded with people getting a glimpse of the Cliffs of Moher, but now, they were alone.

Grayson said nothing as Elinora inched her way to the edge. She extended her arms, and it struck Grayson that she looked like the woman on the bow of the *Titanic* in the movie.

Grayson's body tensed, ready to leap and save this eccentric goddess, immortal, whatever she was, before she went over the cliff.

Elinora turned around and opened her eyes. She looked at Grayson and gave her a challenging look. "Would you save me?"

"Yes."

"Even if it meant you might die, as well?"

"I wouldn't."

"Save me?"

"I wouldn't die and neither would you."

"And how would you be so sure that would not happen?"

Grayson thought for a moment, glancing at her feet still at the edge of the cliff. The wind whipped around them, but something deep in Grayson knew. "I just know."

Elinora smiled. "The knowing."

Grayson remembered how not long ago she stood in that dark dwelling, hearing the whispers of all those who lived before her. All of them telling her of what was and what happened to bring her to this point. She remembered the voice telling her about the knowing. She remembered seeing her mother and Vic, both telling her how she must go on. It was her destiny, she was the true descendant. That all those who lived before her paved the way for this moment. God, how she missed her mother and Vic and the life she knew before all this Celtic mythology and true descendant destiny bullshit.

Elinora shook her head and walked away from the cliff. "You are a stubborn mortal, Grayson MacCarthaigh. It is not bullshit, as you put it. But you have to realize it yourself and believe it. Until then, you a mere mortal who doesn't have the strength or courage to accept the gift that has been given to her. You are a coward."

Grayson grabbed her arm as Elinora started to walk away from her. "What the fuck do you know about this? I lost my wife and my unborn child when Vic gave her life for me. I lost my mother, who gave her life for me." She grabbed Elinora by the shoulders. "I don't want this, do you understand me? I want my fucking life back." She shook Elinora and continued. "And I'm not a coward. So fuck you!"

Elinora, with lightning quickness, pushed Grayson's hands off her shoulders and made an offensive move to strike Grayson, who with equal quickness, fended off not one but two, three, and four blows.

Without Grayson knowing it, Elinora had backed her up to the cliff's edge. For each attack Elinora started, Grayson defended herself. Grayson was not thinking; she was reacting to Elinora and aware of how her heart pounded in her chest, how her muscles and entire body seemed on fire and liquid at the same time, as if she had no body mass at all. Everything was reeling in her mind, but she continued to fend off each blow. Elinora sent a sweeping kick toward Grayson, who sidestepped and blocked it with her forearm. Again and again, they sparred at the cliff's edge.

Finally, Elinora backed off and grinned. Grayson felt like her heart would explode; sweat poured off her body as she stood, feeling the sweat drip into her eyes. Suddenly, she felt her legs shaking with fatigue and fell on all fours, gulping for air.

Elinora reached down and grabbed a handful of Grayson's wet hair, roughly pulling her head back. Grayson swallowed, still trying to catch her breath as she looked up; she didn't like this vulnerable position, but she was too exhausted to fight. She looked into Elinora's deep brown eyes and tried to breathe.

"You are not a coward. Though you have known much pain and loss, you will know more, I am afraid. You are of noble birth. I see the pain, the sorrow, and the joy you have known in life. For some reason, the gods and goddesses have allowed you to keep your mortality. I do not know why, but it is not for me or you to ask. All will be revealed to you in time. But for now, you have done well."

Grayson blinked the sweat out of her eyes. "Can you let me up now?"

Elinora raised an eyebrow; she still had hold of Grayson's hair. "I do not keep you on your knees." She knelt in front of Grayson, who sat back on her heels, her hands resting on her thighs, which were still burning. Elinora smiled. "You are limited by one thing. Yourself."

Grayson ran her fingers through her wet hair. "I know I need to accept all that has happened. It's just so much so fast." She stopped and shrugged. "I'm not feeling sorry for myself."

"No one would blame you if you did. The unfortunate situation for you is you have no time for self-doubt or pity. And for that I am sorry." Grayson looked deep into Elinora's eyes as she leaned forward. "You must go on."

Grayson nodded and grinned. "So I did good?"

"Yes, for a mortal." She stood and offered her hand, which Grayson took.

Grayson groaned painfully and flexed her shoulder.

"You are injured?"

"No," Grayson said and laughed. "I just have never had a workout that intense."

"Stand still." Elinora rubbed her hands together. "Take off your sweater."

Grayson hesitated but did as she was told.

"Now unbutton your shirt." Elinora was still rubbing her palms together.

Grayson looked around but complied. She gasped when

Elinora stuck her hand in her shirt and rubbed her shoulder; her hand felt red hot on her skin.

Grayson winced. "Hey, for chrissakes!" She writhed beneath Elinora's healing hands.

"Do not be such a mortal," Elinora said and continued.

Suddenly, the pain was gone and her shoulder tingled. Elinora pulled her hand away. "There is no more pain."

"Thanks, Mr. Miyagi." Grayson flexed her shoulder and laughed at the confused look from Elinora. "It's from a movie…" She saw the befuddled look and waved her off. "Skip it."

"This is sufficient for now. You have done more than I expected. Perhaps your human emotions will not be such a hindrance." She stopped and put her hand on Grayson's arm. "But make no mistake, you must try and think more like an immortal for your powers to work for you. You were angry when we fought, and you did well, but you must learn and focus your anger and make it work for you. Do you understand?"

"Yeah, I get it. It's just so foreign." Grayson shrugged. "Thanks for helping me."

Elinora cocked her head. "I see an unassuming charm in you. Not the arrogance of the vampire."

Grayson laughed openly. "Well, you know vampires."

"Yes. Although I have not encountered that many in my travels through the centuries, I find them to be very arrogant immortals. It comes from not having to ask for anything. They take whatever they want."

"You sound as though you speak from experience. What has your life been like? Can we sit?" Grayson rubbed the back of her thigh.

"Are you still in pain?" Elinora reached around to touch Grayson.

Grayson scooted out of the way and felt the color rush to her face. "No, no. I'm fine."

For a moment, Elinora seemed confused, then she nodded. "I see. You are attracted to me and are having sexual thoughts."

"Well, you are beautiful," Grayson said, feeling very uncomfortable and not from the pain in her ass. She sat on the stone wall and let out a sigh of relief.

Elinora stood in front of her. "Yes, you are of noble birth. The vampire would be naked by now."

"Well, don't hold that against her." Grayson gingerly sat on the wall. "Where are you from, Elinora?"

Elinora smiled. "And why do you want to know?"

"Why not?" Grayson countered with a shrug.

"It is not a good idea to become familiar with mortals."

"But I'm not just a mortal."

"True, but right now you are more mortal than immortal, and that is a dangerous thing."

"Why?" Grayson picked up a stone and absently threw it down the dirt path.

"You mortals are far too emotional. But what I find odd is the vampire."

"This whole thing is odd," Grayson said. "But why do you find Sebastian odd?"

"For an immortal and the undead, she exhibits human qualities. This is completely reverse behavior from their kind."

"Honestly, I have never come across one, and I thought there was no such thing. Only in the movies and books."

"Oh, there is a whole new dimension you do not even know exists." Elinora waved her hand around. "You must be prepared to believe that which will not come easy to you."

Those words made Grayson stop and think; she heard them before. When she realized, she smiled. "Sister Daniel said those words to me as a young girl when I left Ireland for America."

Elinora nodded in agreement. "In the Celtic universe, she is the mother of us all. Before Brigid, Morrighan, Bran, and the rest known only as mythology, Danu was the first."

"I had no idea Sister Daniel was a goddess all that time."

"You were chosen long, long ago, long before all of them. Sister Daniel was here to see the prophecy unfold. Even she was not sure about your destiny."

Grayson took a deep breath, still trying to absorb all of this. "Will there be more? I mean prophecies?"

"Your historian has the key in the book that was entrusted to him. You must protect him, as well. He has no idea how valuable he is to you and to Ireland."

"Was he chosen, as well?"

"No, Corky is a true believer as was his father and throughout his lineage. We may all have our destiny, but your historian has made his own destiny."

"That's what I mean. Corky loves this shit and lives for it. Why not have him be the true descendant?"

"It is not a popularity contest."

"And what about Neala? You haven't met her yet, but—"

"She's the curator of the National Museum in Dublin. When you met her, you considered her a suspect in a murder case in which you were working. You believe it is all related to this, and she protected the stone, like your mother."

"What else do you know?"

Elinora stopped walking and faced Grayson. "You thought she was a murderer at first."

"Well, yes and no. I thought she knew something about the murders. Turned out she did, but she wasn't the bad guy," Grayson said with a laugh.

When Elinora did not laugh, Grayson said, "It was a joke. Neala's a good guy. Phelan's the bad guy."

Elinora continued to walk down the path. "And you like Neala."

"Well, yeah. She's been through it all with me and Corky. I'm very fond of both of them." Grayson smiled when she thought of Neala; it was true she was very fond of her.

"Do I sense more with this Neala?" Elinora asked.

Grayson did not respond right away. It was a good question. "I'm not sure. It's been a long time for me. And since Vic's death, there's really been no one special in my life. Now enough about me. Nothing more until you divulge a little of yourself. How did you become immortal?"

Elinora was silent for some time. Grayson felt uneasy in the silence. "I'm sorry," she whispered.

Elinora shot a curious look her way. "Why? You did nothing."

"You didn't answer. I thought I had overstepped…"

"It is of no consequence how I came to be immortal. You must prepare yourself and work on your mind and not so much on your emotions."

Grayson laughed, shaking her head as they continued to walk side by side.

"Humor?"

"No. I was just thinking. Back in Chicago, I was told I was too logical and used my mind too much and not enough of my heart. It's all different now."

"Not completely different. As I've said, there's some reason why they allowed you to keep your mortality. You just have to work harder to embrace your powers. Perhaps this is part of your destiny, as well. All—"

"I know. I know. All will be revealed. I'll be old and gray before that happens."

Chapter 12

"Historian, good morning."

Corky spilled his coffee down the front of his sweater when he heard Sebastian's voice. He jumped up and wiped his sweater. "Good Lord, you scared the life out of me."

Sebastian walked into the room and grinned. "So sorry."

Corky looked up then. "Why don't I believe you? Where's Grayson?"

"Sparring with her immortal. I couldn't bear it any further. You might want to call the hospital and reserve a room."

Corky laughed as he mopped up the mess. "For a vampire, you have a very good sense of humor. Now I take it you're here to continue with the letter from Tatiana."

"Yes. I want to get to the bottom of this. It seems Grayson and I are connected on some odd level. And it would appear that connection will be further explained in the book Tatiana left, if we ever get to that point."

"I agree with ya." Corky sat back down. He put on his glasses and opened the letter once again. "It's a good thing Grayson understands this ancient dialect. Almost as if…"

"She was meant to see this letter," Sebastian said absently.

Corky agreed. "Grayson's mother used to say everything and everyone was connected."

Sebastian stood in front of the desk. "Tatiana said the same thing. She said this letter and the book will show me what we were before the dawn and how much we are like the mortals. Though I don't see what it has to do with Grayson."

"I don't either," Corky said with glee. "That's the fun of it."

Sebastian watched Corky with a wary eye. "You enjoy this, don't you?"

Corky laughed. "Grayson asks the same thing. And yes, I do." He took off his glasses and sat back. "There is so much in this universe that cannot be explained. And those who offer an explanation are dismissed as eccentric or just plain crazy. No one wants to believe the fantastic. It disrupts their nice, neat, orderly lives." He looked at Sebastian and winked. "I am neither neat nor orderly." He put on his glasses and continued, "But I am nice."

"And I have a feeling you'll find out what this letter means."

"I hope so. Now let's get back to this…"

They looked up when Grayson walked into the room. "Hi, kids."

"You don't look like you need a hospital," Corky said, hiding his grin.

"It was a close call." Grayson rubbed the back of her thigh.

Sebastian looked behind Grayson. "Everything all right back there?"

"I was going to ask the same thing."

Grayson whirled around to see Neala standing in the doorway, her arms folded across her chest. She then saw Sebastian and frowned slightly.

"Neala," Grayson said. "This is Sebastian." She watched Sebastian carefully.

Sebastian smiled and offered her hand to Neala, who walked into the room and took the offering. "It's a pleasure, Neala. Grayson has talked a great deal about you. I feel as though I know you."

Grayson could see Neala searching Sebastian's face; she saw the blush rise from her neck to her face.

Down, Romeo. Grayson knew, by the slightest smirk on Sebastian's face, she heard Grayson's thought.

"Well, I've heard a great deal about you. Corky is wildly impressed," Neala said, still holding Sebastian's hand. "I will admit this is strange, but with all that has happened in the past few months, I suppose nothing is normal."

"Whatever normal is," Sebastian said with a grin.

Grayson knew she purposely flashed her canines; she nearly laughed at Neala's reaction.

"You'll have to do better than that, Sebastian," Neala said.

Sebastian raised an eyebrow. "Is that a request?"

"Okay," Grayson said quickly and stepped in. "Let's get this letter from Tatiana translated. Neala, can you stay?"

Neala tore her gaze from Sebastian. "Yes, for a little while, then I need to get back. I have yet another board meeting with the directors of the museum. So what have ya found out?"

Corky rubbed his hands together. "It appears that Tatiana left Sebastian a letter that only Grayson could decipher. I couldn't. It's a prophecy of sorts, the same as the one for the residual moon for Grayson." He took the translation and handed it to Neala.

For some reason, Grayson noticed how Sebastian watched Neala while she read. Grayson tried to gauge what was on Sebastian's mind; she couldn't read it at the moment, but she saw what looked like doubt or perhaps a skeptical glance. It confused Grayson as she looked from the sullen vampire back to Neala, who was examining the translated letter.

"What did you figure out so far?" Neala asked.

"Well," Corky said, scratching his red head. "I've been thinking as I've read this. I believe that it makes a little more sense to me if you put the first two lines together, then the last two. Now listen to this." He stopped and cleared his throat before continuing. "In the shadow of the crescent, a mark is cloaked unseen." He took of his glasses. "We figure the crescent has to do with the residual moon from Grayson's prophecy, and the 'mark is cloaked unseen' more than likely means something or someone is hidden, which of course we haven't figured out yet."

Neala concentrated on the paper in her hand; she nodded in agreement but said nothing.

"And the last two lines." Corky put on his glasses. "The traitor's song eclipse the moon, Blackheart betrays the queen. We've gotten the first line of this. We think whoever is betraying the queen is hidden, or at least we don't know who it is. The traitor's song we think is whatever lie is being told."

"Hmm. What does this have to do with Grayson?" Neala asked.

"The reference to a crescent and the moon. And the mention

of a traitor's song we think has to be connected to my dream and Rose Barry's dream of Maeve saying 'liar's moon.'"

Again, Neala nodded. "But how can, I'm sorry, I forgot her name…" She looked at Sebastian.

"Tatiana. You were about to say, how can she know about Grayson and her crescent or residual moon?"

"Yes, I was."

"I don't know," Grayson said. "But for some reason, Tatiana told Sebastian we mortals were somehow connected with the vampires. How I can't imagine."

"Maybe we're going about this the wrong way," Neala interjected. "This letter is from Tatiana. Shouldn't we be thinking of Sebastian's world, not Grayson's?"

"You would think so." Grayson laughed softly. "But with all that has happened, who really knows? We could indeed be deciphering this all wrong. How would we ever know?"

Suddenly, Grayson was filled with doubt. An uneasy, almost queasy feeling swept through her gut. This usually told Grayson something was wrong, out of place, but that was back in Chicago when she was a detective and someone was lying to her. Again, the sick feeling fluttered in her belly. She looked up to see Sebastian watching her. Grayson knew she was reading her mind.

Mendacity is all around you, Grayson. Can you feel it?

Yes.

"How indeed," Sebastian said, looking at Neala.

Grayson caught the look again from Sebastian. Corky let out a deep sigh and tossed his glasses down on the desk. "Neala could be right. We could be going about this the wrong way."

"Let's not get too down here. Something tells me we're on the right track." Grayson put her hand on his shoulder and gave it a reassuring tug.

"Right then," he said firmly. "If we're translating this correctly, then Tatiana somehow knows about Grayson. How, we don't know. Perhaps as we continue with her letter, we'll see a clearer connection."

Neala glanced at her watch. "Saints above, I'll be late if I don't leave now. I wish I could stay." She gathered her coat. "I'll be back over the weekend. Keep at it, and let me know if you figure out anything else."

"Sounds good," Grayson said, and to her surprise, Neala walked over and kissed her cheek.

She turned to Sebastian, who leaned in. Neala smiled and offered her hand once again. "It was nice to meet you, Sebastian. I'm sure we'll meet again."

"I'm sure we will," Sebastian said.

"Call me later, Grayson," Neala said over her shoulder as she walked out of the library.

"I'll walk you to your car," Corky said and followed Neala.

Grayson stared at Sebastian, who was scowling as she watched Neala leave. Suddenly, Grayson didn't like the look on Sebastian's face. It was far too serious. "What's the matter?"

When Sebastian didn't answer, Grayson pulled on her arm. Sebastian looked at Grayson, then down to her hand on her arm. Grayson would not be intimidated. She held on to her arm. "What's the matter with you?"

"You can let go of me now," Sebastian said.

Grayson saw the anger in her eyes and didn't let go. "Look. I don't know what life is like as a vampire, and I'm sure you've had your share of women, but don't get any ideas about Neala."

In a flash that left Grayson pinned to the wall, Sebastian stood nose to nose with Grayson. "Don't test me. I'll take whomever I choose, whenever I choose."

"I'll kill you first."

"You may try."

The anger that stirred deep in Grayson was palpable. With all her might, she let out a low growl and pushed against Sebastian. She was shocked when Sebastian flew across the room and smashed into the far wall.

For an instant, Grayson saw a stunned look; the dark scowl soon spread across Sebastian's face. "Very good," Sebastian said.

"What the hell is going on?" Corky called out. "If you two don't stop this pissing contest."

Grayson stared at Sebastian, whose eyes were dark and her fangs exposed.

"Grayson, stop this," Corky nearly yelled.

Grayson's eye twitched as she watched Sebastian. Both were breathing like bulls. "Just a friendly discussion, Cork."

"Grayson is afraid I'm going to bite Neala." Sebastian nonchalantly brushed off the sleeves of her coat.

"Damn you," Grayson said.

"Is that all?" Corky said. "Sorry, Sebastian. Grayson has first dibs."

Grayson shot Corky an angry glare. When Corky grinned, then started chuckling, Grayson felt the color rush to her face. She looked back at Sebastian. "I-I'm sorry. I…"

Sebastian took a step back. "You're not going to hug me, are you?"

"All right, enough clowning around." Corky pushed up his sleeves. He sat behind the desk and put on his glasses. "Now let's get back to this letter before you kill each other."

Chapter 13

The rain that pelted the window made the outside world seem distorted, as if Kathleen were peering through a kaleidoscope. When the car pulled into the museum parking lot, she sighed heavily. She was sure Dr. Rourke would not be looking forward to this meeting. As she looked at the clock on the wall, she realized Dr. Rourke was running late and Kathleen couldn't blame her. She had rushed to her office, waving a hello to Kathleen.

She knocked on Dr. Rourke's office before opening the door. "Mr. Bradley just pulled up."

"Yes, Kathleen." Neala turned her chair back to her desk and nodded. "I saw him."

"Dr. Norman is to see him first, I'm told." Kathleen walked into Neala's office and sat in the leather chair by the desk. "What will you tell him?"

Neala sighed with a shrug. "The truth. Mr. Tynan took the stone as a safety precaution. He told me he had heard it was going to be stolen. I suppose, given the amount of money he has, he had a right to decide."

Kathleen couldn't hide the doubtful frown.

"This is what Mr. Tynan told me, Kathleen."

Kathleen sat forward. "Then why not bring it back by now?"

"I don't know. But I'm sure he has a good reason." Neala angrily picked up a pen and tapped it against her fingers. She glanced at Kathleen. "What else is on your mind?"

"What about the American policewoman that was here the day Mr. Tynan stole, took the stone? Perhaps she can..." She hesitated before continuing, "…persuade Mr. Tynan to return the stone."

Neala rubbed her temples. "This is for the museum officials to decide. I'm sure they want to keep this as quiet as possible. I know I do."

"But…"

"Kathleen, please. Enough. It's out of my hands," Neala said. "And yours. So let's just go on about our business and let Mr. Bradley and Dr. Norman take care of this."

Kathleen nodded and sat back. "Well, how about some lunch?"

Neala smiled and shook her head. "No, thanks. You go on ahead. As a matter of fact, I'll be tied up all afternoon with this. Why don't you just take the rest of the day?"

"Are you sure?"

Neala laughed at her incredulous tone. "Quite. You've worked hard and you could use the time. Go on now before I change my mind."

"Thanks, Dr. Rourke. Have a good weekend."

"You too. We'll do it all again on Monday."

Kathleen ran to her desk and grabbed her coat.

"You must be hungry," Michael Dornan said, looking up from the file in his hand.

"I have the rest of the day off." She slipped into her coat and picked up her purse. "What are you looking at?" She motioned to the file.

"Oh, nothin'. Just a file on Mr. Tynan," he said absently and leafed through the pages.

"Why are you looking at his file?" Kathleen buttoned her coat. "Tell me."

Michael scratched his chin before answering. "It just doesn't make sense, Kath. Why take the stone? Why not just get more security around it? God knows he can afford it."

"What are ya thinking?" Kathleen came around her desk and took the file out of his hand and leafed through it. "There isn't much here."

"That's what worries me."

Kathleen looked up. "If you don't start tellin' me what you're thinkin', Mick Dornan—"

"Okay, okay." Michael ran his fingers through his hair and looked out at the rainy day. "We both know Dr. Rourke, right?"

Kathleen stood behind him. "Right."

"She's above board and honest."

"Right."

Michael turned around then and pointed to the file. "Then why isn't there more on him being someone with such power and money? Why wouldn't she have more information about him? Look at the file. It's barely the basics on the guy. He's giving over a million euros and we know nothing about him."

"What are ya saying? That Dr. Rourke—"

"No..." he said angrily. "Maybe she's been duped by this guy..."

"Should we go to the police?"

"God, I don't know. Maybe I'm making all this up. I just have a feeling something is terribly wrong here."

Kathleen looked at the folder once again. There were just a few pages. Michael was right; it was basic information. She had never seen the file, never thought it was necessary.

"I see that look in your eye. You're about to do something, and you're scarin' me."

Kathleen took a deep breath and shoved the file in the top of her coat. "I think I know someone who might be able to help."

"Where are you goin'?"

Kathleen smiled and dashed past him. She called over her shoulder, "Don't worry, I'll be discreet. Have a good weekend."

As she ran to the door, she bumped into Neala. Both women let out a small screech.

"Good heavens, Kathleen. Ya gave me a fright." She laughed and held on to Kathleen's elbow. "I know I gave ya the day off, girl, but don't kill anyone." She let go and walked away. "Have a good weekend."

Kathleen laughed and scooted out of her way. "Sorry, Dr. Rourke."

She ran to her car in the back parking lot as the rain soaked her. As she got behind the wheel, she took the file out of her coat and set it on the seat next to her. The windshield wipers sprang to life as she started the car. Just as she put it in gear, she looked through the windshield. There were two people standing far off, out of the parking area, and near the alley.

Through the rain and the wipers, she squinted, trying to get a look. It was odd to see them standing in the rain. One was obviously a man. He was tall, that was all Kathleen could see. The other, she couldn't make out, could have been a woman. Her heart stopped when both turned and looked directly at her. With her paranoia in high gear, she quickly drove out of the parking lot and onto O'Connell Street. Her mouth was bone dry as she shifted gears and glanced in her rear-view mirror. Heading out of Dublin, she took the northwest road.

As she neared the small town of Dungarin, she remembered Neala talking about the American's birthplace. When she arrived in Dungarin, she stopped by the tavern, not exactly sure why. She rolled down her window; luckily, the rain had stopped.

"Excuse me," she called out. Two men and a woman turned to her. "Do you know Grayson MacCarthaigh?"

The old woman peered into the window. "And who might you be?"

"My name is Kathleen Moore, I work with Dr. Rourke. I was wondering if you knew where she lived."

"I do."

Kathleen waited, then hung her head. "Can you tell me where?"

"Take this road, about a mile out of town. It's the only thatched cottage."

"Thank you." Kathleen started to roll up her window.

"She's not there now."

Kathleen stopped and looked to the heavens. "Can you tell me where she is? No, let me rephrase that. Would you please tell me?"

"She's with the historian."

"Tim Kerrigan?" Kathleen asked. The old woman nodded. "Fine, I know where Tim lives. Thank you."

It was later in the afternoon when she drove through County Clare. She took the coastal road north and headed for Tim Kerrigan's. She hoped Grayson MacCarthaigh could help shed some light on Phelan Tynan.

Chapter 14

With her head against the cushion, Grayson stared at the ceiling while Corky looked over her translation. Sebastian sat on the windowsill, looking out at the gray day.

"Did you take your serum?" Grayson asked.

"Yes, Mother. How else could I be sitting here in the middle of the day?" Sebastian countered. She looked at Corky who was once again hovering over the book. "So tell us what we know."

"Well," Corky said. "We have a traitor, or liar, who is marked, perhaps the same way as you, Grayson. This person is more than likely someone we know, and to put it bluntly, right now we're being duped."

"What about the blackheart betrays the queen?" Grayson asked, still staring at the ceiling.

"I would have to say the blackheart is our liar. And the queen? I don't know. But look at this next stanza. Let me read it." Corky looked over the translation and continued. "One emerges from the night, at the behest of ancient call. A star falls from a distant realm, uniting and revealing all."

Grayson turned her head and looked at Sebastian, who shrugged.

"Okay, keep an open mind here, both of you," Corky said. "One emerges from the night, at the behest of ancient call. I think that's you, Sebastian, emerging from the night. And the ancient call might be Tatiana. She gave you the book, and this letter knowing you had to come here to have it translated."

Grayson sat up and turned around to Corky. "That sounds plausible."

"It does indeed." Sebastian stood by the desk. "Go on."

Corky adjusted his glasses. Grayson could see he was trying to contain his excitement. She walked over and stood next to Sebastian.

"Right then. A star falls from a distant realm, uniting and revealing all." He looked up, waiting for a response. "Don't ya see?"

"No," Sebastian and Grayson said simultaneously.

"Oh, for godsake, you're immortals." Corky groaned and took off his glasses. "The star from a distant realm. Elinora. And what did she say to you, Grayson? All will be revealed."

"You're right," Grayson said in awe. "I'll be damned. So we can eliminate Elinora from our list of liars?"

Corky absently pulled at his eyebrow. "I wouldn't do that too fast."

"She could be the one who reveals our liar by being the liar," Sebastian said.

Corky agreed. Grayson groaned deeply. "So we're back to square one."

"At least we have something more to go on. I believe I'm right on this, though."

This time, Grayson agreed. "If you say it's so, then I believe it." She glanced at Sebastian, who had a very doubtful look. "What's the matter with you?"

"Do you remember when I told you someone is lying and asked if you felt it? You said yes."

"Right. I still do. What's your point?" Grayson asked.

"I find it curious that I cannot read any thoughts from Elinora. I get no read from her at all."

"She's immortal," Corky reminded her. "And she's been around for quite some time. Perhaps she's good at concealing her thoughts."

Sebastian was hesitant to agree. "Perhaps."

For some reason, Grayson agreed with Sebastian, which she was not willing to openly admit. She turned bright red when Sebastian quickly looked at her and grinned. "You can admit it, Grayson."

"Shut up," Grayson said. "And quit reading my—"

125

"Ladies, please," Corky begged.

Several sharp raps at the door had Corky jumping up to answer it. "Liam."

"Corky, is Grayson here?"

Corky stepped back as Liam quickly entered, taking off his cap. "You must come quick."

Grayson heard the urgent tone; he seemed petrified. "What's wrong?"

"I-I found something, someone. I left Dolan with her. I... Come quick, please."

By the way Corky was breathing, Grayson figured they should have used the car, but she had no idea what Liam was talking about. They all took off in a mad dash after him. It was then Grayson saw it on the side of the road—a car with the driver's door opened. She noticed Dolan standing by, frantically looking around. She also noticed Sebastian was nowhere in sight.

"What's happened?" Grayson asked, taking a quick assessment of the area: no one in the car, the motor stopped, but the keys still in the ignition, a purse on the floor of the passenger side.

"Over there." Dolan pointed away from the road, toward the oak trees that lined it.

She saw Sebastian then, looking grim, but then she always looked grim. She stood by a tree, looking at the ground.

"Who is that?" both men asked as they looked at Sebastian.

"A friend," Grayson said over her shoulder.

She saw the thick trail of blood from the side of the road through the grass and followed it to where Sebastian stood.

"This is not pleasant." Sebastian motioned to the ground.

Grayson sucked in some air when she saw the woman lying on the ground. As far as she could tell, her throat had been ripped out. Images of her mother lying in the path that night flashed through Grayson's mind. She looked up at Sebastian. "Your handiwork?"

Sebastian's anger was evident. Grayson saw the clenched fists and regretted her words. "If it were, there would not be this mess," she said in a dark voice. Grayson thought she heard a trace of sadness, as well.

"That's Kathleen Moore," Corky said; he then looked away. "Neala's assistant."

"Are you sure?" Grayson asked.

Corky just nodded as he now stared at Kathleen's body.

Grayson looked back at Liam. "Tell me exactly what happened."

Liam took a deep breath before starting. "Dolan and me were comin' back from town when we saw the car. Then the blood."

"Did you touch anything?" Grayson studied the surrounding area. All the concentration of blood was right here, except for the gruesome trail.

"Nothing."

"You sure?"

Both men nodded.

"Why did you come to me instead of the police?" Grayson asked.

Liam glanced at Dolan. "Because we know the way of it, Grayson."

Corky, Grayson, and Sebastian shared curious glances. "What do you mean?" Corky asked.

"We know what happened to your mother. God rest her," Liam said. "We remember your grandmother, as well. When the villagers had a curious problem, we'd always go to Deirdre first. It was just the way of it. So now with you here…"

Grayson wasn't sure what he meant, but it appeared Corky did. He nodded in agreement but said nothing.

"Well, we're going to have to call the police. Damn it," Grayson said.

"I'll make the call." Liam motioned for Dolan to follow. "We'll wait by the car."

"Mind where you walk," Grayson called after them.

Corky waited until the men were back by the car. "Are you thinking it was Phelan?"

"Who else could it be?" Grayson angrily ran her fingers through her hair. "Fuck."

"I take it it's your shape-shifted friend," Sebastian said.

Grayson nodded. "Corky, you'd better get in touch with Neala and let her know. It'll take her a while to get here from Dublin."

"Why do you think he killed her, Grayson?" Sebastian asked as Corky pulled out his cell phone.

"I have no idea. What was she doing out here?" Grayson looked back at the car. "Why do it that way, though?" she asked absently.

"What do you mean?"

"Her car. There was no blood. No signs of a struggle."

"So?"

"How did he stop her?" Grayson asked, then quickly went back to the car.

She looked at the road from the back of the car. She looked inside the car once again. Sebastian and Corky said nothing as she walked around the area. "No blood around the car at all. The keys are still in the ignition, but the car was turned off." Grayson looked behind the car. "If she came upon Phelan in his wolf state, she would have come to a screeching halt, I would think."

"Your point?" Sebastian asked.

"No tire or skid marks." Grayson absently scratched at her brow. "Now why would Kathleen just stop, turn off the car, and get out, but leave the keys in the ignition and her purse on the seat? Why would—"

Dolan and Liam called to her as they came back. "They said not to touch anything. They'll be here shortly along with an Inspector Gaffney."

Grayson hung her head. "Shit." She was not looking forward to this.

"Hmm," Inspector Gaffney said as she crouched near Kathleen's body. She looked up. "Another wolf?"

Grayson stood outside the crime scene the police had taped off. Inspector Gaffney did not wait for an answer. She snapped off the rubber gloves, handing them to the forensics officer.

"I'm assuming you didn't touch anything," she said.

"No, we didn't."

"And those two villagers found the car and the victim."

"Yes, ma'am."

"Have any idea what she was doing out here?" she asked as she looked around the area.

"No, I don't."

"And you say she was Dr. Rourke's assistant at the museum..." she said absently, checking her notes.

"Yes, she was." Grayson fought the anxious feeling that swept through her. For the first time in her life, she understood how the bad guys felt—and she wasn't even one of them.

Inspector Gaffney looked at Sebastian. "And you are?"

"A friend of Grayson's."

"And a name?" Inspector Gaffney asked.

"Oh, pardon me. Dr. Sebastian."

Inspector Gaffney nodded. Grayson hoped she would not pursue any more questions.

"A doctor of what?"

No such luck.

"Hematology," Sebastian said.

Grayson silently begged Sebastian: *Knock it off.*

She's an infuriating mortal. It's far too late, my friend. Sebastian smiled slightly, never losing eye contact with the inspector.

"Well, all this blood should be right up your alley," Inspector Gaffney offered.

"One would think," Sebastian agreed emphatically.

Grayson closed her eyes and counted to ten in Gaelic.

"Ms. MacCarthaigh," Inspector Gaffney said. "What is your take on this?"

Grayson shrugged. "I don't know. I wouldn't want to speculate. And I know what you must be thinking. It's coincidental this is like my mother's death."

"I've learned long ago that nothing is a coincidence. As I'm sure you agree, given your years of being a detective in Chicago." Inspector Gaffney looked at her notes. "Which you left abruptly."

Grayson felt her anger rising as she stared back into the cool blue eyes. "To come here to take care of family business."

Ancient family business, you mean.

Grayson vaguely heard Sebastian in her mind while she continued to stare into Inspector Gaffney's eyes. She found it difficult to look away, which irritated her, and wondered if the inspector had the same difficulty. Given the fact Inspector Gaffney was still looking at her, Grayson could only surmise. She was also keenly aware of Sebastian's intense scrutiny.

She's quite fetching, for a mortal.

"Will you shut up?" Grayson said to Sebastian, who raised an eyebrow and looked at the inspector.

Inspector Gaffney gave Grayson and Sebastian a cautious look but said nothing.

"Look, Inspector, I'm not sure what you're getting at, but my previous line of work means nothing here."

"There's no reason to be upset."

"Who's upset? I'm not upset." Grayson stopped and rubbed her forehead.

Inspector Gaffney raised an eyebrow. "I can see that. Well then, all right. I'll be in touch if I need anything more. If you see any stray wolves, you let me know." She nodded to Sebastian, who bowed slightly as she walked away.

"She's rather attractive," Sebastian said. "I wonder what she looks like under that trench coat. I would assume she would be very fit and—"

"Will you shut up?" Grayson said loudly. "Christ, you're annoying. This is serious, you undead vampire."

"That's redundant. A vampire—"

"I can't tell you how much I hate your guts right now." Grayson grumbled and walked away. She glanced back and Sebastian was gone. "Good."

Grayson lingered for a few minutes, trying to piece this mess together. Damn it, she thought, what was Kathleen doing out here? Phelan had to see her; she must have had something, some information Phelan did not want known. As she walked back to Corky's, Inspector Gaffney was nowhere in sight. Grayson took the opportunity and stood by the area on the road where they had found Kathleen's abandoned car. She walked into the grassy area where the heaviest concentration of blood was found.

"This is where you killed her," Grayson said, then followed the trail of blood. "Then you dragged her off the road and left her by the tree." She stood by that tree and crouched down. "Why, Phelan? Why kill her? What did she know?"

Kathleen had left the keys in the ignition and her purse on the floor; perhaps it slid off when she stopped the car. There was no blood anywhere near the car. "She saw you, stopped, and got out. That's why there's no blood by the car. She came to you, and you morphed and ripped her throat out."

"Morbid curiosity?" Grayson whirled around to see Inspector Gaffney standing behind her. She swiped her dark wind-blown hair away from her face. "Once a detective?" She almost smiled— almost.

"Something like that," Grayson said, feeling uneasy around this woman. "I thought you left."

"I was about to when headquarters called. I'm staying in town for this." She motioned to their surroundings. "Apparently, this is one wolf or rabid dog bite too many for Dublin. So I'm relegated to the country until this is solved."

"And you don't like the country?"

"I have nothing against it. I'm just a Dubliner," she said. "I detect a slight brogue. Were you born here?"

"Don't tell me you didn't find that out?" Grayson heard the sarcasm in her own voice.

Inspector Gaffney heard it, as well. "I suppose I could have." She pulled the collar of her coat around her neck. "I'm off duty, Ms. MacCarthaigh. Can I buy you a drink?"

Caught completely off-guard, Grayson nodded. "Sure."

This was so not a good idea.

Grayson brought two pints of Guinness to their table, situated under the window of the pub. They were secluded for the most part; Grayson wasn't sure if that was a good idea or not.

"Thanks, but I said I'd buy you the drink."

"You can get the next round," Grayson said, sitting opposite her.

"Sláinte." She raised her glass. Grayson did the same. "Now tell me why you were at the crime scene." She took a drink.

Grayson hesitated, then took a very long drink from the pint. "As you said. Morbid curiosity."

The inspector smiled slightly and nodded. She leaned in. "Ya want to know what I'm thinkin'?"

"Not really." Grayson took another drink.

Inspector Gaffney went on as if she didn't hear Grayson. "I think you know a little more than you either let on or than you realize. You're a detective, and I can't imagine you think these killings aren't related."

"You're like a dog with a bone."

"As you would be, I'm thinking."

It was this truth that irritated Grayson. Actually, she would be more insistent than Inspector Gaffney of the sparkling blue eyes. At any rate, Inspector Gaffney was not going to give up, and Grayson would try to keep ahead of her and anticipate her moves. However, in the end, Grayson knew she would run out of time. And if she didn't stop nosing around, the attractive inspector would see more than she bargained for, and that worried Grayson.

Out of everything, Grayson wanted to keep a low profile and not draw attention to herself, the monastery or... Oh, God, she thought, please don't let her see Elinora. It was bad enough the inspector met Sebastian. Inwardly, Grayson laughed: an immortal and a vampire.

"Ms. MacCarthaigh?"

Grayson blinked. "Oh, I'm sorry. What?"

"I asked you if you had any idea what the victim was doing out here."

"I honestly don't know."

The inspector nodded and sipped her beer. "So tell me, what made you became a police officer?" Inspector Gaffney finished her pint and stood. She took Grayson's empty glass. "I'll give you a minute or two to think about it." She almost smiled again as she walked away.

Grayson watched her hips as she walked to the bar. She filled out her black slacks very nicely. Though the inspector was a tad on the short side, she ... Grayson stopped herself. "Geezus, MacCarthaigh," she chastised herself. "Get a grip." She looked up when the inspector came back with two fresh pints of Guinness.

"This will be my limit," she announced as she sat down. "Have you had enough time?"

Grayson was stumped for a moment. "Oh. My father was a beat cop." She saw the curious look and grinned. "A patrolman, on the streets. I wanted to be like him, I suppose." She took another long drink. "How about you?" Anything to take the conversation away from me, she thought.

"If there is anything in DNA, I can't say. I didn't know my biological parents. I was adopted."

"I'm sorry."

"Oh, no need, I loved my parents, but thank you. They both died a few years back. They were on holiday and were in a car accident. I must admit, for a time afterward, I thought of finding my biological parents, but I never did." She stopped and took a long drink. "I became a detective because I loved to read detective novels as a young girl and thought myself Agatha Christie, I suppose."

"And you love it," Grayson said, staring at her glass.

"Yes," Inspector Gaffney said softly. "As you did?"

Grayson looked up and nodded. "Yes, I loved it."

"And you left it that easily to take care of family business?"

"Not easily, but yes. Being in Ireland is more important right now."

"To take care of your mother's affairs?"

Grayson heard the soft concern in her voice, and for a moment, she sounded like Vic. "Yes, she was born in this area. So was I."

"I am sorry."

Grayson nodded and drank her beer. Inspector Gaffney did the same as they sat in silence.

"These two deaths are connected. You know that," Inspector Gaffney said. She ran her fingertip around the rim of her glass. "And I will find out how."

"I know you will. You should, you're a police officer. It's what you do."

"And you would do the same. If you had any ideas, I would appreciate a call."

"Sure," Grayson said and finished her beer.

Inspector Gaffney finished her pint, as well. "I'd best be going. I'll be in touch."

As Grayson started to rise, the inspector put her hand on her shoulder. "Don't get up. Good day, Ms. MacCarthaigh."

"Good day, Inspector." Grayson watched as she weaved in and out of the late afternoon crowd.

She won't give up until she finds out who killed my mother and Kathleen, Grayson thought. "This is not going well."

Chapter 15

Corky and Grayson met Neala at the coroner's office the next morning. Neala looked pale and tired as she identified Kathleen's body.

"It's just too gruesome," Neala said while they walked toward her car.

Grayson put her arm around Neala's shoulders. "I know. I'm sorry you had to do that. Does she have any family?"

"Yes," Neala said. "In Tipperary. They've been notified by the museum. I believe they're making the funeral arrangements now. It's just so sad. Do you really think it was Phelan?"

"Who else could it be?" Corky yanked off his tie, shoving it in his jacket pocket. "We all saw the marks. Just like Maeve. What was she doing there? Damn him to hell."

Grayson patted him on the shoulder. "And now we have Inspector Gaffney to contend with. With two killed the same way, it'll be impossible to explain it."

"Are we going to try?" Corky asked.

"No. I don't see why. As far as we know, my mother was attacked by an animal."

"I—" Neala stopped and leaned against her car.

"What?" Grayson asked.

Neala shook her head. "I don't know. It's just that…"

"That what, Neala? C'mon, don't hold back now," Grayson said.

Corky agreed. "Tell us what's on your mind."

"It's just that, well, I know the common denominator is Phelan, but it could also be our new vampire friend."

Grayson cocked her head in contemplation. "But she wasn't around when my mother died. And she was with Corky and me when Liam came about Kathleen."

"Grayson, remember when Sebastian brought you to my house? It took a matter of minutes," Corky offered.

"That is true. She can travel like the wind," Grayson said. "I suppose she would have time to kill Kathleen, then zip right over to us."

"And she was already standing over Kathleen's body when we got there, and we all left together," Corky said quietly.

"How long was she with you? Let's not forget she's a vampire, and initially, she did show up in Corky's book. And now she's come back with a book of her own and some ancient letter. It just appears too coincidental to me is all I'm saying."

They stood by Neala's car in silence. Grayson pondered this new piece to the puzzle. Anything is possible now, she thought. She longed for the time when the lines were clear. Good guys and bad guys. You worked the clues and evidence. You caught the bad guy. Now...

"What in the world are you thinking?" Neala asked, placing her hand on Grayson's forearm. She caressed up and down her arm.

"Just all this Celtic mythology and mystical mumbo jumbo."

"Which is not mumbo jumbo," Corky said, leaning against the car.

"I wish it were." Grayson sighed and did the same.

"If wishes were fishes..." Corky's voice trailed off. "What does that mean?"

Grayson glanced at Neala and all three laughed. "Who knows," Neala said and opened the car door. "I have to get back to the museum. You two stay out of trouble."

"I thought you'd at least take the day off. This was such a blow," Grayson said.

Neala smiled and touched her cheek. "It was, which is why I need to keep busy."

"Neala." Grayson placed her hand on Neala's arm. "You've been running back and forth from Dublin to the monastery and back again. You're exhausted. And now with this."

"I know, Gray," Neala said. "But I have to be at the museum. I'd love to take a vacation, but it would look too odd with everything that has happened." She looked into Grayson's eyes. "I'd rather travel the distance and stay for just a little while than not see you at all."

"And me too?" Corky added.

Grayson smiled as she looked into Neala's eyes. "Yes, you too, Corky," Neala said.

"Why don't we meet for an early dinner?" Corky suggested. "We can take in Dublin and meet you, say, around four?"

"Yeah. That's a good idea. No arguing, Neala. You'll need a break." Grayson held the car door open for Neala, who rolled her eyes and got in.

"We'll meet at Darwin's, ya know, on Aungier Street," Corky said.

"Fair enough. I won't argue with either of you," Neala said. "See ya there at four."

Grayson and Corky watched her pull away. "Okay, now what?" Corky asked.

Grayson slapped the back of his shoulder, and in doing so, another vision flashed. She grinned evilly. "We go find Caitlin Delaney."

Corky seemed stunned. "W-what? Why? I mean—"

"Timothy Kerrigan. Are you afraid?" Grayson asked, still grinning.

"I am not," Corky said with an air of indignance. "I'm cautious."

"Whatever." Grayson pulled him along. "Now where did you say she—"

Corky grinned. "*Irish Times*. She's a reporter. It's on Tara Street."

"Hmm. Good thing you don't know much about her anymore."

"Oh, shut your gob," Corky said and pushed Grayson.

They stood in front of the *Irish Times* office on Tara Street. Grayson glanced at Corky and saw the forlorn look on his face.

For an instant, she thought he might walk away. Grayson quickly reached over and straightened his tie. She then winked; Corky nodded.

"Let's do this before I lose me nerve," he said.

Grayson opened the door and grinned as Corky walked into the building. The receptionist looked up with a friendly smile. "May I help ya?"

Corky cleared his throat before asking, "I'm lookin' for Caitlin Delaney. I'm an old friend."

"And your name?"

"Tim Kerrigan."

"Certainly. Let me see if she's in the building."

Corky glanced at Grayson while the woman was on the phone.

"I'm not sure this was a good idea, Grayson," Corky whispered.

"Don't worry. It'll be fine."

"She'll be right with you, Mr. Kerrigan," the receptionist said.

"Thank you." Corky stretched his neck, then ran his fingers through his thick red hair.

"You look very handsome," Grayson whispered. "She'll swoon."

Corky glared at her. "Will you cut it out? She'll probably not even remember me. It's been so—"

"Corky," a woman's voice called softly.

Even Grayson heard the tenderness in her voice. She looked up to see an attractive woman with coal black hair cut short and just as unruly as Corky's red mop. She wore black framed glasses that contrasted the creamy white skin and rosy cheeks. Grayson inwardly grinned. This woman was adorable, she thought. And by the stunned yet grinning face on Corky, he felt the same.

"Hello, Caitlin," Corky said with equal tenderness.

"My Lord, it's been a long time." She walked up to him and wrapped her arms around him affectionately.

With Corky's back to her, Grayson saw Caitlin close her eyes and smile as she held on to him. Corky pulled back and held her at arm's length. "You look wonderful. Time has been good to you."

"And to you, Corky. Still the same smiling green eyes."

Suddenly, Grayson felt out of place. As if sensing this, Corky quickly turned to her. "I'm sorry, Grayson. Caitlin, this is Grayson MacCarthaigh, a good friend."

Grayson offered her hand, which Caitlin took. "It's a pleasure to meet you, Grayson."

"Same here."

They stood in silence for a moment until Caitlin said, "Well, I have nothing major planned for the afternoon." She looked at both of them.

Corky looked at Grayson, who offered a solution. "Why don't you two go? I'm sure you have a lot of catching up to do." Grayson went on before Corky could object. "I've got a few things to check out. Caitlin, if you're not doing anything, we're meeting a friend for an early dinner in a few hours at…"

"Darwin's," Corky said. "And you are very welcome to join us."

"Let's see how the afternoon goes. You may decide it wasn't a good idea to look me up," Caitlin said, nervously adjusting her glasses.

"Whatever you decide," Grayson said, extending her hand. "It was nice meeting you if I don't see you later."

"I'll meet you at four," Corky said as Grayson walked out of the building.

"Okay, so now what should I do for the next couple hours?" Grayson said as she walked down Tara Street.

As she strolled with no purpose in mind, Grayson found herself at the O'Connell Street Bridge. The day had turned sunny and warm with the white billowy clouds drifting with the breeze. She walked down the boardwalk, then stopped and rested her forearms on the thick metal railing that overlooked the River Liffey. She leaned farther, feeling like a little kid as she peered over the side.

"Don't jump. It's not high enough."

Grayson whirled around to see Inspector Gaffney standing nearby. She's haunting me, Grayson thought.

"You'll only get wet, and I'll be bound to jump in after ya." The inspector walked up to her and looked over the side, as well.

"I've had to pull many a drunk off this ledge, let me tell you."

Grayson tried to hide her grin. "Really? The drink does that to a person. I thought your superiors relegated you to Dungarin."

Inspector Gaffney leaned on the railing and nodded. She swept the windblown dark hair from her face. It was then Grayson noticed her noble profile as she gazed at the river. The inspector had a firm jaw; inwardly Grayson smirked—more stubborn than firm, she thought.

"I have been. I needed to be in court this morning, and I wanted to talk to some of Ms. Moore's coworkers."

"And did you?" Grayson tried not to sound too interested, which she was.

"I did. Mr. Bradley and Dr. Norman, they are on the board of directors at the museum. They had no clue and couldn't offer any explanations. However, I spoke with Michael Dornan. He's Dr. Rourke's assistant, as well."

Grayson was itching to find out but said nothing. She looked at the inspector, who was smiling slightly. "Would you like to know what he said?"

Grayson gave a noncommittal shrug. "Up to you."

"Ms. MacCarthaigh, you're dying to know. He couldn't shed any light, as well. But it was not what he said. It's what he didn't say."

Grayson knew exactly what the inspector was doing. The first thing Grayson did when interviewing someone was to concentrate on what the person was not saying. It was that hesitation in his voice, that slight hitch that told Grayson there was something else. She knew Inspector Gaffney did the same thing.

"He's protecting someone, I think."

"What makes you say that?"

"Would you like something to eat? I'm starving."

Completely taken aback by the abrupt change of topic, Grayson stammered, "Uh, no, no…"

She watched as the inspector walked over to a street vendor and made her purchase. In a moment, she came back with a small order of fish and chips. She grinned at Grayson. "It's the malt vinegar that does the trick."

Grayson chuckled along. "So why do you think he's protecting someone?"

"It's the vague way he answered. I also noticed him glancing at the file cabinet while I asked questions."

"File cabinet," Grayson said absently. She leaned against the railing and looked out at the river. "What files are in there?"

Inspector Gaffney ate a bit of the fried fish. "I don't know. So I asked Dr. Rourke."

"And what did she say?"

"She was very nice. Said they were financial profiles on patrons who contributed to the museum. And personnel files."

"Hmm."

Inspector Gaffney offered her fish and chips. Grayson absently took a fry and popped it into her mouth. "Wonder if any files are missing."

"I wondered the same thing. So I asked Dr. Rourke to take a look. And she said nothing was missing."

Grayson heard skepticism in her voice while she munched on the fried fish.

"You don't believe her?" Grayson asked.

"Yes. I don't have any reason to think she would lie." She looked at Grayson then. "Do you? How well do you know Dr. Rourke?"

"Well enough to know she's not a liar." Grayson felt the anger rising. This line of questioning was not a good idea.

Inspector Gaffney finished her impromptu lunch and tossed the remnants into the trash can. "Well, I need to get back to my flat to pick up a few things. Mrs. O'Toole runs a very nice bed and breakfast in your village. It's a peaceful village, Ms. MacCarthaigh."

"I think you can call me Grayson if you like. I have a feeling you're going to be—"

"A pain in your arse?"

Grayson did laugh at that. "I wasn't going to say that."

"I don't blame you, Grayson. And you may call me Megan since I'll be such a bother to you."

Grayson's body reacted when she heard her name from this

woman. Her body tingled and her heart rate increased. Even the hair on the back of her neck tingled—she immediately scratched said area.

"But I have to be a bother." She turned to Grayson then. "Because there is something going on and I will find out."

Grayson searched her blue eyes and saw the determination there. She almost envied the inspector's strength of purpose and love of her job. Grayson remembered those feelings. "I know you'll do what you have to do, Inspector, uh, Megan."

"I should be going." She smiled at Grayson. "I'd like to talk to you further. Are you heading back to Dungarin?"

"Later this evening. I'm meeting some friends for an early dinner."

Grayson wasn't sure what was going through her mind as Megan searched her face for a moment. She seemed to be considering a question. Grayson was grateful when Megan merely nodded and said, "I think I'll mingle with the folks of Dungarin. Have a good evening. I'll be in touch."

"You too." Grayson watched as Megan walked away from her. She watched until she was lost in the afternoon crowd on the boardwalk.

Grayson looked up into the midday sun and sighed. It was then she noticed a hawk lazily flying overhead. Immediately, she thought of the first day she, her mother, and Neala came to Ireland when that woman picked them up at Shannon, whose name escaped Grayson, and noticed a hawk flying overhead. And then again, when they met Corky, he noticed them, as well. What did he call them?

"Messengers," she said as she watched the hawk. Grayson wondered if this hawk was just a plain ole hawk or some messenger from the gods.

Knowing she was not going to get an answer, she shook her head and made her way back to the O'Connell Street Bridge. As she crossed the bridge heading to the restaurant, she did not need to look up to know the hawk was still circling above her.

It was nearly four when she got to Darwin's. She noticed Corky sitting at a table by the window and stopped for a moment.

He looked lost in thought as he stared at his pint of Guinness. At this point, she was glad she did not possess the ability to read minds without physical contact. Although, right now, her left palm itched incessantly while she watched the pensive look on her friend's face.

For another moment, Grayson regarded this quirky Irishman, who quickly had become a good friend. She smiled remembering how they first met, when Corky realized Grayson was indeed the true descendant of the Tuatha De Danann—the one who would protect the power and magic of the ancient ones. It was too fantastic to Grayson, but to Corky, it was real, almost a religion to him. He believed every word and never denounced the possibility of even the most outrageous ideas. He was a true believer, and Grayson often wondered why the gods and goddesses did not choose Corky for this. But that is not the way of it, she thought. Her mother, Maeve, and her wife, Vic, fulfilling their destiny on this earth, gave their lives so Grayson could be at this point.

She looked down at the three rings on her finger. Again, she remembered her time in that ancient dwelling where she saw Vic and Maeve. Though only in spirit, they helped her see exactly what her destiny was. She saw all the women throughout time who lived and died to bring all of this to fruition—to fulfill the prophecy of the residual moon and reveal Grayson as the true descendant. So many had to die, she thought, still looking at the rings. They will not have died in vain, she promised them. Taking a deep breath to hold back the tears, she looked up to see Corky waving to her. His big Irish smile and green eyes sparkling, he held up his pint glass.

Grayson laughed and walked into the restaurant. "Couldn't wait for me?" she asked as the server came to their table. "I'll have the same."

"The thirst got me," Corky said.

"I can imagine," Grayson said. "No Caitlin?"

Corky shook his head. "She had to get back to work."

Grayson noticed his smile. "I take it, it went well?"

"Yes. She's a grand gal. And seeing someone." He took a long drink of dark beer.

Grayson's smile quickly faded. "Shit."

"Over here we say shite," Corky mumbled into his glass. "But it means the same."

"Well, she's not married. Is she engaged to this guy?"

"No."

"So she's only dating, so don't give up."

Corky laughed. "This is the first time I've seen her in years. We had a nice chat, and it was very friendly as if we had seen each other every day. She's a good friend."

Grayson snorted. "I saw the way she hugged you, pal."

"Who's hugging who?" Neala said, walking up to the table. Corky and Grayson stood and pulled out her chair. "Well, thank you."

"Corky saw an old girlfriend earlier. And they had a nice chat."

"That's wonderful, Corky. Who is it?"

"Caitlin Delaney."

"The reporter from the *Times*?" Neala asked.

Grayson saw the look of concern on Neala's face. So did Corky. "Yeah, what's wrong?"

Neala put the napkin in the lap. "She was at the museum last week asking questions. She's doing a series of articles about the Book of Kells, and supposedly she wanted to interview someone at the museum. It would figure this would happen now."

"We can't catch a break with this." Grayson picked up a menu. "So much for staying out of the limelight."

"It would appear there's no way around it. I talked to one of the directors, and he's steering her away from the recent activity and keeping her in the archives. So he gave the interview, then sent her to Trinity College to see the Book of Kells. We hope this will keep her busy for a while, at least until things quiet down at the museum."

"If that ever happens," Corky interjected.

"Do you feel like talking about Kathleen?" Grayson asked; she reached over and placed her left hand on Neala's arm.

"Sure," she said with a smile. "It's such a sad thing."

"I understand you had a visitor today."

Neala impatiently waved her hand in the air. "Oh, that inspector is tenacious."

"Ya had to figure she would come and see ya," Corky said.

"I know. She talked with Michael first. Then asked me about the files. I don't know why."

"I think Megan was trying to figure out why Kathleen was all the way over in our neck of the woods."

"Megan?" Corky asked with a sly grin. Neala raised an eyebrow, as well.

Grayson glared at Corky. "Shut up."

"Can you think of what she was doing out there?" Corky asked.

"I don't know why she would come to see you, Grayson. I really don't. I talked to Michael, who didn't know where she was going." Neala stared at her water glass. "I just don't know what it was or why Phelan killed her."

"What makes you think she came to see me?" Grayson asked.

Neala hesitated. "Well, I don't know, really." She shrugged and drank her water. "It had to be something." Neala went on, "I know Phelan is crazy, but I can't imagine he would want to bring attention to this."

Grayson noticed Corky was silent during this. He was looking across the room at the bar. Grayson watched his intent stare when suddenly he bolted up and walked over to the bar.

"What is he doing?" Neala asked as they watched him.

"I have no idea," Grayson said. "He can't be that thirsty."

She and Neala laughed as they watched Corky talk to the bartender. He then took some money out of his pocket and handed it to him. With his back to her, Grayson couldn't see what Corky picked up.

"What the hell..." Grayson whispered; she and Neala watched him walk back to the table holding what Grayson thought looked like a hunk of concrete.

"I think I have an answer to one of our problems." Corky placed the triangular jagged stone on the table. He looked from Grayson to Neala, whose frown turned to a smile.

"Corky, that will not work."

"What?" Grayson said. Then it dawned on her.

"It looks like the stone," Corky argued as he examined it. "The bartender said his grandfather found it while plowing the fields. It looks ancient."

"And he was so attached to it," Grayson said dryly. "How much for his loss?"

"Thirty euros, shut up," Corky said without looking at her.

"But there are no markings of the Ogham alphabet." Neala picked up the stone. "Though it does seem to weigh the same."

"Neala, you must have photos of it," Grayson said. "Can it be altered?"

"Sure it can," Corky said. He sounded so enthusiastic, Grayson laughed. "Let's get it back to the museum. We can look at the photos and make the Ogham etchings on the stone."

"You know someone will notice it's not an ancient piece of archaeology, that we got this off the bar at a restaurant."

"Don't be a dud, Grayson," Corky said.

"This is the craziest—" Grayson stopped and shook her head. "What am I saying?"

Corky laughed and pulled Neala out of her chair. She grabbed her glass of Guinness and took a huge gulp. "I thought we were going to eat."

"This will never work," Grayson said, and Corky pulled her along, as well.

Chapter 16

Megan pulled in front of the bed and breakfast and parked. She noticed some townspeople gathering outside the pub a few stores down. "Good place to start," she said and locked the car.

"Good afternoon," she said with a smile.

Two men standing near the door nodded and tipped their caps. "Good day," one said. "Are ya lost?"

Megan raised an eyebrow. "No. I do have a few questions if you don't mind." She showed her badge. Both men peered down at her ID, then exchanged glances. "I'm a bit thirsty. Would you like to join me?"

"Well, now, Inspector. Maybe for one."

When she walked in ahead of them, a few patrons turned but said nothing. She walked up to the bar as the young man behind it smiled and wiped off the area in front of her. "Good day, miss. What'll it be? It's not often we get such a pretty face here," he said with a wink.

"Thank you. I'll have a Guinness, and please buy these two gentlemen a drink." Megan looked at the two others at the end of the bar. "I'd like to buy you a drink, too."

"Very good," he said and stuck out his hand. "Denis Reed."

"Megan Gaffney." She shook his hand. "Inspector Megan Gaffney."

Denis's smile turned to a frown as he looked at the two men. "One pint comin' right up."

Megan watched as Denis poured the thick stout for her and the whiskey for the men. She could see him gauging his comments.

"So," he finally said. "What brings you to Dungarin?"

"Murder," she said, taking a drink.

One man choked on his whiskey.

Denis laughed nervously. "Well, then. Um…"

"How well do you know Grayson MacCarthaigh?" She looked around the bar.

The man on the far end slowly pushed his drink away from him. He put on his cap. "I'll be goin' now, Denis."

Megan watched him as he walked around the bar. "I'm sorry, sir. Did I say something?"

He smiled and shook his head. "No, miss."

"Do you know Grayson?"

"I do. And I knew her mother and father. And old Deirdre."

"How well—?"

"And I don't talk about my friends in a pub. Good day, Inspector." He tipped his cap and walked out.

Megan turned back to the bar and drank her Guinness.

"What are ya after?" another man asked.

Megan heard the harshness in her voice. She recognized this man as Liam O'Toole, one of the men who found Kathleen's body. He owned the bed and breakfast with his wife.

"Just gathering information, Mr. O'Toole, nothing more. How well do you know Grayson MacCarthaigh?"

"Not very well. She left Ireland with her parents when she was a young girl."

"Did you know her parents?"

"I did. They were fine people, as were her grandparents. Deirdre had a way about her with the village folk."

"What kind of way?" Megan asked.

Liam glanced at Denis and shrugged. "Just a way of kindness."

Megan knew that was not all; she could tell by the dismissive tone in Liam's voice. He quickly put on his cap. "It was a horrible thing what happened to that girl."

"And to Maeve MacCarthaigh," Megan interjected softly.

"Yes," he said. He looked at Megan then. "They've been in this village for generations. They've helped many a farmer and villager. They are…" He stopped.

"They are what, Mr. O'Toole?" Megan asked.

"They just are," he said in a low confident voice that Megan thought had a hint of challenge in it. "It's just the way of it. Good day to you, Inspector."

When Liam walked out, so did the other patrons, each of them leaving their drinks untouched.

"Well, I certainly know how to clear a room."

Denis chuckled and cleared the bar. "It's nothing personal, Inspector. The Grayson-MacCarthaigh family is much respected here. The villagers tend to be very protective, that's all."

"Why should they feel protective?"

Denis shrugged and tossed the towel over his shoulder. He then poured himself a stout and leaned against the bar. "You're not from around here, are ya? You have the tone of a Dubliner about ya."

"Very good. I am from Dublin, though I don't know what difference it makes. I understand loyalty, Mr. Reed."

"Denis, please. And it's more than loyalty." He looked around the pub. "My grandfather started this place. My uncle and father then took it over. Now it's my turn. We tend to keep things in the family in Dungarin." He took a long drink of the black beer and continued, "Now I'm too young to remember Deirdre and only have a vague recollection of Maeve and Grayson. But my Aunt Rose, she knows the entire family."

"Do you think she'll talk to me?"

"I doubt it," Denis said, finishing his beer. He laughed then. "I'm sure she will. Aunt Rose loves to talk. Her name is Rose Barry. She lives on the edge of Dungarin. Ya can't miss it. Big red front door."

"Thank you, Denis." Megan reached into her pocket.

Denis held up his hand. "I've got this. You can get the next one."

Megan walked to the other end of Dungarin. It did not go unnoticed that everyone she came across had the same look: You're a stranger here.

Now more than ever, Megan wanted to know why this

village protected the Grayson-MacCarthaigh clan so much. She saw the house Denis described at the edge of the village. As she approached the door, she saw a woman standing in the road about a hundred or so meters away. Megan took in her appearance as best she could: tall, long dark hair, Irish sweater, wool slacks. This woman was standing there, seemingly watching Megan.

Megan looked away when she gently knocked at the door. When she looked back, the woman had disappeared. Megan searched the countryside as the door opened.

"Can I help ya?" An old woman with a skeptical eye peered at Megan.

"Rose Barry?"

"Yes. And you are?"

"Inspector Megan Gaffney, from Dublin. I'd like to ask you a few questions—"

"About?"

Megan slightly cleared her throat. "Grayson MacCarthaigh."

Rose Barry raised an eyebrow, still giving Megan a cautious once-over. But she stepped back, allowing Megan to enter her home. She followed Rose to the living room where Rose offered her a chair.

"I just put the pot on to boil. We'll have tea in a minute."

Megan sat down. "Thank you."

"Now what is it you want to know about Grayson?"

"Anything you can tell me. I'll be honest. I'm investigating the death of a young woman. She was found the other day by some villagers. That coupled with Maeve MacCarthaigh's death a couple of months ago had Dublin thinking they might be related."

Rose sat back and nodded. "I've known Grayson all her life. Her mother was my best friend."

"I'm sorry."

Again, Rose nodded. "I knew Deirdre very well. She was a grand woman. Are you thinking Grayson killed this woman or her own mother?"

Megan frowned deeply. "No, I'm not. However, we can't deny the similarities in their deaths. This latest victim was killed in the same fashion. It appears to be an animal of some sort. Forensics seems to think perhaps a wolf or rabid dog. They're not quite sure. As you can imagine, Mrs. Barry—"

"Rose, please."

"Thank you. As you can imagine, Rose, it's hard to believe a wolf in Ireland."

"True. What does Grayson have to do with it? I mean, other than Maeve was killed this way."

"I'm just gathering as much information as I can. I'm trying to figure this out before anything else happens."

"It could possibly be a rabid dog, and wolves are not that unheard of. You've got something else on your mind."

Megan regarded this old woman. What she liked was that Rose Barry looked her right in the eye when she spoke. "What was Grayson like as a child?"

Rose smiled then and rocked in her chair. When the whistle started on the tea kettle, Megan rose. "I'll get it."

"Thank you," Rose said, clearly surprised. "The teapot is on the table. Cups in the cupboard."

Megan smiled as she found what she needed in the kitchen.

"And there's some bread on the table, along with the jam, if ya have a mind for it."

After preparing the tea, Megan placed a few pieces of soda bread along with the jam on a plate.

"Thank you," Rose said again as Megan poured the tea.

"Not at all. I have ulterior motives."

Rose let out a genuine laugh before sipping her tea. "Yes, Grayson as a child. She was an adorable child. Coal black hair, blue eyes, and a smile that lit up a room. Oh, she had the devil in her, as well. But she was a happy child."

"Liam O'Toole said her grandmother, Deirdre, had a way with the villagers. Can you elaborate?"

"Deirdre was a kind and generous woman who loved this village, as did the generations before her. Oh, she had her moments." She laughed and sipped her tea. "One day, I remember as if it were yesterday. Maeve and I were playing out in the field. Well, we got too close to the woods. Deirdre had told us to stay away, but ya know how children are, they don't listen."

Megan heard the wistful tone as Rose continued. "So there we were laughing and chasing each other in the woods. And all of the sudden, there she was."

"Deirdre?"

"Yes. Oh, how angry she was. It was Samhain, you understand and…"

"Samhain?"

Rose blinked, apparently realizing what she had said. "Yes, the harvest festival, ushering in the winter months. The dark half."

"Oh, yes. I have a friend who is into all that."

"All that?" Rose said with a laugh and set her teacup down. "Ya don't believe in 'all that'?"

"I'm a grown woman. I understand the ways of the old…" She felt her face get red hot. "I didn't mean…"

"I know. The old ways and old beliefs have faded much. But if your friend is into it, as you say, then perhaps all is not lost."

"You really believe all that? The festivals, the rituals."

"I do. Why not?"

"I don't know, really. I never thought about it. It's not something we're taught in schools."

"No, it isn't."

Megan heard a bit of sadness in Rose's voice. "What do you believe? I mean about all that. Did the Graysons believe in it?" She felt she was close to something here. "Liam said she helped the farmers and the villagers. How?"

"I don't think I'm tellin' ya anything you couldn't find out on your own. I have a feeling you're a persistent woman. Deirdre had a gift, I think. She was able to help the farmers with their planting. She helped many villagers with…" She hesitated, seeming to find the right word. "Troubles, I suppose is the word for it."

"Troubles? What kind of troubles?"

"Anything they might need help with. Compassion and kindness can take many forms."

"Why do I have the feeling you're being vague?" Megan asked. When Rose did not answer, she went on, "I'm not trying to harm Grayson if that worries you."

Rose looked at Megan then, which caused the hair on the back of her neck to bristle. "Ya can't harm Grayson. I would not allow it. And neither would anyone in Dungarin. It's just the way of it."

"That's what Liam O'Toole said. Just the way of what?" Megan took a sip of her tea, realizing she hadn't touched it. It was ice cold as she set it back on the table.

"You're a smart woman. Have you talked to Grayson at all?"

"Yes. I saw her in Dublin earlier today. She's as vague as everyone else," she said irritably. "I'm not trying to hurt Grayson. I'm trying to do my job."

"Grayson was a policewoman in America. I'm sure you know that."

"Yes. From what I can get out of the Chicago police, she was a decorated officer and made detective sergeant very early. They had said she was injured and her partner was killed."

"Yes, when Maeve called and told me, I cried for days. I don't understand the lesbian part of Grayson. But I understand Grayson. She was deeply in love with this woman, who was pregnant, as well. I met Vicky only once. They came back here for a vacation along with Maeve and Dermott. Grayson was so happy and so content. Now with Vicky and Maeve gone..." She stared at nothing in particular.

Megan sat in silence, absorbing all this information. She had the report on Grayson MacCarthaigh. She did not know the personal side of her life, however.

Her thoughts wandered back to her relationship with Anne. After five years of living in fear, wondering if Megan would come home in one piece after her shift, Anne couldn't take it anymore and Megan couldn't blame her. Being in a relationship with a police officer was not an easy task. It took more than Anne had, though she tried. It was a sad realization for both of them. Now Anne lived in Cork in a nice, comfortable, safe relationship with a woman who was a lawyer. She and Anne had called and e-mailed for a while, but then the communication became less and less. She heard from Anne two years earlier. Just a line to say she was doing well and happy. That was enough for Megan.

"Grayson held that woman in her arms when she died," Rose was saying.

Megan blinked, shaken from her reverie. "What?"

"Vicky was a hostage negotiator, I believe is the term. Grayson had already been shot and two other policemen killed. When the man started firing in Grayson's direction again, Vicky leapt in front of him, taking all bullets meant for Grayson." Rose stopped and put her head back as she rocked. "She was going to give it up when she found out she was pregnant. Grayson said she had a law degree and wanted to be a judge. They had it all planned."

"That's horrible," Megan whispered.

"Yes, it was."

"Then to have your mother die the way she did," Megan said, almost to herself. She wasn't sure how she would handle something like that.

"It's a tragic thing, that's for sure." She looked at Megan then. "So ya see, Inspector, why we keep Grayson close to our hearts?"

"Yes, I do. But I still have to do my job."

"Ah, you're a stubborn one. But I suppose I understand."

"I'll know more when the lab results come back. We'll see if it's a wolf or dog or something or someone else."

She stood and held out her hand. Rose smiled and shook it. "You're a grand gal. Are ya single?"

Megan laughed. "Yes, I am."

Rose beamed. "And are ya a lesbian?"

Megan, clearly caught off-guard, stared at Rose for a moment, then she nervously laughed and held up her hands. "Scotland Yard could use you, Rose Barry. Good day. Thank you for the tea and the insight."

As she walked back to the bed and breakfast, Megan realized she indeed had great insight to Grayson MacCarthaigh. However, despite Grayson's losses, Megan was bound to her duty. She took comfort in believing Detective MacCarthaigh would do the same. It was little comfort.

Chapter 17

"This is as good as it will get," Corky said, examining the stone.

Neala agreed. "I'll take it and call Dr. Norman."

"What will you tell him?" Grayson asked. The stone did indeed look like the original, but she wondered if the professionals at the museum would believe it.

"I'll tell him I picked up the stone from Phelan, who decided it was in better hands with Dr. Norman. That will give Dr. Norman an ego boost, which hopefully won't make him concentrate on examining the stone. Maybe I can get it in the glass case in the exhibit before he can do that."

"That's a good idea," Corky said. "Ya know, I've been thinking about Sebastian's letter. The second stanza. I might have it figured out."

"Can you remember it?" Neala asked.

Grayson laughed. "I'm sure he's got it memorized."

"I do. So here it is." He cleared his throat first. "One emerges from the night, at the behest of ancient call, a star falls from a distant realm, uniting and revealing all."

"Okay. Give us your idea," Neala said, carefully wrapping the stone in a linen cloth.

"I think it's Sebastian from the night, and Tatiana is the ancient call. Elinora is the star that perhaps Danu, being the distant realm, sent here. That's my thought."

Grayson pondered this for a moment, as did Neala. "That sounds very plausible." She looked at Neala, who didn't seem convinced. "Neala?"

"I'd feel better if we knew who Elinora really was. She seems to talk in vague innuendoes. I understand Grayson needs a good deal of faith to go on with this, but someone could cut her some slack." She looked at Grayson then and whispered, "You've been through so much. I just don't want you to be hurt anymore."

Grayson smiled and took her hand. "I'll be all right, but I like the way you think."

Neala laughed and picked up the stone. "Well, I should be going. Wish me luck."

"I think it'll be fine. You'll be fine," Grayson said. She placed her hands on Neala's shoulders.

Neala grinned. "I believe you."

For a moment, they looked into each other's eyes. Grayson leaned in and lightly kissed her on the lips. She heard a small gasp from Neala, who seemed to melt into the kiss. Grayson pulled back.

"All right then," Corky said, clearing his throat.

"I'll talk to you in the morning," Grayson said.

Neala nodded. "Good night." She backed up. "Good night, Corky."

"Good night, Neala. It'll work. No worries."

Neala left, leaving Grayson and Corky standing in silence.

"Well then, let's go. It's a long ride back," Corky finally said.

After promising Corky to meet him at the monastery in the morning, Grayson slipped into bed. She let out a deep satisfying groan as she stretched.

"Don't fall asleep yet."

Grayson flew out of bed so fast, she forgot she was naked. It was Elinora, sitting on top of the dresser.

"Damn it. What the hell is the matter with you?" Grayson yelled. She scrambled for her jeans and shirt. "What are you doing here?"

"I have been waiting for you. We need to talk."

Grayson balanced on one foot as she struggled into her jeans. "About what?" She tried to ignore the fact she nearly had a heart attack.

"Your reaction just now. I have told you to embrace this gift and you are not trying. You should have been able to sense my presence. You cannot be caught off-guard so much. Use your abilities."

"It's nearly midnight."

"Time is of no importance to an immortal."

Grayson sat on the bed. "Well, at least my heart rate is back to normal." She looked back at the dresser, and Elinora was gone. Then the tingling sensation started in her left hand and traveled up her arm.

Concentrate.

She heard Elinora's voice in her mind; she closed her eyes and took several deep breaths. She felt it then, or more accurately, she sensed it. She knew exactly where Elinora was. Walking to the closet, she opened it and there stood Elinora, a big grin spreading across her face.

"Very good."

"Get out of the closet." Grayson laughed and stopped when Elinora cocked her head in confusion. "It's a gay joke. Skip it."

"Ah, humor again. Were you funny in your previous life?"

Grayson glared at her. "I always thought so."

"You did well. You must practice and concentrate. It will be slow going, as I have said, due to your being a mortal, as well. However, it will come. Now," Elinora walked out of the room, "tell me of this police officer."

"What for?" Grayson followed her into the living room. She flipped on the small lamp on the desk.

Elinora stretched out on the couch, raising her hands above her head. Grayson had to admit, she was a beautiful woman.

Not woman—immortal.

Whatever.

"So what about Megan?"

"First names? Yes, I sense duplicity in this woman."

"You've met?"

"No, but I saw her earlier today. She was at the house of Rose Barry after she visited a public house."

"What did she want with Rose?"

"To find out about you, of course. She is not what she seems."

"How do you mean?"

"I know all about Maeve and your woman visiting your friends in their dreams. Liar's moon."

"What do you know about it?" Grayson asked. "Tell me what you know."

"I am not here to answer questions. It will be as it is written."

"Written by whom? Why is it such a secret? You know, but you won't tell me."

"It is not why I am here. I am here to teach you and help you with your powers."

"If I knew what the fuck was going on, I might be able to handle my powers better."

Elinora smiled. "A valiant attempt, but you are to do this on your own. I cannot hold your hand. You must travel this road on your own, but not alone. It's who you choose to travel with you that will define you."

"And Megan Gaffney is not someone I should choose?"

"I cannot say."

"Shit. You're driving me nuts." Grayson ran her fingers through her hair and sat down. "I'm just asking for a little help. And if you knew me at all, you'd know that's not an easy thing for me to do."

She looked up when she felt Elinora's hand on her head. "Nothing will be easy. However, once you truly embrace who you are, it will ease the burden. Call upon the instincts you had when you were a police officer. You were confident and true. You will be again." She ran her fingers through Grayson's hair. "You must believe that. No one can do this for you for your strength and sense of righteousness will see you through."

"You make me sound like Gandhi."

"No one is like Gandhi," Elinora told her. "Not even Gandhi."

Grayson did find that amusing. "See, you have a sense of humor. So why tell me about Megan? Is there anyone else?"

Elinora knelt in front of her. Grayson looked into her brown eyes and waited. "Someone is lying to me. I know it."

"Grayson," Elinora nearly pleaded. "Stop thinking with your head. Everyone has mendacity in their heart. Even the holy ones."

"So I was right about Sister Gabriel?" For the first time, Grayson felt like she was getting somewhere with this convoluted mess. "Fine, a nun. I'll go to hell."

Elinora chuckled; Grayson thought it sounded purely childlike and chuckled along. "You will be praying for forgiveness for centuries."

Grayson continued to laugh. "The rosary will get a workout."

Elinora then placed her hand on Grayson's knee. "The vampire is the key."

"Sebastian?"

"And I have said too much. I will compromise your destiny if I say anything further."

"Okay. Sebastian's the key, eh? Tatiana told her that we're connected. The prophecy from this ancient vampire has reference to the crescent moon. If she's correct, then Tatiana knew Sebastian and I would meet."

"It is written, you will see in the coming months how correct Tatiana is. Now you must rest." Elinora walked to the window and peered into the night. "The moon is nearly full." She turned back to Grayson. "The liar's moon is at hand."

"There's not much time, and all we know is there's a liar and they're marked." Grayson looked down at her palm. "Like me."

"No. Not at all like you. Their mark is evil. Remember that, no matter who it is, remember that."

Grayson watched Elinora as she gazed out the window. The soft moonlight drifted across her face as the clouds shrouded the moon. "You're telling me something here. I can feel it."

"Good." Elinora then faded and was gone.

Remember.

Chapter 18

"I need to rent your boat," Grayson said as a blast of cold Atlantic air nearly swept her off the dock.

"Do ya know how to handle one?" the old man asked as he puffed on his pipe.

"I need to rent your boat and you." Grayson pulled her collar up around her neck.

The old man smiled slightly. "I'm not cheap."

"No doubt. How much?"

"Where is it that you want to go?"

"Aran Islands, Innishmore." Grayson waited for his reaction.

He showed no sign of surprise as he banged his pipe on the heel of his hand. "Now why would a beautiful woman want to cross the Atlantic on this blustery spring day to go to Innishmore?"

Grayson pulled out her wallet with a sigh. "How much?"

He watched as she sifted through the bills. He reached over and grabbed three. "This will do ya, lass. Get in."

Grayson stepped down into the hull of the sailboat. "Is this thing going to make it?"

"It'll get ya there." He reached out his hand. "Seamus Malone."

Grayson took the offering. "Grayson MacCarthaigh."

For an instant, he frowned. "And your father?"

"Dermott MacCarthaigh."

He smiled then. "I knew him. I knew your mother, too. So they gave ya her name?"

Grayson sat on the narrow bench and leaned back. "Yep."

"Hmm," he said with a grunt and untied the boat from the

dock. He pushed off the dock and started the small engine. "Better than a sail. The Atlantic is a wee bit restless today. I suppose you're not going to tell me what your business is on Innishmore."

"Nope."

"Hmm. And do you have people on the island?"

"I do not."

"Well then, how will you find your way around?"

"I'll manage." Grayson closed her eyes and lifted her head toward the afternoon sun. After a moment, Grayson could feel him watching her. "What would you like to know, Mr. Malone?" She stretched her legs out in front of her.

"Just Malone if you please. And nothin'." He cleared his throat. "It's none of my concern. I just wouldn't want anything to happen to you."

Grayson opened her eyes and grinned. Corky felt the same way that morning when she told him where she was going. He thought she was crazy for going all the way to the islands.

"I appreciate that." She sat forward and brushed the hair off her face as the wind tossed the sailboat. She looked over the side, sincerely hoping they made it to the island. "I need to find a convent."

For an instant, Malone looked stunned. Then he let out a hearty laugh. "And you want me to believe a woman as yourself wants to be a nun?"

Grayson chuckled along. "No. There is a cloistered convent on the island. One of the nuns just came to St. Brigid's Monastery. I'm just curious."

"And your curiosity has you sailing across on a windy day?" He reached his hand inside his breast pocket and pulled out a small flask. With one hand on the helm, he deftly opened the flask, taking a healthy drink. He then offered it to Grayson, who declined. "I think it's more than curiosity," he said and took another swig. "But then, it's none of my business."

"This is true." Grayson turned her head to avoid laughing. She knew the old man was itching to know what she wanted on Innishmore, the largest of the three Aran Islands.

They were desolate places, with some villagers only speaking

Gaelic. It was as if time had forgotten them, and they couldn't care less. Innishmore had a bigger population and was better for the tourists than the other smaller islands. And it was here that Sister Gabriel spent her life since she was seventeen. Grayson wanted to know how she came to be there and why. She couldn't put her finger on it, but there was something odd and secretive about Sister Gabriel. It unnerved Grayson, and with everyone dreaming about a liar's moon, she wanted to know. When Grayson held her hand, she saw flashes of a young woman standing in what looked like a field surrounded by rocks and a small church. If her hunch was right, that vision she had was the convent on the island.

"I know of this convent. Not many from the mainland know if it."

Grayson looked at Malone, who smiled. "And I suppose you'd take me there for a price."

"Well, there is an expense for petrol and all."

Grayson shook her head and dug into her pocket while Malone puffed on his pipe. "It'll be an adventure, so to speak," he said, blowing out a stream of pipe smoke.

It took the better part of an hour to sail to the islands. As they motored up to the dock, there was no one around—anywhere. A light fog had settled on the island, shrouding the village of Innishmore. "This figures."

Malone chuckled as he tied the boat to the mooring and jumped out. He offered his hand to Grayson, who took it and jumped onto the dock, as well. "Okay, lead on."

Malone scratched his head as he peered through the fog.

"Do not tell me you don't know where this place is," Grayson said in a threatening voice.

Malone laughed again. "Oh, hold your horses, lass. It's been years since I've been on these islands. But I swear—"

"Ah, ah, Malone. Watch what you say." Grayson walked ahead of Malone and off the dock. In the distance, she heard the shorebirds screeching, but through the fog, she couldn't see one. "I don't suppose we can get a car."

"I doubt it," Malone said, looking around. He then smiled and pointed. "But I'll wager we can use that."

Grayson looked in the direction and saw a cart with a lone horse. In the cart was a large metal container.

"It's a milk cart," Malone said as if reading her mind. "Let me go and see if the owner is around."

"Do not steal that cart," Grayson called quietly as he walked away.

She heard him laugh as he waved his hand in the air. She watched as he disappeared into the stone building. As she looked around through the fog, she shook her head. "This was such a dumb idea. What the hell kind of an immortal am I anyway?" She shoved her hands in the pockets of her jacket and absently kicked at the sand pebbles and seashells. She looked up when she heard Malone call to her and jogged over to the horse-drawn cart.

"We're in luck," he said, beaming.

Grayson gave her a wary glance. "I'll be the judge of that."

"Don't be pessimistic. The gentleman who owns the cart has to deliver this milk to the house down the road. I convinced him we would do it for him and rent his cart for the day."

"That's awfully nice of him..."

He held out his hand, and Grayson hung her head and dug once again in her pocket. Malone plucked out two bills and walked back into the store.

"There is someone who might know more about the sister." Malone jumped into the cart. Grayson got in the opposite side. Malone gently slapped the rein against the horse.

Grayson waited and waited as they rode the milk cart down the road. "Are you going to tell me?"

"There's an old woman at the other end of the island. She worked at the convent for many years."

"Do you think she'll talk to me?"

"I doubt it." He gave Grayson an innocent look. "Unless, of course, I was to go with ya."

"And if I paid you enough."

"True, true."

"Whatever it is, I'm sure I don't have it on me. I can get it to you when we get back. You thief."

"I think you're good for it. Let's go."

Malone rode through town, then down the narrow road that hugged the edge of the island. Grayson was captivated by the rugged Atlantic as the waves lapped onto the rocky shoreline.

"What's this woman's name?" Grayson asked as they raced down the road.

"Her name is Abigail McGill, she goes by Irene."

"But everyone knew her as Nancy."

"N-no, Irene."

"Skip it."

He slowed down as he pulled up to a very old-looking cottage. The thatching seemed new, but it needed a good coat of paint. "Let me do the talkin' first," he said as he got out of the cart.

"Fine." Grayson followed him up the path to the front door.

"Who's out there?" a gravelly voice called out.

"It's Malone, Irene."

"Who's that man with you?"

Grayson raised an eyebrow and Malone chuckled. "This is Miss Grayson MacCarthaigh. She has a few questions about the nuns at the convent. Can we come in?"

He stepped back when the door opened. An old woman poked her head out, nearly causing Grayson to laugh at the owl-like expression. "Come in then."

Like most Irish cottages, it had that earthy aroma of a peat fire. It was a small cottage. The living room consisted of two cushioned chairs and a table in between with a lamp on it situated in front of the fireplace that nearly took up the entire wall. Grayson could see the old woman used that as an oven, as well. A black pot hung over the burning peat bricks. Grayson smelled the aroma of bread; her stomach reminded her she hadn't eaten all day.

The old woman was about five feet tall if that. Her stark white hair was quite a contrast with the black wool shawl draped around her shoulders, covering the dark wool dress. But Grayson took notice of her eyes. They were crystal blue and sparkling.

Irene and Grayson regarded each other for a moment. It was then Grayson knew—she knew this woman.

Irene narrowed her eyes in speculation. "You seem familiar to me, young lady." She glanced at the confused look on Malone's face. "Come into the kitchen. There's more room." She leaned on her cane and led them down the small hallway.

Grayson followed without question. Malone trailed behind.

"Sit down," she ordered. "I just put the kettle on for tea. Malone, get the cups if you would." She sat and let out a tired groan, then looked at Grayson, but said nothing. She turned to Malone and spoke in Gaelic.

Grayson inwardly grinned as she listened to Irene ask Malone where Grayson was from and why she wanted to know about the nun. Before Malone responded, Grayson spoke to the woman in Gaelic, telling her who she was and where she was from.

The look of surprise on Irene's face was satisfying to Grayson. "We can continue in Gaelic if you like."

"You're a smart one," Irene said with a laugh.

Malone brought the teapot to the table with three cups. "The bread is in the pot over the fireplace. It should be done."

"I'll get it, Irene."

He came back with the cast iron pot and put it on the counter. The heavenly aroma filled the kitchen as he took it out and placed it on the board.

"Thank you, Malone." Irene poured the tea for each. "We'll let it cool. Now tell me why ya want to know about Sister Gabriel."

Grayson toyed with the teacup and took a drink of the strong tea before answering. "She might be involved in something at the monastery, and I would like to know more about her. Like how she came to the convent here and why."

Irene exchanged glances with Malone; so did Grayson. Irene leaned in. "Before I tell ya anything, I want to know exactly who you are."

"Fair enough." Grayson looked at Malone. "I'm worried to involve anyone in this. But I will tell you all I can." She looked down at her left palm and ran her fingers over the crescent-shaped scar. How in the hell could she tell them about this? Where would she start?

She looked up to see Irene staring at her left hand. "Malone. Leave us, please."

He looked startled. "Are you sure, Irene?"

"Yes. Go now and do not come back here. It will be night soon and not safe to drive."

"But what about Grayson…?"

Irene looked at Grayson, who felt the hair on the back of her neck bristle from the intense look in Irene's blue eyes. "She'll be fine. Go on with ya now."

As Malone stood, Irene reached over and touched his arm. "Thank you, Malone."

"Not to worry. I've got a pail of milk to deliver anyway. I believe I'm leaving ya in good hands." He looked at Grayson and nodded. "I will be at the dock tomorrow to take ya back to the mainland."

"Thanks." Grayson shook his hand.

Then he was gone, and they sat in silence.

"I know who you are," Irene said in a low voice.

"How do you know?" Grayson asked, knowing full well how. She rubbed the fingers of her left hand against her palm, trying to ignore how her entire body tingled.

"I sat by the fire the other night and had what I expect was some sort of vision. You were making coffee in a pot by the fire, and we looked right at each other. I asked who you were, and the vision faded like the morning fog. It was you, wasn't it?"

"Yes, it was."

"And you have these visions often? Because I never have. It terrified me, let me tell you."

Grayson hesitated, not knowing how much to tell this woman.

Irene touched the loaf of bread. "It's ready. Would you please get the butter and jam on the counter, plates in the cupboard?"

"Sure." Grayson collected the items and watched as Irene cut thick slices of the brown bread and prepared one for each of them.

"This is heaven," Grayson said as she bit into the warm bread.

"Thank you. Now tell me about the mark." Irene motioned to Grayson's hand.

"It's a long story," Grayson said.

"We have all night."

Grayson proceeded to tell Irene about the stone, the prophecy, her mother, and Phelan Tynan. She recounted her visions, her time in the rock dwelling where she saw all the women who had gone before her. She told Irene of the knowing and her place as the true descendant. She looked down at her left hand and presented her palm. "This is the birthmark, which I thought was a scar. Apparently, according to the prophecy, I was chosen, and when everything aligned under the residual moon, I stopped the ancient wizard and saved the power the gods placed in the stone." She laughed then. "It sounds so silly."

Irene was silent throughout, sipping her tea and eating the bread. "It sounds ridiculous." She laughed, as well. In a moment, both were laughing like children. Irene put her hand to her mouth to quiet herself. "We're both daft, crazy as bedbugs, my mother used to say."

Grayson dried her eyes. "I feel like I'm insane."

"Oh, Grayson. Sad truth is, we're not crazy. Ireland is an ancient country. Everyone thinks it started with St. Patrick and Christianity. And it's easier and safer to believe that so you don't sound insane."

"But not true," Grayson said and drank her tea.

"No. It is not true."

The crack of thunder would have anyone else jumping. Irene stared at Grayson and appeared not to notice the thunder or the blinding flash of lightning that followed. Grayson then thought of getting in touch with Corky or Neala; she realized there was no way. A cell phone was of no use on this island, and Irene McGill had no phone. It was now that Grayson wished she had honed her powers of communicating telepathically—not that anyone would hear her except Sebastian. And that was all she needed Irene to see, a vampire on a stormy night. That'd be enough to send the old woman over the edge.

"I think you're finding out just how old this country is." Irene leaned forward. "I sense a goodness about you. You seem steadfast and true. And a wee bit out of your league."

Grayson chuckled at the understatement. "You don't seem

surprised by what I've told you. If I came up with a fantastic story like this back in Chicago, they'd have thought I was nuts."

"There are many in this country who would feel the same. It's hard to believe such a fantastic story."

"But you do," Grayson said. "Why?"

Irene concentrated on her coffee cup. "Some believe by faith alone. Some need to see before they believe. I have both."

"What have you seen?"

"You've come across the sea to a desolate island in the middle of the ocean to see about a nun. You must think she is somehow involved with all this."

Grayson scratched her head. "When you put it that way, it does sound odd."

"What are you after?" she persisted.

"I don't want you unnecessarily involved in—"

"In what?" Irene didn't wait for an answer. "It's a little late for that anyway." She reached over and took Grayson's left hand, exposing her palm.

Grayson looked into her blue eyes, and for a moment, she was lost. The low hum in her ears made her rapidly shake her head. Suddenly, she saw two young women, the same women she saw when she held Sister Gabriel's hand when they first met. Though, now the vision was clear: Two women stood in a dark room; Grayson felt the dampness around her. One woman started crying, holding her stomach. She bent over and sobbed uncontrollably while the other woman put her arm around her.

Grayson then heard the sobbing woman cry, "It can't be. It can't be." Just then, another woman entered the room; she was older and a nun. To Grayson, she seemed terrified, but it did not seem her fear was aimed at either woman. She blessed herself, then led the sobbing woman out of the room. The vision clouded over and vanished.

"What in God's name just happened?" Irene asked as she released Grayson's hand. Her eyes grew wide then. "Did you have a vision?"

"Look, Irene…"

"You did. What did you see?"

Grayson hesitated for a moment. "I saw two young women, one of them sobbing. They were in a room, then a nun walked in and took the crying woman out. Then the vision faded."

Irene lost the rose tint in her cheeks, making her look far older than her age. She sat back and blessed herself.

Grayson knew then. "You were the nun."

Irene looked as though she might faint. Grayson quickly got a glass of water and handed it to her; she felt horrible when she saw Irene's weathered hands shake as she drank.

"I thought it was over," she whispered. "So long ago."

Grayson quickly went to her when Irene stood. "Let's sit by the fire."

"Sure," Grayson said; she led her to the living room and the comfortable chair.

Grayson strategically added a few peat bricks to the fire to keep it burning. "Would you like more tea?"

"No, thank you. Please sit. We need to talk. It's been over thirty years and it isn't over."

"What happened thirty years ago?"

The rain started. Grayson could hear it pelting against the window. Within a moment, the wind started and blew the back door open. Grayson jumped up and closed the door against the wind and rain.

"That came up fast," she said, wiping the rain from her face.

"It's the way of it on the island. There's no warning. No warning at all."

Grayson shivered, not knowing if it was from the wind and rain or the desolate tone in Irene's voice. She was also aware that Irene had not answered her question. Grayson drank the remains of her tea, noticing the large leaves in the bottom.

"Do not disturb those leaves," Irene said in a cautious voice. "Hand me the teacup with—"

"Not you, too." Grayson groaned. "My left hand. I know. I've had this done already."

"Grand, then you know what to expect. What was the last reading?"

"Oh, no, you don't." Grayson wagged her finger at Irene.

"A non-believer." Irene took the cup and peered into it.

Grayson watched in silence as she cut another slice of bread. "So…?"

Irene put her hand up to quiet her. After a moment, she sat back; the deep frown caused some concern for Grayson.

"I take it I'm not coming into some money?"

Irene tried not to smile. "No, you're not." She leaned forward then. "You will have much trouble to contend with very soon. There is a great deal of deception all around you, woman."

"Rose said the same thing." Grayson pushed the plate of bread away from her and leaned forward. "A few people have had dreams."

Irene raised an eyebrow. "Dreams of what?"

"Rose, she knew my mother and grandmother, recently had a dream of my mother, who said 'liar's moon' and not much else. Another friend, who is a historian, had a similar dream. My mother and Vic came to him in his dream and said the same thing. But with no explanation of what liar's moon meant."

"Who is Vic?"

"She was my wife." Grayson saw the raised eyebrow and the nod.

"I take it both women are deceased," Irene said.

"Yes. Both of them died saving me. Vic was pregnant." Grayson looked at her ring finger and gently twirled the three rings.

"An interesting arrangement." Irene motioned to Grayson's hand.

"It's our wedding rings and my mother's," Grayson said softly. "They gave them to me when I was in the dwelling. They said they'd always be around…"

"You're very lucky. To have them come to you like that."

"So what is your take on this liar's moon? My friend, the historian, told me about the liar's moon in the almanac. And how the haze around it shrouds the truth."

"I don't know about this liar's moon. But in your reading, there is much dishonesty in your near future."

"Tell me what you've seen. Tell me about Sister Gabriel."

"Let's go by the fire. It will be a long night, Grayson MacCarthaigh. And I've held on to this for over thirty, nearly forty years. It's time. If you're asking about Sister Gabriel, then it isn't over. And by what you've told me, it's just beginning."

Chapter 19

Well, Irene scared the crap out of me, Grayson thought, as she stoked the fire, adding several bricks of peat. She took a spot on the hearth, watching Irene, who sat in the chair that Grayson had pulled close to the fire. Grayson felt bad when she saw Irene's eyes glistening in the fire's light.

"She was sixteen when she came to Our Lady of Sorrows convent." Irene let out a deep breath as if it took a great deal out of her just to say those words. "She was alone in the world and pregnant." Irene looked at Grayson and whispered, "And terrified. And when she explained her story, I was terrified, as well. You might not believe what I'm about to tell you. I didn't at first, nor did I during the entire pregnancy. But after that child was born..." She shook her head in what Grayson thought was disbelief.

"Irene, trust me. I'll keep an open mind. I've experienced some bizarre things in the past couple of months."

Irene nodded. "Sister Michael was at a convent in Galway where they met. It was Sister Michael who came to me with the story. I was the abbess here. And after hearing from Sister Michael, we decided to bring Mary here." She stopped and looked at Grayson. "That was her given name. Mary Reardon, poor child."

"So Sister Michael brought her here? Why? I mean, thirty, forty years ago, it was the 1970s. I know Ireland is very Catholic, but I would think she could have had some help back in Ireland. And to become a cloistered nun. Something's not sitting right with me." Grayson saw the doubtful look on Irene's face and smiled. "I was a cop back in Chicago for many years. I suppose I'm a little jaded and suspicious."

Irene nodded. "Well, in this case, I'd say you were right to be so. On the surface, it does appear to be an extreme thing to do."

"I suppose it's just a coincidence that she's now at the monastery."

"You don't believe that. There are no coincidences. Only a string of predetermined events that have yet to happen."

"Okay, it's time to tell me why it's not a coincidence and why Sister Gabriel is at St. Brigid's Monastery right now. It's not as simple as her being alone and pregnant."

"No. It's not. It's who the father of her child was. Or more accurately, not who he was, but what."

"What he was? What do you mean?" Grayson asked, not sure she wanted to know, but somehow, in the back of her mind, perhaps she already knew.

"Mary told us of a fantastic story of a man she fell in love with, who promised her the world and everything in it. For a sixteen-year-old with no one, how wonderful that must have sounded. It's not an unfamiliar story, but what happened after that is the fantastic part. He was a member of the IRA. A gunrunner, from what Mary said. He was wild and free, and Mary gave herself to him and naturally got pregnant. She told us at first, it was heavenly. He adored her and kept her. Then one night, she saw what he really was and it terrified her."

"He wasn't Catholic?" Grayson tried to lighten the mood.

Irene chuckled sadly. "Oh, if that was only it. No, from what Mary said, he was not human."

Grayson knew she had an incredulous look; her mind was reeling at this point. She let Irene continue without interrupting.

"She said she saw him performing some ritual. She thought it was some coven, but he was alone as he knelt in the woods, looking around at the trees, as if he were talking to them. At first, she thought he was just a lover of nature. Mary said she desperately wanted to think of him that way. However, when he changed…"

Grayson knew then. "Into a wolf."

Irene nearly fell out of her chair when she leaned forward. "How in God's name do you know that?"

Grayson was sick to her stomach at the thought of him doing this to a young woman. She felt her anger rising, thinking of all Phelan had done throughout the centuries. She shook her head to bring her back to the situation at hand. "The ancient wizard I told you about. Phelan Tynan."

Irene sat back in stunned silence. "That's not the name Mary told us. She said his name was Padraic Thomas."

"I doubt he'd use his real name. Not if he was running guns for the IRA. Please go on."

"When she witnessed this transformation, she was terrified. She ran and didn't remember how she got to the convent and Sister Michael. She only knew she needed to be far away from him. As far as she could get. So she was brought here. At first, she wanted an abortion. I will tell you, I didn't believe this story in the slightest. But when Sister Daniel contacted me—"

"Sister Daniel from the monastery?"

"Yes. I was very surprised she knew of this. Sister Michael said she had only mentioned it to Sister Daniel but did not mention Mary's notion of him being a changeling. I don't know how she knew."

"I do. Sister Daniel was a big part of all that has happened. She knew everything from the beginning."

"I always thought she was involved somehow. Especially when she said the child must live. Mary must give birth and give the child up for adoption. Then she said something very odd. She said to me, 'so it is written, so shall it be.' She never explained that to me. And I, of course, did not ask. You just don't question the Mother Abbess of a famous monastery. We advised Mary, and she agreed. I don't believe she ever wanted to abort the child."

"When did you start to believe Mary's story?"

"When Sister Daniel entered the picture. She took a great interest in it and swore Sister Michael and me to secrecy, not to speak of this to anyone. We gave our word, and I have never told a soul. Once the child was born, we immediately took her to the proper channels, and I believe a very good family adopted her."

"It was a girl?"

"Yes. And to answer your hopeful look, I don't know what family adopted her. Just a wealthy family from Dublin. And after that, Mary became Sister Gabriel, and it was never spoken of again. Soon afterward, I left Our Lady of Sorrows. I asked to be sent far away, and I was granted that request. I was sent to a convent in Scotland. And now, I'm old and I suppose you could say I'm retired. My brother owned this house and the land. It was left to me when he died ten years ago. Coming back here was very hard, and when I found Sister Gabriel still here, virtually alone, it broke my heart. I tried to see her on many occasions, but she would not see me. So I stopped, but I always had one of the sisters let me know how she was doing. It was through them I found out she went to St. Brigid's, and hearing what you've said, I can see why."

"Yes, I'm sure she knew about my mother's death. Phelan's name has been in the news off and on for decades. He's no stranger to the limelight. I think he likes it, the asshole." Grayson turned bright red. "Sorry."

"No need. I feel the same. So tell me now what will happen."

"I have no idea. I was just trying to satisfy my curiosity about Sister Gabriel. This is something I didn't expect." Grayson stood and placed more peat on the fire. She stared down at the glowing fire. "What happened to the little girl, I wonder."

"I don't know. But if that man, Phelan, is still around, perhaps he knows."

"It's amazing he never found Mary after all these years. He could not have known."

"Perhaps he didn't care."

Grayson laughed. "No. If he knew where Mary was, he would have done something about the child and Mary, trust me."

Though the wind and rain had stopped, Grayson heard it, thinking it was her imagination; she hoped it was. But when she saw the look of fright on Irene's face, Grayson knew she hoped for too much.

"What was that?" Irene asked, looking toward the kitchen.

"Just the wind," Grayson said, patting her shoulder as she walked by. "I'll go check."

They both heard the noise at the front of the house now. It was a low growl, more guttural. Grayson stopped, and for a moment, her heart stopped, as well. She saw the latch to the door unlocked. Without breaking into a dead run, she quickly bolted the door.

Irene stood, leaning on her cane. "Look there. At the window."

Grayson looked where Irene was pointing. At the front window, a shadow of someone, something stood outside. It looked as if it were trying to open the window. For a moment, the window rattled, causing Irene to let out a terrified scream; she stood perfectly still behind Grayson, who glanced back to Irene just in time to see her bless herself. Say one for me, Grayson thought.

She watched as the figure disappeared and instinctively put her hands on the front door and listened. When she put her ear to the door, she heard the guttural breathing; she could almost feel the hot breath through the door. A shiver ran down her spine when the growl turned to laughter.

"Mother of God, what is that?" Irene whispered.

"I'm not sure. I—"

The force sent Grayson reeling backward, but in the next instant, she flew back at the door, her weight full against it. She struggled for a moment, then feeling a surge of energy through her body, she pushed the door with all her might. She now heard more than the growling; something else was outside, as well.

Grayson, aware of poor Irene whimpering behind her, still listened. It sounded like two animals fighting, one snarling at the other. Then, as quickly as it started, it stopped with a high-pitched squeal. Grayson and Irene stood in silence.

"Grayson." She heard someone call her. "Grayson. It's Sebastian."

"Who's Sebastian?" Irene asked. "Don't let them in."

"Irene, it's okay." Grayson opened the door.

Sebastian stood in the shadows and did not move. Grayson could tell she was breathing heavily.

"What are you doing here? Was that you out there all this time?"

"No, but you seem to have a wolf problem," Sebastian said.

"Well, get in here."

"I can't. I must be invited."

"Are you shitting me?" Grayson asked, putting her hands on her hips.

"I shit you not."

Grayson shook her head. "Irene, it's okay. Would you please invite my friend in?"

"Are ya sure?" When Grayson nodded, Irene said, "P-please come in."

"A gracious invitation," Sebastian said. "Thank you, madam." She stepped over the threshold and into the living room.

Grayson was astounded when she saw the blood on Sebastian's face and her fangs protruding. When she heard Irene screech again, Grayson was at her side with lightning speed just as she fainted.

"Oh, dear." Sebastian raised an eyebrow as Grayson glared at her. "I seem to have that effect on women."

Grayson easily picked up Irene and gently placed her in the chair. "You scared the shit out of her, the poor thing, coming in here all bloody and fanging…"

Sebastian called after Grayson, who disappeared into the kitchen, "Do not test me."

Grayson came back with a towel for Sebastian. "Wipe your face before she wakes up. I hope she hasn't had a heart attack." Grayson then put another cold cloth on Irene's forehead; she immediately moaned.

Sebastian wiped her face. "I just had a run-in with a very large wolf outside, which seems to be following you around."

Grayson's head shot up. "What do you mean?"

"I had a feeling you were in trouble."

"A feeling? About me?"

"Yes, it nagged at me all day. It was annoying," Sebastian said with a scowl.

Irene moaned again; her eyes flickered open. "Okay, lose

the fangs, she's waking up." Grayson gently wiped Irene's brow. "Hey, you with us?" she asked softly.

Irene smiled and looked up at Sebastian. "I'm not dead, am I?"

"No, madam. I am—" Sebastian's last word came out as a painful grunt when Grayson quickly stood, pushing her out of the way.

"How do you feel, Irene?"

"I'm fine. It just scared the wits right out of me." She laughed and put her head back. "What was that, Grayson?"

"Just an animal, madam," Sebastian said.

Irene gave Sebastian a skeptical glance. "Who are you?"

Grayson and Sebastian exchanged quick glances. "A friend of mine," Grayson said quickly when Sebastian started to speak. "She scared away whatever animal was out there."

"Thank you," Irene said, but Grayson knew Irene didn't believe her. Irene kept her eyes on Sebastian.

"My pleasure," Sebastian said with a bow, much to Grayson's ire.

"You don't know what type of animal it was?" Irene asked.

"I believe it might have been a wolf."

Grayson closed her eyes and hung her head.

"We don't have any wolves on this island," Irene said to Sebastian.

"Perhaps not now," Sebastian said.

"What Sebastian means, Irene, is—"

"We both know what she meant," Irene said, still watching Sebastian. "Where are you from?"

Sebastian seemed to ponder the question. "From a distant land."

"Why don't I believe you?" Irene asked.

"I don't know."

Grayson rubbed her temples before turning to Irene, who spoke first. "It was him, wasn't it?"

"Irene…"

"God help us," Irene whispered. "How do we know he isn't still out there?"

Grayson quickly knelt next to her when she heard the terror in her voice. "We don't know what that was. And I won't let anything happen to you. Sebastian and I will stay the night." She glanced back at Sebastian, who was now scowling deeply.

After Irene finally fell asleep, Grayson and Sebastian stood by the fireplace.

"It was Phelan, right?" Grayson asked.

"Is there another shape-shifter you're not telling me about?"

"No." Grayson heard the doubt in her voice. Apparently, Sebastian heard it, as well.

"You don't sound convinced. Why?"

"Irene and I had a very interesting conversation."

"About?"

"Sister Gabriel. It seems before she was Sister Gabriel, she was Mary Reardon, and at the impressionable age of sixteen, she fell in love with a gunrunner for the IRA and got pregnant."

"Something tells me there's more to this story."

"Oh, yes." Grayson glanced at Sebastian's curious face before continuing. "It appears the gunrunner was Phelan Tynan. Mary Reardon found him in the woods one day, shape-shifting."

"And ran screaming into the night, heading for a nunnery to become Sister Gabriel."

"Yep."

"And she gave birth to this child?"

Grayson nodded. "A girl, immediately taken and given up for adoption." She watched Sebastian shake her head. "And to answer your next question…no, we have no idea what happened to the child."

"I can see why you don't sound convinced. What are you feeling, Grayson?"

"I don't know."

Grayson looked at Sebastian; their gazes locked.

What is it, Grayson?

I'm not sure.

You feel something, someone else, don't you?

Yes.

Trust these powers. Trust what you feel.

Grayson nodded and flopped back in the chair by the fire. She was aware of Sebastian's scrutiny. "Tell me."

"I'm not sure. I had an overwhelming feeling there are others or more exactly, one other. I-I don't know why."

"It's been my vast experience, where there is one, there are many."

Grayson looked up and groaned. "Please don't say that."

"It's true. Tell me, what did Phelan look like when he morphed into a wolf? Did he look human? Larger than an ordinary wolf? Did he walk upright or as a wolf?"

"He looked exactly like a wolf. No human aspects at all. No, he did not walk upright." Grayson gave Sebastian a wary glance. "Please don't start with werewolves."

Sebastian laughed outright. "Don't worry. I know one when I see one."

Grayson's jaw hit the floor. Sebastian cocked an eyebrow. "Let's not go there right now."

Grayson waved her off. "Let's not. Phelan morphed into a brown-eyed black wolf."

Sebastian's head shot up. "Black?"

"Yeah, big, well over a hundred pounds and black with a gray muzzle, why?" Grayson felt the hair on the back of her neck bristle so much, she shivered uncontrollably.

"Are you sure?"

"Yes. We got up close and personal a couple months back. Now tell me why you ask."

"Because the wolf I tangled with was much smaller and gray with blue-green eyes. I sensed it was—"

"Female."

"Yes. I take it you did, as well."

"And I don't know why," Grayson said. "This is getting worse. Is it possible we have two shape-shifters?"

"It would make sense if Phelan spawned a child, it would have his genes, hence some of his capabilities."

"Make sense?" Grayson asked angrily.

"I certainly understand your anger and resentment. I too am

in a position I wish not to be. But you'd best get over this petulant anger, and in your own vernacular, grow the fuck up."

Grayson quickly rose and stood in front of Sebastian, who held her ground. "Look, no one asked you to be here, you ghoul."

Sebastian sighed. "So much for not being childish," she mumbled. "What is it that you want—your life back? You can't have it. Trust me. I spent the better part of three centuries in search of it. It can't happen. Your life as you knew it back in Chicago is over. Just as mine in Romania nearly five hundred years ago. At least you have memories. Imagine," she said and looked into Grayson's eyes, "not remembering your wife, your mother, your childhood. And knowing you had all of it."

Grayson said nothing while she absorbed what Sebastian said.

"So what say you live right now and move forward? Because if all you do is piss and moan about what you don't have, you'll miss all you possess and your sense of purpose."

Grayson remained silent as she stared at the peat fire.

"You absolutely hate it when you're wrong, don't you? You're so human."

Grayson hid her grin and shook her head. "I'm sure you're the picture of maturity when Alex brings it to your attention."

Sebastian didn't flinch. "We're talking about you."

"How is Alex, by the way? I only met her once, and that was a couple years ago. She was dating a detective at the time. Alex seemed very nice. Too good for Carey Spaulding, as I recall. I expected them to break up, but not in my wildest dreams did I think she'd go for a vampire. She must have been so distraught she'd go to anyone and—"

"Let's ride this maniacal train to its destination without derailment. We were talking about wolves."

Grayson grunted and stood. "Okay, so now what? We have two wolves? How can we know who it is?"

"Well, we did scuffle. I believe I got a good bite in."

Grayson grinned. "And if you did, it would leave a mark?"

"Perhaps. I know I heal quickly. But I have no idea about shape-shifters. Perhaps your historian can shed some light. If he knew about vampires, he may know about Phelan and his kind, as well."

"In the morning, we'll go back. I'm staying here with Irene tonight. I don't want the poor woman to wake up alone. Not after what she went through."

"I will not be here in the daylight."

"No serum?"

"I…"

"You forgot your serum? I'm not sure I want to be associated with a forgetful vampire."

Sebastian's fangs dropped. "Good night, mortal."

"Good—"

Sebastian had already disappeared.

Chapter 20

"Look after Irene for me, Malone," Grayson said as she handed him the folded bills.

Malone gently pushed the money back toward Grayson. "Won't take your money, but I'll do as you ask. I've known Irene for many years. I shouldn't stay away as long as I have. I won't let anything happen to her."

Grayson shook his hand. "Thanks. If you ever need anything, anything at all, you know where to find me."

"I do." He held her hand tighter. "You're a good woman. If I can be of any help to you, anytime, you do the same."

"I will. Thanks."

Grayson hopped onto the dock and waited as Malone maneuvered his boat and headed back to the Aran Islands.

Once back at the monastery, Grayson wondered what in the world to do next. Gratefully, Corky was already in the office studying over his book. He looked up when Grayson walked in.

"Good morning. Where in the world have you been? I've been worried sick." He sat back and laughed then. "Although I thought you'd gone to Dublin after you went to Innishmore to see Neala and…" He wriggled his eyebrows.

Grayson chuckled and sat by the fire. "No such luck." She held her hands up to the fire to warm them. "Was, um, Neala worried?"

"I dunno. I haven't been able to get in touch with her, either, hence my thought of you two being together."

Grayson nodded but said nothing, though she smiled at the idea of being with Neala on a personal level. It beat this god and goddess crap completely.

"So where were you? You have my full attention." Corky tossed down his pen and waited.

"Well, in a nutshell, I was right about Sister Gabriel."

Suddenly, her palm itched. She quickly scratched at it with her other hand and looked around. "Let's go for a walk."

"Sure," Corky said cautiously and grabbed his jacket.

They walked away from the monastery down the dirt path. Grayson formulated all that had happened. "It appears before she was Sister Gabriel, she was Mary Reardon. At the tender age of sixteen, she fell head over heels for some IRA gunrunner and found herself pregnant. It's after she found out who this charming terrorist was that Mary became Sister Gabriel."

"Who was he?"

"One guess."

Grayson nearly laughed at Corky's incredulous stare. "No."

"Yes. Apparently, she saw him morph during some ritual and made a beeline to the nearest convent. It was Sister Michael who took her to the Aran Islands and Our Lady of Sorrows Convent. The baby was born, a girl, and was adopted by a family in Dublin. But they don't know what family. Mary Reardon became Sister Gabriel and lived the last thirty years or so in seclusion."

Corky shook his head slowly, as if absorbing all Grayson had said. He then scratched his chin. "Then Sister Michael lied to us, and Sister Gabriel lied. That means we have two more for our liar's moon. It's disheartening to find this out. Who told you?"

"Another nun. She was in a vision I had the other night. But this was the first time a vision actually talked. She looked right at me and asked who I was, as if she saw me, as well. When I met her—her name is Irene, by the way—she recognized me. So she did see me in her vision."

"How did she know Sister Gabriel?"

"She was the Mother Abbess of the convent back then. She told me everything." Grayson looked out at the green sloping hills, reveling in the quiet and solitude she knew would not last.

"How do you know she told you everything? She could be another liar."

"I know. I suspect everyone now," Grayson said angrily. She

felt Corky watching her and saw the hurt look. "No. I don't suspect you or Neala." She laughed and said, "I don't even suspect that scowling vampire. Though I probably should."

Corky laughed along. "You two are connected somehow. I truly believe that."

"The other night, Elinora was in my room. She told me Sebastian was the key to this, and she hinted about Sister Gabriel. This is why I went to Innishmore. Sebastian did show up last night. Out of nowhere. She said she felt something was wrong. Don't ask me how she knew where I was. I haven't a clue. Must be some psychic vampire shit she has."

Corky chuckled as Grayson cleared her throat and glanced at him. "There's something else."

He stopped laughing and immediately frowned. "I don't like the tone in your voice. What else?"

"There was someone or something outside Irene's cottage last night. Sebastian tangled with it. She said it was a wolf."

"Phelan?"

"No, I don't think so. When Phelan morphed into the wolf, it was big and black with dark eyes. The wolf Sebastian encountered was gray, with what she thought were blue-green eyes and smaller. She also got a good bite in."

Corky ran his fingers through his red hair. "This is interesting."

"Interesting? That's putting it mildly, my friend. It scared the crap out of me, and you find it interesting. You amaze me."

"Do you suppose this wolf was Phelan's daughter?"

"I knew you were gonna say that. I hate this."

"I know, but it makes sense. If Phelan can shape-shift, his offspring could, as well. But how did she know where you were? And who is she?"

"I have no idea."

"Well, look at the bright side," Corky said with enthusiasm that scared Grayson.

"There is one?"

"At least we know it's a woman we're looking for. And last night, I figured out another piece of this letter from Tatiana."

Grayson felt a ray of hope. "What?"

"Let's get back to the monastery. I want to show you what I think."

Corky sat behind the desk with Grayson hovering over him.

Corky put on his glasses. "Let's start at the beginning. In the first stanza, what do we have figured out?" He opened Grayson's translation and started. "In the shadow of the crescent, a mark is cloaked unseen. The traitor's song eclipse the moon, Blackheart betrays the queen."

"Okay, we know Tatiana knows about me, and we have a traitor or a liar among us. What else?"

"The word blackheart and the phrase 'in the shadow of the crescent, a mark is cloaked unseen' were curious to me. So I did some digging in my book. And look what I found." He reverently turned the pages of his book, then pointed to a certain passage.

Grayson peered over his shoulder and looked at the drawing on the page. "What is that? It looks like a black circle with a line bisecting it. I'm sure it's more than that."

"It's a rune, I believe, but doesn't seem to have anything to do with the Celts. There is a mythical—"

Grayson hung her head. "God, not again."

Corky smiled and continued. "I won't go into it, only to say it's Germanic in origin but that rune means 'shadow' or 'darkness.' Now if you read further, look..." He pointed to the passage.

Grayson leaned closer and read. When she finished, she looked at Corky, who sported a superior grin. "I'll be damned."

"Yes." Corky read aloud. "This mark is upon the one with a blackheart who will betray the queen." He took his glasses off and rubbed his eyes. "So it is my belief that whoever our liar is has this mark on him, well, her. If we believe Phelan had a daughter and she is the liar. I still don't know who the queen is. It could be you."

"Me? Well, I guess that would make sense since it references the crescent."

"And the liar will be exposed at the full moon. But right now, 'the traitor's song eclipse the moon,' so we don't know who he is or what his intentions are. Whoever this is, Gray, is very, very clever and devious and one more thing…"

"What's that?"

"It's someone you know."

Grayson thought for a moment and groaned. "Inspector Gaffney."

"Why would you think it was her?" Corky took off his glasses.

"For one, she's a woman and about the right age. And two? She's from Dublin and adopted."

"How do you know?"

"We had drinks the day we found Kathleen's body." She stopped and chuckled. "That sounded ghoulish. You know what I mean. She asked why I became an officer. I explained about my father, then asked her the same question. That's when she told me she was adopted by a family in Dublin."

Corky whistled and walked over to the window. He pushed the long window open and took a deep breath. "Now what?" he asked as he gazed out at the morning.

"Now I have a little conversation with the inspector. But first I'm going to have a chat with Sister Gabriel."

"Well, you couldn't pick a better time. She just walked out into the courtyard. Look. She's talking to Sister Michael."

Grayson quickly stood by Corky. "The two of them. Thick as thieves."

Corky nodded. "I wonder what they're talking about. Perhaps they don't know any more than Irene told you."

"I doubt it. This is all too coincidental for me. Really, what are the odds of all this?" Grayson turned and walked out. "I'm going to talk to them. Are you coming?"

"Are ya daft?" Corky nearly tripped over the chair to keep up with her.

"Good morning," Grayson called out as they approached the two nuns. "Are we interrupting your morning meditation?"

"No, not at all," Sister Gabriel said.

"What do you need, Grayson?" Sister Michael asked.

For a moment, Grayson didn't know what to say or how to start. She glanced at Corky, who looked like a little kid who lied about going to Mass. This was not going to be easy.

"I need to talk to both of you," Grayson finally said.

Sister Gabriel watched Grayson. "Perhaps we should go to your office."

It wasn't a request. Sister Gabriel walked away with Sister Michael right behind. Grayson and Corky followed without a word.

Sister Gabriel sat in the uncomfortable high-back chair. Corky sat behind the desk, while Sister Michael sat in the chair by the fire. Grayson stood.

"What is it you want, Grayson?" Sister Michael asked.

Grayson heard the trace of sadness in her voice. "I went to Innishmore yesterday. And found Irene McGill."

Sister Michael quickly looked at Sister Gabriel, who watched Grayson with a mix of concern and sadness. "Did you now?" she asked softly. "And what did you find out?"

"I think you know, Sister," Grayson said. "But I'd like to hear it from you."

"Grayson—"

"No, Sister. It's time." Sister Gabriel held up a hand to silence Sister Michael. "If you went to Innishmore, then you know how I came to be there and why."

"Yes. But what I don't know is why you're here at this time." Grayson sat on the edge of the desk. She watched Sister Gabriel, whose face showed little emotion. "We have a bit of a problem, Sister. I hope you can shed some light."

"When Sister Michael brought me to Our Lady of Sorrows, I thought it would be over. I would repent for my promiscuity and subsequent pregnancy. The child would be cared for and loved in a good family. For this, I prayed and devoted my life to God and God alone. I never heard from him again and assumed my prayers were answered. I lived my life at Our Lady, and I was content and sure I had done the right thing by my child.

"It was not until Sister Daniel came to see me after your mother died that I realized he was still in Ireland. Being cloistered, I did not know what was happening in the outside world. Sister

Daniel explained that because of him, your mother died, and it was time I joined the world. She said it was written this way that I would come here, and when the time came, I would assist you. She would not say how or when, only that I would know when it happened. I suppose this is the time." She stopped and looked at Grayson. "What has happened?"

Grayson didn't know how to explain Sebastian, so she decided not to try. "Corky and Rose Barry had a dream. My mother came to them and said liar's moon. We didn't know what that meant, but now we have a letter that indicates this liar's moon is at hand. And that someone, someone I know, is lying. They're marked as I am. But I'm told they are evil, and I should remember that."

"Who told you this?" Sister Michael asked.

Grayson was aware Sister Gabriel watched her carefully. "Sister Michael, you don't believe in what Corky, Neala, or I are doing. I respect that…"

"There is too much that has happened. Although I may not believe in it, I cannot deny its existence. While I have not seen firsthand, I trusted Sister Daniel. I pray every day for God's help. I will listen to what you have to say."

"This mark you were speaking of. How do you know this? Where did you get this letter?" Sister Gabriel asked.

"It was given to a colleague of mine. Suffice it to say, the letter was written by a very, very old…woman who never met me. What we find curious are references to me and to this." Grayson held up her left hand, exposing the crescent-shaped scar that bisected her palm. "It also references a liar, or traitor, and the moon. This is what Corky and Rose dreamed of, liar's moon. We believe now that this letter is more of a prophecy. And now, with Neala's assistant being killed the same way as my mother and the information from Innishmore, things are getting a little out of control."

"You mentioned this person being evil and marked. In what way marked?"

Grayson looked at Corky, who put on his glasses and held up Grayson's translation. "It says the mark is cloaked unseen. It's hidden from sight."

Sister Gabriel nodded and looked at Sister Michael, who was about to faint. "Do you have any idea what this mark looks like?" Sister Gabriel asked. "And I pray you do not."

Corky leafed through his book. "We believe it looks like this." He presented the page to both nuns.

They leaned forward and peered at the page. Grayson knew which picture Corky had shown them: the black circle with a line bisecting it.

"My God," Sister Michael whispered.

Grayson said slowly, "My God, what, sisters?" She looked at Sister Gabriel, who looked so despondent; it nearly broke Grayson's heart. "Sister?"

"On the small of her back, on the left side, she had a tiny birthmark," Sister Gabriel whispered. "I remember seeing it after she was born. It was fleeting, as they took her away quickly, but I saw it. It was the mark in your book."

The loud hissing of the fire broke the silence that hung in the air.

"The evil that men do lives after them," Sister Gabriel whispered.

Grayson saw the tears glistening in her eyes when she looked at Grayson. "He is evil."

"Yes, ma'am. He is," Grayson said, her heart aching at the forlorn, helpless look.

"And he has spawned evil. And God forgive me, I helped him."

The truth in Sister Gabriel's statement was hard to argue.

"What is he, Grayson?" Sister Michael asked.

Grayson looked at Corky, who sported an incredulous look. "Tell them."

"All of it?" Corky's voice came out in a squeak.

"Now's not the time to be timid, Timothy," Sister Michael said. "I'll have a pot of strong tea made."

We're gonna need more than tea, Grayson thought.

"Do you know where Neala is?" Corky asked.

Grayson shrugged. "I assume the museum."

"I'll call her. Maybe she can drive over. She really should be here." Corky pulled out his cell phone.

"Come to think of it, where's Sebastian?" Grayson asked, mostly to herself. She didn't like that vampire running around the village of Dungarin.

She tried to ignore the sudden anxious feeling when she thought of Sebastian. Elinora said Sebastian was the key to this. When Grayson thought further, actually Elinora said "the vampire" was the key. Perhaps it was Tatiana. Confusion hit her like a wave; nothing seemed certain now—she could not shake this unsettling feeling.

Chapter 21

Sebastian stood in the shadows of the museum exhibit. She watched as Neala talked to several men, gesturing to the stone encased in glass as if explaining. The men definitely looked relieved; one man mopped his brow with a handkerchief and nearly hugged Neala.

As they seemed satisfied with whatever Neala had told them, they walked out of the exhibit room, leaving Neala standing there alone, staring at the glass case.

"An odd-looking thing," Sebastian said from behind her.

Neala turned. "It's an archaeological find. May I ask what you're doing here?"

Sebastian grinned. "Grayson bored me. So I thought I'd take in Dublin. It's an old city."

"And you were around for its conception?"

Sebastian raised an eyebrow. "Very good, but no. I was not present for the ribbon cutting. I do, however, know many who were."

Neala smiled and nodded. Sebastian searched her face; certainly, she was a very beautiful woman. "You didn't have the usual reaction when you discovered I was a vampire. Even Grayson, with all she has been through, and who is an immortal of sorts, was unbelieving when we first met."

"Grayson unfortunately has disbelieved much."

"And you don't?"

"As you say, much has happened in the past few months. Our lives have changed, as the rules. Nothing is what it seems."

"And standing here with a vampire is one of those things."

"I suppose it is. I certainly wouldn't believe that Grayson

could walk through a stone wall and experience all she did." She stopped, and as she raised her hand to brush the hair from her face, she winced. "So I suppose you're not the scary vampire you might want to be."

"I can be very scary if the situation warrants. Let's hope it doesn't come to that."

"I agree. Tell me about this serum. I understand you now can stay in the light of day."

"Not indefinitely. It has its limits."

"What's it like?" Neala asked.

"The serum or being the undead?"

"That sounds so sad to say it that way."

"Perhaps it is sad," Sebastian said, watching her. Neala was indeed a beautiful woman. She could see the attraction Grayson had for her. "It is not an existence I would choose."

"Now you sound like Grayson."

"We have that in common."

"You must have a feeling of power, knowing you can have anyone you want."

Sebastian noticed her staring at her lips, so she grinned ever so slightly, allowing her fangs to protrude. Yes, there is a great deal of power, Sebastian thought as she watched the artery in Neala's neck throb. She took a step closer to Neala, whose breath caught in her throat as she backed up. "Power takes many forms, Neala. I thought I had infinite power until I met Dr. Alex Taylor."

"Who is she?" Neala whispered.

"My savior. The one who discovered the serum."

"And you're in love with her? She's human, correct?"

"Yes, on both counts. She is beautiful, much like you. Grayson is a lucky woman."

"Grayson and I are not—"

Sebastian closed the distance between them. "Then Grayson is a foolish immortal."

Sebastian saw the crimson color rise from Neala's neck to her cheeks. "Thank you." She walked away; Sebastian grinned and followed her as they left the exhibit room. "It was very sad about your assistant. I wonder what she was doing."

"I don't know, and yes, it was very sad. She was a friend, as well as a colleague. And I miss her."

Sebastian glanced at Neala, who looked deep in thought. "She must have known something for this Phelan to kill her."

"I know, but I can't think what it was. I don't know why she was going to see Grayson."

"What makes you think she was going to see Grayson?"

Neala stopped. "I don't know what other reason she would be in that area. Grayson lives there, Corky. The monastery is there. I suppose I just assumed it had to be one of those reasons. She had some information, something."

Sebastian could see the frustration within Neala. "What's your take on this liar's moon?"

"Again, I don't know. It's annoying. But we think Tatiana knew that you and Grayson have some connection. I wish everything wasn't so cryptic."

"I agree. Nothing is easy. However, we are very fortunate to have Corky," Sebastian said as they walked into Neala's office.

Sebastian looked around while Neala leafed through some papers on her desk. Neala looked up to see Sebastian watching her. "What's wrong?"

"Wrong? Nothing, really. I just find it odd that I can't read you."

"Read me? What do you mean?" Neala sat and signed a few papers. "I'm an open book. What would ya like to know?"

Sebastian leaned against the file cabinet. "How is it that you came to know Grayson and her mother?"

"I knew Maeve for a few years. We shared a love of Irish history and mythology. We also believed the Tuatha De Danann was not a myth, just as Corky believes. Grayson is a little slow in that department." She laughed while she concentrated on her work. "I met Grayson in Chicago. We had the exhibit there. One of the women who guarded their portion of the stone was killed by Phelan. Grayson suspected I was involved somehow."

"And you were," Sebastian said, watching her.

Neala looked up. "Yes, I was."

Their gazes locked for a moment. The soft knock at her door

had Neala looking away. "Come in." She groaned audibly when Inspector Gaffney walked in.

Sebastian grinned once again. "Inspector. How nice to see you. May I call you Megan?"

"No," Megan said and looked at Neala. "Is this a bad time? I just have a few nagging questions about the victim."

"She has a name, Inspector." Neala angrily shuffled the papers on her desk.

"I'm sorry. Would you like me to come back?" Megan asked. Sebastian heard the softer tone.

"No, no. Please sit down." Neala offered the chair in front of her desk.

"Should I leave?" Sebastian asked.

"Please stay." Megan flipped open the small notebook. "Have you given any thought as to why Ms. Moore would drive across the country when she lived in Dublin? You say you had just given her the afternoon off, and it was Friday. If it were me, I suppose the first thing I would do is go home. Did she have friends or relatives in Clare?"

"I don't know," Neala said.

Megan glanced at Sebastian, who said, "I never met the woman."

"Dr. Rourke, you said there were personnel files and files on your contributors. But you found nothing missing?"

"No. All the files are there. But to be honest, we've had so many contributors and employees that have come and gone, it truly is hard to keep track. And I don't work in that department. I'm curator, not human resources."

Sebastian listened to Megan's calm voice and couldn't blame Neala for sounding irritated. She watched both women—Neala, the fiery redhead, and Megan Gaffney, the cool, collected brunette. Grayson had two women in proximity. Sebastian fought the primal sexual arousal.

"Well, I think I'll be going," Sebastian said quickly and headed for the door. She noticed the stunned look from Neala and the smug curious look from Megan. "Good day, ladies."

"What are you doing, vampire?"

Sebastian saw Elinora at least a hundred yards away from her. In a flash, Sebastian was at her side. "What do you mean?"

"I observed you with the doctor and the inspector. Your sexual appetite hasn't changed over the centuries."

Sebastian nearly laughed. "I wondered if you remembered. Your name was not Elinora back then, Melaina."

"That was long ago, Sebastian. We were both much, much younger then and our time together fleeting. We are as ancient as Greece."

"We're not that old."

"Do you remember?"

"Yes. I remember."

"You were persistent," Elinora said.

"You were desirous."

"I can see your ego tells you our time together is the reason for my celibacy."

Sebastian heard the sarcasm in Elinora's voice. "It is not?"

"No, it is not. Now onto my previous question. What were you doing with the doctor?"

"There's something about her and I cannot figure it out. It's unusual, as if…"

"As if what? You seem disconcerted, and that is unlike an immortal, with the exception of Grayson MacCarthaigh, who seems constantly unsettled. Perhaps if you get your insatiable libido out of the way, you can figure it out."

Sebastian raised an eyebrow. "My libido is just fine. But I appreciate the interest."

"Is your human Dr. Alex Taylor as interested?"

"I had forgotten for a moment you were immortal. Reading minds is very invasive, Melaina. Oh, pardon me, Elinora."

"I love my powers. I hope to help Grayson with hers, as well. She is a good choice to be the keeper of their power and magic. It flows through her now, though she is so reluctant to accept it."

"Perhaps she just wishes to be human," Sebastian said.

"As you know, that cannot be. As much as you wish it so," Elinora said in a soft voice. "We all have our destiny."

Sebastian scowled but nodded in agreement. Elinora smiled and gently touched her cheek. "You fight it, as well, vampire. I know of your place in your world and what you must do."

"How much do you know?"

Elinora swiped the dark hair from her face as the wind blew across the green hills. "Much." She looked at Sebastian then. "And you must keep your distance for now. As much as you want your book deciphered, you must not interfere."

"Interfere with what?"

"With Grayson's destiny under the liar's moon."

"What will happen to Grayson?"

"Is that affection I hear in a vampire's voice?"

"No."

Elinora laughed. "You care for this mortal. It is good. But you must not interfere."

"If I can help—"

"It is not your destiny. And I will stop you."

"If you are able."

Elinora grew serious. "I am here for one purpose, and I will see it through."

"If you harm Grayson or anyone else..."

"You know better than to threaten me. I will not succumb to you or anyone. I know my purpose here."

"You are being purposely vague. It's because of this that I don't trust you."

"I do not care if you trust me or not. This is not about you, remember that."

They regarded each other for a long moment before Sebastian spoke. "You know who this liar is. You are not being forthcoming. Another reason for my distrust. Perhaps you are the liar. Should I or Grayson believe her gods sent you to aid her? Or someone else to stop her?"

Elinora showed no signs of emotion. "Be warned, vampire."

And then she was gone.

Chapter 22

Elinora stood on the edge of the cliff. With her head lifted skyward, she closed her eyes and flexed her neck and shoulders. Gaining strength from the wind and the earth beneath her feet, Elinora smiled as she floated from the ground and rose higher and higher. Her outstretched arms became wings and her body now that of a hawk soared above the trees.

In this state, she had felt no other feeling of freedom than this. She felt the wind through her wings as the world below her drifted by while she traveled inland from the shore. With the monastery below, the green sloping hills of this ancient country beckoned to her free spirit of a hawk in flight. In all the other forms she had been, nothing appealed to her more than this.

She was free, if only for a few moments, before she was once again bound to the earth and to the duty at hand. Elinora did not like this part of being immortal; however, the decision was not hers. It was out of her hands.

Trying to ignore what she had to do, she soared higher and farther out to sea, leaving the monastery far behind. Elinora allowed her mind to drift to another time. And now she remembered Sebastian. Although she told the vampire it was not because of their time together Elinora chose to no longer have relations with anyone, she knew it was a lie. Though their time was a mere grain of sand in this universe, it changed Elinora's existence completely.

"*You want this,*" *Sebastian whispered against her neck.*

Melaina shuddered. "As do you, Sebastian. You have waited long enough."

Sebastian pulled back and ran her fingertips across the top of Melaina's shoulders, then down her arms. On the way, she slipped the straps of her white gown down her arms. Melaina sighed as Sebastian easily stripped the silken material from her, her olive skin glistening in the moonlight. Melaina stepped out of the gown and lay back against the pillows. The summer breeze blew the long sheer curtains; Sebastian gazed as she shivered. "You are beautiful, Melaina. Your gods have favored you and me."

"You are unlike any immortal I have known, though my life as an immortal is relatively new."

Sebastian slowly undressed as she gazed at Melaina, who raised her arms above her head. She quickly slipped beside Melaina, kissing her neck, feeling the pulsating artery against her lips. "Beautiful," she mumbled and sensually licked the area with the tip of her tongue.

"I was advised not to have sexual relations," Melaina whispered. She sighed as Sebastian lips traveled down her neck to the top of her breast.

"Why is that?" Sebastian lightly placed kisses up and down the valley between her breasts.

"It is a distraction." Melaina ran her fingers through Sebastian's long dark hair.

Sebastian shivered when she felt Melaina's nails scraping her scalp. "A most sought-after distraction."

"Yes, but a distraction nonetheless." Melaina laughed, then gasped when Sebastian's fingers traveled across her breast, toying with her nipple.

Sebastian's hand wandered down to her belly, her fingers dancing through Melaina's arousal. "You do indeed want this."

Melaina said nothing as she parted her legs. Sebastian took the offering and slipped her fingers inside. Melaina arched her back, her inner muscles contracting around Sebastian's insistent fingers.

As Sebastian brought Melaina over the edge, her fangs dropped; she plunged them into the soft olive flesh just above Melaina's right breast. Melaina cried out as the pleasure and the pain swirled around her. She heard the vampire snarl and move over her, dominating her completely, and Melaina welcomed the possessive posture. It was a surreal feeling for her; never had she felt so vulnerable and out of control. In the back of her mind, Melaina knew this is what the goddesses advised her against. An immortal could not lose control at anytime.

When Sebastian pulled back, Melaina saw the blood on her lips. Though she was completely sated, Melaina shook her head. "This cannot happen again."

Sebastian licked her lips. "An immortal with a conscience. This is my luck." She rolled away and lay on her back, breathing heavily.

Melaina walked over to the table and poured water from the ornate pitcher into the bowl. Taking the towel, she gently washed the blood away from her neck and shoulder. She did not move when she felt the towel taken from her hands; she stood still while Sebastian bathed her. The vampire's touch was exquisitely gentle, causing Melaina nearly to forget her own words, as she leaned back into the strong body behind her.

She then turned around. Taking the wet cloth from Sebastian, she gently bathed her face and neck. "A vampire with a romantic, sensual touch. Just my luck."

Sebastian scowled. "I am not romantic."

"And I have no conscience."

Sebastian sported a toothy grin. "One more go?"

Melaina laughed openly and wrapped her arms around Sebastian's neck. "Your Tatiana was correct. You are the devil."

Elinora would never let the egotistical vampire know she was the reason for many changes in her existence—many changes.

Chapter 23

"Neala is on her way. She left nearly an hour ago," Corky said to Grayson. "And she had another go around with Inspector Gaffney."

"Damn it," Grayson whispered. "Why don't you start, Cork? It'll take Neala a while to get here."

"Right then." Corky put on his glasses as he leafed through the book. He waited until the young nun wheeled the teacart in, poured the tea, and left. "From the beginning. I'll give you the short version and expand on it when needed, right?" When both nuns nodded, he started, "You both know a little Irish mythology, I hope. The Tuatha De Danann?"

"Yes, Corky, we're familiar with them," Sister Michael said.

"Well, in a nutshell, when Danu, the goddess of them all, realized their existence in the real world was about to end with the battle of Teltown, she instructed the druids to encase all the power and magic they possessed in a stone marked with the Ogham alphabet. The marking depicted the exact time when the true descendant would be called upon, if need be, to claim the power and protect it and Ireland. The stone was then broken in three and each piece given to someone different—a sorcerer, an alchemist, and a healer, so no one entity had all the power. They were to protect their section of the stone throughout the centuries until that time. Figol, a wizard, was the sorcerer. Unfortunately, he was an ancient wizard of evil and decided he should have all the power. On the night of the ritual, he murdered the ancient ones and gave his section to his son, who stayed in the real world in quest of the other two sections of the stone. When he found the other two sections, he would reunite all three sections under the residual moon and capture all the power and magic.

"From the prophecy I had been working on for years, I ascertained the exact time when all this would happen, but I never found who the true descendant was." He stopped and glanced at Grayson. "Until I met Grayson. You see in the prophecy, the true descendant was marked with a crescent shape. Grayson has such a mark on her palm, which she thought was a scar. The crescent shape is also on the stone. According to the prophecy, Niamh, daughter of Manannan, Celtic god of the sea, had a child with a mortal. In future generations, Grayson proved to be the true descendant." He stopped to get the reaction from both nuns.

Sister Michael was enthralled but disbelieving, Grayson could tell. Sister Gabriel seemed more open-minded. When neither nun said a word, Corky continued.

"Grayson had been investigating the murder of three Irish women in Chicago. Neala was in Chicago at the time with the latest exhibit. A triangular stone with ancient markings on it. It was to be the final section of stone from the Tuatha De Danann. Neala safely transported it back to Ireland where it was subsequently stolen by—"

"Phelan Tynan," Sister Gabriel whispered.

"You cannot believe all of this, Sister Gabriel," Sister Michael exclaimed. "This is pure nonsense. Whoever heard...?"

Sister Gabriel reached over and placed her hand on Sister Michael's forearm. "Let him finish, Sister."

Corky cleared his throat and glanced again at Grayson who smiled. "Go on, Corky."

"Right then. Yes, Sister, it was indeed Phelan Tynan who took the stone from the museum. He killed Maeve, thinking she was the true descendant, thus Maeve fulfilling her part of the prophecy, as well. Her destiny was to give her life for Grayson." He looked at Grayson.

Grayson raised her left hand, presenting her palm to both nuns to examine. "It's true, as much as I would like it not to be. Sister Daniel showed me the ancient rock dwelling. Upon entering it, I had a visitation for lack of a better word. It was my mother and my wife." She looked down at the three wedding bands on her ring finger. "They showed me all those who had lived and died to bring me to this point. I had visions of Phelan throughout his existence, lying, cheating, and killing anyone to get the stones. I saw ancient rituals that I still don't understand. But I now had what Sister Daniel called the knowing."

"The knowing?" Sister Michael asked with a good deal of skepticism.

Grayson nodded. "Sister Gabriel, you asked where I learned the ancient Celtic dialect. When I was in that rock dwelling, I heard women speaking in a language I understood but never learned. All of the sudden, I just knew it. I can't explain how. I don't want to go into too much, but I do have certain abilities." She looked down at the palm of her hand. "I'm not sure to what extent, but I'm learning about them. Trust me, this is all new to me, and I see the look on your face, Sister Michael. Believe me, we are not doing anything against nature or God.

"You know, my mother believed all things were connected. From Christianity to paganism from practicing Catholicism to Wicca. You may not agree with her philosophy, but no one can argue her love or her faith. The one thing she instilled in me was to be true to myself and what I believe and never forget where I came from. I didn't ask for this, but here it is. All that Corky has told you is true." She stopped and looked at both nuns, willing them to believe her. "There is evil out there, and it is in the form of Phelan Tynan."

"And perhaps his offspring," Sister Gabriel said.

Corky interrupted. "I know this is hard for you, due to the fact it is not sanctioned by the church and probably goes against all you believe in. But it is happening, and we wanted you to know since you are both involved in this. Please be careful whom you trust."

"When is this liar's moon?" Sister Michael asked. Grayson still heard the disdain in her voice.

"When the moon is full. Two nights, if that," Corky said.

Sister Gabriel rose along with Sister Michael. "Let me know

if I can do anything. What that may be, I surely do not know. I need time to absorb all of this."

Grayson could see the tears welling in her eyes as they walked out of the office, just as Neala walked in. "Good evening, sisters," Neala said as they walked past. Neala looked at Grayson and Corky. "What's happened?"

Corky tossed his glasses down on the desk. "We told them everything. And we have something new." He looked at Grayson.

"What? Tell me. I hate that I'm missing what's going on," Neala said.

"Are they gone?"

They all turned to see Sebastian in the doorway.

Grayson groaned. "Are who gone?"

"The sisters have gone, yes." Corky waved Sebastian into the room. "You're safe."

"If someone doesn't tell me what's been going on…" Neala said in a threatening voice.

Grayson noticed Neala walked away from Sebastian and stood by the window. She also noticed Sebastian's smirk; she instinctively knew something had transpired between them.

"Grayson found out the reason behind Sister Gabriel's cloistered life," Corky said.

"I took a trip to Innishmore and long story short, found out that before she was Sister Gabriel, she was Mary Reardon, a sixteen-year-old girl who was basically seduced by an IRA gunrunner. She found herself pregnant with his child."

When Neala said nothing, Grayson chuckled. "Did you hear me? I'd think you would have a reaction to this."

"I'm stunned. It's unbelievable. But that's not all, is it?" Neala asked.

"Nope." Grayson rubbed her hands over her face. "It seems Mary Reardon happened to be in the woods one late afternoon and learned something quite disturbing about the lover and father of her unborn child. It seems the gunrunner was also an ancient Celtic, shape-shifting wizard."

"Are ya sayin' that Sister Gabriel had Phelan Tynan's child?"

Neala asked slowly, as if trying to register what Grayson had just said.

Grayson looked at Sebastian. "That's what I'm saying, isn't it?"

Sebastian nodded. "It is." She smiled then. "And I thought you and I were the only immortals. This country seems to be crawling with them."

"What happened to the baby?" Neala asked.

"She gave it up for adoption, then stayed at the convent, devoting her life to God in solitude." Grayson watched Neala, who now looked out the window, her arms folded across her chest.

Neala turned back into the room. "And she has no idea what happened to her daughter?"

Grayson shook her head. "No. Only that she was given to the proper Catholic agency and apparently adopted. But that is not substantiated."

"By whom?" Neala asked.

Grayson told them of Irene and her story. Once again, Neala listened completely enthralled. "So that's where we stand."

"Sister Michael was in on this from the beginning?" Neala asked.

"Another participant in our liar's moon. That makes two." Corky looked at Grayson, who nodded.

"Three. Inspector Gaffney told me she was adopted by a family in Dublin."

As they sat in silence, Grayson gazed into the fire, listening to the quiet hiss as the flames flickered around the glowing peat bricks.

"What do we do now?" Sebastian asked, breaking the silence.

"We?" Grayson grinned slightly, and Sebastian scowled. "Are you offering your help?"

Sebastian's smirk produced two sharp canines. "You can't possibly think you can handle this alone."

Grayson's grin faded quickly. "I've done all right lately, you ghoul."

"True, but you still aren't very good comfortable with your new abilities."

Grayson grunted. "And I'm sure you handled being the undead perfectly from day one."

Sebastian raised an eyebrow. "Good point. So what are you going to do with this information about darling Megan?"

Grayson ignored the sarcasm. "I'll talk to her next. It may be a coincidence."

"One thing is ringing true with all this," Corky said.

"What's that?"

"It would appear there is some truth in the tea leaves. There is great deception around you."

"I, for one, don't blame Sister Gabriel for this lie." Grayson scratched the back of her head before continuing, "But I'd sure like to know what else she knows. And why she came to the monastery now. She has to know what's going on with Phelan."

"Perhaps she has followed him throughout the years," Sebastian suggested.

"Kinda hard being cloistered. They don't have access to the outside world. And I doubt she'd do something to bring attention to herself and have Phelan find out where she is."

Corky closed the book and leaned back. "Do ya suppose Phelan doesn't know he has a daughter?"

"Something tells me, Corky, he knows. But does she know her father is an ancient wizard, shape-shifting asshole?"

Corky winced at the anger in Grayson's voice.

Sebastian showed no emotion at all. "A bigger question might be, does this woman have any of his shape-shifting abilities and was she the one who was outside Irene's cottage?"

"I can't help but feel sorry for Sister Gabriel," Corky said. "Neala, you should have seen the way she nearly broke down when we confronted her. I can't imagine finding out something like that and giving birth to a child."

Neala, still looking out the window, said, "No, Corky. I can't imagine it at all. I too feel very sorry for Sister Gabriel."

Sister Gabriel knelt in front of the crucifix hanging on the wall in her room. Bowing her head, she gathered her rosary beads and began to pray. "Dear Lord, I pray I'm doing the right thing."

She looked up, wiping the tear on her cheek. "I've lived my life repenting my sin. Help me to understand what You want me to do next, Lord. I know Your will be done. I pray I may serve You one last time."

As she continued to pray, she heard the mournful baying of an animal off in the distance, and her heartbeat quickened. She shut her eyes tight, mumbling her prayers over and over as she held the sacred beads in her hand. "He cannot know. He cannot know," she chanted and prayed.

She jumped when she heard the soft knock at her door. "Come in." She blessed herself and stood.

Sister Michael walked in, quietly shutting the door. Sister Gabriel offered her the chair, then sat behind her desk. "Good evening, Sister."

"Did you hear it?" Sister Michael asked.

Sister Gabriel nodded, frowning deeply. "I suppose it would be too much to think it might be a wolf."

"Because we have so many in Ireland," Sister Michael said.

"It was only a thought."

"What will happen, Sister?"

Sister Gabriel tiredly rubbed her temples. "I don't know," she said softly. "I have prayed this day would never come. That he would never find me. I fear he has. When I heard what had happened here months ago. When you called and said Sister Daniel was transferred, I knew it. I knew he was back." She looked at Sister Michael, who had tears in her eyes. "He has been such a vile entity all these years. My only hope is that he has not found our child, and she is far from here, safe and sound." She took a deep, saddened breath. "So many years of lying and repentance. I have tried to do God's work and pay for my sin."

"You did nothing wrong, Sister."

She smiled sadly. "Yes, I have. I pray God will forgive me and keep my child out of harm's way, wherever she is."

"I'm almost glad Grayson found out about this," Sister Michael said. "So many years of keeping this in, hiding it. Perhaps she can find your daughter and keep her safe."

"I prayed for that, as well."

"I hope she is…" Sister Michael stopped.

Sister Gabriel understood. "I too pray she is not like him. I have prayed with every fiber of my being." She put her arm around Sister Michael's shoulder. "You have been a good friend all these years. I remember how I came to you and how you helped me unconditionally. You saved my life and the life of my child."

"I pray that is enough."

Deep in her heart, Sister Gabriel knew it was not.

Chapter 24

It was the sound from the living room that woke Grayson. Her head shot up as she listened. Grayson then heard it again. It sounded as if someone was walking around in the living room.

Damn Elinora, she thought, and flew out of bed. She crept out to the living room, amazed how the moon lit up the room. Grayson peered through the eerie darkness, fumbling for the lamp on the desk, and turned it on.

There was no one in the living room, though now she heard something in the kitchen. "I'm gonna kill that immortal if she's raiding my refrigerator."

As she pushed the swinging door open, she nearly had a stroke when she saw a woman sitting at the kitchen table. Her heart pounded in her ears, and her left hand itched so incessantly, she immediately had to scratch at her palm. The woman had long coal black hair that hung in thick waves around her shoulders, and white, almost alabaster skin and rosy cheeks. She looked up and smiled when Grayson walked into the kitchen.

"Hello, my sweet baby," the woman said.

Grayson felt as if she were in a dream. Her grandmother used that term for her all the time when she was a little girl.

"Who are you?" Grayson asked.

The woman smiled. "You know who I am, Grayson Fianna."

"You-you can't be."

"Of course I can. You only remember me as old and gray, with rheumatism. I like me better this way, don't you? Sit, darlin'."

Completely stunned, Grayson obeyed and sat opposite her

grandmother, who lovingly looked around the kitchen. "Oh, how I miss this cottage. You used to sit right there and wait but not patiently while I made bread. Maeve would hold you in her lap, and we'd talk and talk all mornin'. Do you remember how it was?" she asked softly.

Grayson's bottom lip quivered as she nodded. "I miss you, Grandma. I miss Ma..." Grayson hung her head and tried desperately not to cry.

"Oh, darlin'," Deirdre whispered. "We're right here for ya. Always."

Grayson looked up. "Am I dreaming?"

"No, sweet baby. You're not dreamin'. I'm here to warn you. You must use the gift, the knowing. As I helped the villagers and the farmers, so must you. It's in your blood. You're the last of us, and it's your time. There is great evil here. I know you can feel it. Rose Barry was right. The tea leaves never lie."

Deirdre leaned over and grasped Grayson's left hand. Grayson was amazed how warm and soft her grandmother's hand felt. "Look at me, Grayson."

Grayson looked up into the dark blue eyes. "He has help. He will never do anything alone. You know who it is. Use your logic now. When the time comes, use the knowing."

"How will I know?"

"The evil that men do..."

"Lives after them," Grayson said, remembering what Sister Gabriel had said. "The one who is marked. His child?"

"A mark is cloaked unseen," Deirdre said, repeating the line from the prophecy. "You know your vampire was sent by her maker, just as Danu sent Elinora. Maeve was right, darlin', we're all connected. You will see as you grow."

"I need to figure out the rest of the prophecy." Grayson rubbed her eyes.

Deirdre rose and walked over to Grayson, who looked up through teary eyes. Deirdre ran her fingers through Grayson's hair. "So much like your mother." She bent down and kissed Grayson on the forehead, then easily sat on Grayson's lap, pulling Grayson's head to her chest. "Close your eyes now."

Grayson did as she was told, nuzzling her head against her grandmother. "Do ya remember the song I used to sing to you when you were my sweet baby?" Deirdre whispered.

She nodded, clinging to her grandmother when Deirdre softly sang, *On the wings of the wind, o'er the dark rolling hills; angels are coming to watch over thee.*

"I wanted the chance to sing this to my child," Grayson whispered as her grandmother sang and rocked her gently in her arms. Visions of Vicky flashed through her mind, when Vicky told her she was pregnant. Grayson never saw such beauty in her life than when she looked into Vicky's eyes that night.

Hear the wind blow, love, hear the wind blow...

Soon, Grayson fell into the most peaceful sleep she had ever known.

When she woke, she was in bed.

She walked to the kitchen and looked at the table. "Was I dreaming last night?" she asked and opened the refrigerator. She took out the carton of juice and took a drink.

Grayson felt very refreshed and rested. "Thanks, Grandma," she said and headed for the shower. "Now I see Megan Gaffney."

Rose Barry greeted Grayson as she walked into Dungarin.

"Good afternoon, Grayson," she said, sweeping the front doorstep.

"Hey, Rose." Grayson kissed her cheek.

"What's put you in such a good mood?" Rose asked, leaning on her broom handle.

"I had a dream last night or maybe she was really here," Grayson said thoughtfully.

"Who?"

"My grandmother. I dreamed she was in the kitchen. She looked young and beautiful. We talked about..." Grayson shrugged. "Stuff."

"A dream was it?" Rose asked.

Grayson laughed at her doubtful tone. She scratched her head. "It did seem real."

Rose leaned against the door. "And do ya not think it was?"

"I suppose."

"Where are you off to?" Rose asked.

"I need to see Meg, er, Inspector Gaffney. I have a few questions for her."

"I spoke with her yesterday."

Grayson did not hide her irritation. "Why was she bothering you?"

"Hold on to that temper of yours. You're like your father. She was only asking after you. I think she wanted some insight."

"What did you tell her?" Grayson asked. "I'm so afraid of this answer."

Rose laughed. "We talked about your mother and Deirdre. Things like that." Rose stopped and grinned evilly. "I think the inspector is cut from the same cloth as yourself."

Grayson glared at her old friend. "What? We're both detectives?"

Rose laughed again. "Ya know what I mean. She's single." Rose wriggled her eyebrows.

"You're a wicked old woman, Rose Barry." Grayson walked away. "I'll talk to you later."

Grayson walked down to the bed and breakfast at the other end of the village. Mrs. O'Toole greeted her when she walked in.

"Good day, Grayson. What brings you here?"

"Is Inspector Gaffney in?"

"I assume so. She came in very late last night and hasn't been down yet."

"What room is she in?"

Mrs. O'Toole raised an eyebrow. "End of the hall on the left."

"Thanks."

Grayson gently knocked on the door and heard a mumbled, "One minute, please."

She stepped back when the door finally opened and hid her grin. "Good afternoon."

"If you insist," Megan said in a coarse voice. "What time is it?"

"Almost noon."

"I'm not a morning person." Megan pulled her robe around her and ran her fingers through her long hair. "I don't get up with the cows or sheep or whatever is roaming outside my window." She looked at Grayson for the first time. "How did you get past Mrs. O'Toole? I'm not sure it's appropriate for you to be in my room."

"I have my ways."

"I'm sure you do." Megan sat on the edge of the bed. "What's on your mind?"

"I understand you talked to Rose Barry yesterday."

"Yes, and I talked to Denis at the pub and a few villagers. Is there something wrong with that?"

"No, not really." Grayson watched her for a moment. "What do you want to know? I'll tell you, if you ask."

"I did ask," Megan said angrily. "You're very tight-lipped, Ms. MacCarthaigh."

"Grayson..."

"And so are your friends. I'm not trying to harm you or anyone else. I'm just trying to find out who murdered your mother and Dr. Rourke's assistant." She stood and pulled her robe tighter around her. "Because you and I both know they were murdered. And not by some wolf or rabid dog."

Grayson sighed and stood. "Get dressed. I'll meet you in the dining room. Maybe Mrs. O'Toole can make us some tea."

"You're a bossy woman, Grayson."

"Yeah, I know. See you in twenty."

Grayson walked out and heard a small irritated groan as Megan shut the door. Mrs. O'Toole met Grayson at the end of the hall.

"I heard yellin'. Is everything all right?" she asked.

"Fine. Is it all right if we sit in the dining room?"

"Of course it is. Go on, I'll bring some coffee or tea." She gently pushed Grayson toward the dining room.

Grayson gratefully accepted the pot of coffee and poured a generous cup. She wondered how she would explain what had happened or if she even should. However, she had to find out about Megan Gaffney. The fact that she was adopted by a couple in Dublin could be a coincidence. Kids are adopted all the time. How in the hell would she find out if she had the mark on her back? That might be kinda hard to explain. Excuse me, but can I see your ass? Grayson laughed openly.

"It does not bode well that you're alone and laughing," Megan said as she sat.

Grayson knew her face was red. "Coffee?"

"Only a pot full," Megan said as Grayson poured her a cup.

Mrs. O'Toole scurried over to the table. "Now it's late, but what would ya like for breakfast?" She looked at Megan. "The same as yesterday?"

"Please. It was delicious," Megan said between gulps.

"I'm good with the bread, thanks," Grayson said.

When Mrs. O'Toole hurried back to the kitchen, Megan sat back. "So what's on your mind?"

Grayson had a mouthful of brown bread that she washed down with coffee before answering. "I'm not sure how to explain this to you, and I'm not sure I should be." She wasn't sure if she was grateful or not when Megan didn't respond. Now she didn't know what to say. Mrs. O'Toole bought her some time when she came back with Megan's breakfast.

"You going to eat all that?" Grayson asked.

A plate of eggs, sausage, bacon, and a bowl of oatmeal sat in front of the beaming inspector. "Yes. A healthy breakfast is the most important meal of the day."

"Never mind that it's lunchtime."

Megan ignored her. "Now you've had enough time."

"When I tell you what's happening, I'm not sure what you'll do with the information. That's my big concern. I know you're a police officer, and you know I respect that."

Megan ate her oatmeal without a word while Grayson talked. She finished the porridge and started on the other plate. She looked up. "You know I can't give you any promises, Grayson. You were a detective back in Chicago. A respected detective, who followed the law." She took a mouthful and shrugged. "You know you're going to tell me. It's your nature."

"You don't know my nature, Megan."

"I believe I'm a good judge of character, and you, Detective MacCarthaigh, are honest. I can see it in your eyes. Sorry," she said and picked up the rasher of bacon.

Grayson glared at her. "You eat too much."

Megan continued eating. "I'm waiting."

"Okay, here goes nothing. Get the net." Grayson leaned her elbows on the table and buried her fingers in her hair. She wanted to pull it out. "I'm the true descendant of the mythical race Tuatha De Danann. When the goddess Danu realized her race was to be exterminated, they took all the power and magic and encased it in a stone, broke it in three pieces, and gave each section to an alchemist, a sorcerer, and a healer.

"Figol, the sorcerer, was evil and wanted all the power, so on the night of the ritual, he killed the druids and tried to take the stone. He only got his section and gave it to his son, Phelan, who took his section and spent the next thousand years trying to find the other two, murdering anyone in his path. He also has obtained unbelievable wealth, so he has the appearance of being above reproach. He's also a shape-shifter, and Corky thinks his shape of choice is a wolf. He killed my mother, who was fulfilling an ancient prophecy, protecting me. We think Phelan killed Kathleen, as well, though we're not sure why. She must have known something, but that has nothing to do with the prophecy, which according to that prophecy, I was to battle Phelan under the residual moon several months ago. I won, so to speak, and now I'm the keeper of the power as it were. Not my choice, but there you have it.

"Because of this, I'm an immortal but still human, too, but I have abilities that Elinora, who is a real immortal, is here to assist me with. Phelan is real and very evil. We haven't seen him at all, but he's out there. And now we find out he had a child, a girl, about thirty years ago when he was a gunrunner for the IRA. We don't know who this woman is since she was given up for adoption to a couple in Dublin. But we know from another prophecy that she has a marking on her that is on the small of her back on the left side. We're hoping she's human with no knowledge of any of this, but the downside is she's a shape-shifter like her father and she's in league with him and just as evil." She stopped and took a deep breath.

The entire time, Megan stared at Grayson, blinking occasionally to show she was listening. Grayson knew she sounded ridiculous and knew exactly how Megan felt. It was the same way she felt when Neala first told her about Phelan and the stone—she thought Neala was nuts.

Megan sat back and took a deep breath. She drank her coffee and wiped her mouth on the linen napkin. Grayson watched her with a cautious eye. Megan set the napkin on the table and leaned forward.

"Are you insane?"

Grayson's gaze darted around the room. "If you had asked me a few months ago, I'd say yes, without a doubt. Now? I only wish I was. It would make it a hell of a lot easier all the way around."

"I have no response to this. How in God's name do you expect me to believe this?"

"Because it's true." Grayson leaned in. "Megan, you said you were a good judge of character. Do you think I could make this up? Why? For what reason? Shit, I couldn't come up with something like this if I tried."

"You expect me to believe you're some descendant of a mythical race and you've saved the world…"

"Just Ireland."

"From this Phelan wolfman who spawned another shape-shifter who is marked and given up for adopt…" Her voice trailed off.

Grayson winced but said nothing when she saw Megan's anger show in her blue eyes. "Don't tell me. Do not tell me you think I'm the daughter of this, this…"

"Well, there's one way to find out, um," Grayson said.

Megan leaned over the table, Grayson leaned back. "I may have been adopted, but I am not…" She angrily stood. "Come with me."

"What?"

"You heard me. Get up."

Grayson followed her down the hall to her bedroom. "Um…"

"Shut up and get in here." Megan pulled Grayson in her room

and shut the door. "Where was this so-called mark again?"

"Uh, on the small of the back, left side. It's a dark circle bisected by a line and..." Grayson was shocked when Megan stripped off her sweater and quickly unbuttoned her blouse. "Uh..."

"You want to know. Well, here's your chance."

Megan took off her blouse; Grayson knew she was staring at her breasts, which were exquisite, even though hidden by the black silky bra. "Uh..."

"You already said that." Megan had her hand on her hips. She then turned around. "Help yourself."

Grayson cleared her throat, trying not to show her hands shaking. She looked down her back, there was nothing there. However...

"Uh, your slacks are..."

Megan quickly unzipped and pulled her slacks down over her hips. Grayson nearly had a stroke when she saw the waistband of the black thong.

"Well?"

"Huh? Oh," Grayson said in a coarse voice. She quickly shook her head. "There's nothing there."

Megan turned around and pulled up her slacks. "Satisfied?"

"I'm sorry. I...I'm sorry," Grayson said; she picked up her blouse and handed it to her.

Megan gently took the blouse from her and put it on. She walked up to Grayson, who frowned deeply. "Was this just a ploy to get me out of my clothes, Detective MacCarthaigh?"

Grayson swallowed and laughed nervously. "Uh, no. And I'll probably slap myself later on for not thinking of it."

Megan chuckled and buttoned her blouse. "So if this insanity is true, you believe I'm not Phelan's daughter. And why does that name sound so familiar?"

"Phelan Tynan. I told you he had immense wealth. Have someone look him up. You won't find much. I didn't, and I had a very good researcher. All we came up with was he owns Cian Enterprises which he founded in 1920. Nothing personal, no birth records. We found photos of him with Neville Chamberlain."

"The prime minister of England before World War II?"

Grayson laughed at Megan's incredulous tone. "The very same. There was also a picture of him with Sir John Quigley who, as I found out, was a descendant and kept his section of the stone. He then gave it to Nan Quigley, a granddaughter or niece, I can't remember. You'll find she was one of the victims I was investigating. She had her portion of the stone, and Phelan, the shape-shifting asshole, murdered her for it."

Megan sat on the bed, shaking her head in disbelief. "I don't know what to make of this. It's too fantastic to believe. But almost too fantastic not to."

"I wish it were all a dream." Grayson stood by the window. She watched the sloping green hills sectioned off by familiar stone walls that epitomized the Irish landscape. "If it was, my mother would still be alive."

Grayson felt Megan standing behind her. "I'm sorry for that. And for your wife."

"Thank you," Grayson said, still looking out the window. "She was pregnant." She closed her eyes when she felt Megan's hand on her shoulder. She turned then. "So what will you do?"

Megan looked up into her eyes. "I can't tell this story to my superiors. They'll lock me up and throw away the key."

"I hear ya." Grayson walked away from her. It was getting too close, too personal for her.

"I should go to Dublin to do a little research on Mr. Tynan." She grabbed her sweater and pulled it over her head.

"I hear a 'but' coming." Grayson rubbed her temples.

"But I'm not. You're going to take me to your friends." She grabbed her service revolver and clipped it to the waistband of her slacks, pulling the sweater over it. "And they'd better have the same ridiculous story because if they don't, Grayson MacCarthaigh, you will be my first suspect." She opened the door and waited.

Grayson shook her head and obediently walked out of the room.

Chapter 25

Megan drove as Grayson phoned Corky and had him meet her and Grayson at the monastery along with the sisters. As they pulled up to the monastery, Grayson turned to Megan.

"Please remember this is a very old and respected place, Megan. These nuns—"

Megan tuned off the car and unbuckled her seat belt. "I'm a Catholic, Grayson. I understand the sanctity of the church and its history," she said in a clipped voice as she got out of the car.

"This is not going to go well," she heard Grayson mumble.

"What did you say?"

"Nothing, nothing."

She watched Grayson struggling with her seat belt. Grayson looked up to see Megan standing by the door, one eyebrow raised. "I would think an immortal could figure out a seat belt," she said and opened the door.

Grayson unlocked the belt and got out, saying nothing as they walked through the courtyard.

Corky and Neala met them at the door. His eyes grew wide; Megan saw myriad emotions flash across his face.

"No introductions necessary, we all know each other," Grayson said.

Corky smiled weakly. "Inspector. Good to see you again."

Megan smiled. "I highly doubt that, Mr. Kerrigan, but it'll do for now. Dr. Rourke."

"Hello, Inspector." Megan heard the professional tone from Neala and couldn't blame her.

Corky looked as though he wanted to throw up. He glanced at Grayson, who shrugged. "Where are the sisters?"

"At morning Mass. I-I didn't want to, well, I…they were already in church." He looked back and forth from Grayson to Megan.

"We can wait." Megan sat by the desk. "So, Mr. Kerrigan."

"Corky, please."

"Corky," she said. "I won't ask where you got the nickname. Please sit."

Corky quickly sat next to her. Megan looked at him and motioned to the chair behind the desk.

"Oh, right then," Corky said and took his place.

Grayson sat on the windowsill, her back against the window frame as she looked out at the sunny, peaceful morning. Neala stood close by Grayson.

"Corky, Dr. Rourke, Grayson just told me a fantastic story." Megan leaned back.

"She did?"

Megan heard the squeak in Corky's voice. "Yes, I'd love to hear your version."

"All of it?"

She watched both of them as Corky looked at Grayson, who smiled and nodded.

"Right then." Corky adjusted his glasses and leaned forward. "I don't know what Grayson told you, where would you like to start?"

"The beginning would be too obvious, I suppose," Megan said; she heard the chuckle from Grayson.

"Right. Well, I've been a historian all my life, it seems. I grew up—" He stopped when Grayson cleared her throat while she shook her head. "Oh. Right."

Corky proceeded to tell the story, just as Grayson had told her. The only difference being Corky Kerrigan spoke almost reverently when he told of Grayson's destiny, as he put it. Megan had to admit, he had a way of talking about this fairy tale. Megan found herself mesmerized and lulled by his thick Clare brogue. She watched him as he gently placed his hands on the thick leather-bound book, as if it were a bible. Megan realized, to Corky, it was exactly that. Timothy Kerrigan believed every word he said, and every prophecy he spoke of, he believed in it.

Megan had taken a course or two in Irish history, and her best friend Bess, who was as nutty as they come, believed in all this. She'd love to hear her take on this chaos.

"So, Inspector, that's it in a nutshell." Corky took off his glasses and rubbed his eyes. "It's fantastic and surreal, but true."

Megan looked at Neala. "Anything to add, Doctor?"

"No. And you can call me Neala. It's just as Corky said, and I'm sure Grayson, as well. It is fantastic, I know."

"I have to deal in facts," Megan said.

"So did Grayson." Corky looked fondly at Grayson, who stared out the window. "She still does."

"It's a fact that my mother and Kathleen were murdered in the same way," Grayson said. She looked down at the palm of her left hand. "And this is a fact, as well."

Megan took a deep patient breath. "Grayson, that birthmark—"

"Birthright," Corky gently corrected her.

"Can be anything," she insisted.

Corky looked at Grayson and shrugged. He grinned as he pushed the new stapler to the edge of the desk. Grayson shook her head; Corky nodded.

"All right. What's going on?"

Never taking his gaze off Grayson, Corky said, "Grayson is going to show you."

"Show me what? You two are beginning to irritate me, and it's not a good idea to irritate me at this point."

Grayson glared at Corky and raised her left hand, exposing her palm. Megan watched Grayson take a deep breath, showing a fierce look of concentration and what Megan thought was hopefulness. Out of the corner of her eye, she saw Corky lean back. Neala stepped away from Grayson and stood by Megan.

"What...?"

With that, the stapler flew off the desk in Grayson's direction and crashed through the window. Grayson dodged out of the way as the shards of glass flew all over.

"Damn it," Grayson said angrily as she looked out the window.

"All clear, thank God," Neala said.

Corky gleefully clapped his hands. "You're getting better. At least you almost caught it."

Megan sat there stunned, listening to their banter. Corky leaned over the desk. "It's not 'anything,' Inspector. It's Grayson's birthright. She is the true descendant of the Tuatha De Danann. The powers that the gods and goddesses bestowed on her just have to be honed, that's all."

Megan didn't know what to say; she tried to take this in. "There are people who have telekinetic powers. That doesn't make you immortal, some freak—"

"Hey," Grayson said indignantly.

"You're a stubborn one, Inspector," Corky said happily. "I love provin' ya wrong. Grayson, touch her."

As Grayson walked over to her, Megan instinctively leaned back. "Let me remind you, I have a gun."

Grayson placed her left on her shoulder. Megan felt a tingling sensation through that part of her arm while she watched Grayson. In a moment, Grayson pulled back and smiled. "You shouldn't have jumped that fence. It left a nasty scar on the back of your thigh."

Megan's back stiffened. No one knew how she got that scar. She looked up into Grayson's deep blue eyes—eyes that smiled affectionately. "But I would have done the same for my friend," Grayson whispered and patted her shoulder. "Whether you believe this or not, Megan, it's all true."

They looked up when Sister Gabriel and Sister Michael entered the room. Megan inwardly laughed as the room took on a solemn overtone. Nuns still had that effect on some people. Catholicism at its guilt-ridden best.

As Grayson made the introductions, both nuns looked taken aback at the word inspector. Megan enjoyed the childish sense of "gotcha" when both nuns looked decided guilty. The police had that effect on some people.

With both nuns seated, Megan leaned against the desk, facing them. "Grayson and Corky have told me an incredible story, which I'm sure you know, so I won't go into any more detail." She looked at Sister Gabriel. "She also told me of how you became a nun, Sister. You've had no contact with your daughter or this Phelan Tynan in all these years? Not one letter, one phone call. You have absolutely no idea where they are or who your daughter is?"

"No, Inspector," Sister Gabriel said. "On all counts."

"And you saw Mr. Tynan change into a wolf?"

"Yes." Sister Gabriel went on before Megan could ask, "And no, I was not imagining it. I was not drinking or doing any type of hallucinogen. I was cognizant of what I was doing and where I was. I may have been sixteen, but I know what I saw."

"I do not doubt you, Sister. But you must understand I'm trying to make sense—"

"Make sense?" Sister Gabriel asked. She offered a sad smile. "I wish you luck in your endeavor."

Sister Michael rose. "Will that be all, Inspector?"

"Yes, thank you," Megan said; she watched both nuns as they walked out of the room. "You believe them?"

"What's not to believe?" Corky asked.

"I had a thought perhaps they knew more than they were letting on, but I don't know," Grayson said. "My gut tells me they're telling the truth."

Megan nodded but said nothing.

"What next?" Corky asked.

"Where is Dr. Sebastian?" she asked.

Corky glanced at Grayson. "We're not sure where she is," Grayson said.

"And why is that?" Megan looked Grayson in the eyes. "What is her business in all this?"

Corky opened his mouth, then shut it. Megan waited patiently.

"She's a colleague of mine. We're working on something together. She's not..."

"You're lying, Grayson. I can tell."

Grayson pinched the bridge of her nose. "Please trust me on this for now."

"Why should I?" she asked, clearly annoyed.

"I have no good reason why you should."

Megan heard the tone of resignation; she felt a wave of compassion for Grayson MacCarthaigh. "Fine. What about this Elinora? Or should I trust you on this, as well?"

"It would be helpful if you did."

"Extremely," Corky added with a weak smile.

Megan glared at both of them. "You two are really irritating me now."

"Do not be irritated, Inspector Gaffney. I am Elinora."

Megan whirled around to see an absolutely gorgeous woman standing in the doorway. She was tall with silky long dark hair and dark eyes. Her olive-colored complexion was flawless.

Megan was aware of two things: she was staring and Grayson MacCarthaigh was groaning.

Chapter 26

"Go away," Grayson said through clenched teeth as Elinora ignored her. All she needed now was Sebastian to make an appearance. She sincerely hoped the vampire ran out of sun juice and was sleeping in some dark cave.

"Everything they told you is true," Elinora said as she walked into the room. She looked at Megan, who was rubbing her temples. "What is the matter?"

"Nothing. Just looking for the rabbit hole."

"I realize none of it makes sense," Elinora said.

"True," Megan said. "But it's consistent. That's a plus."

"You have a sense of humor. This will serve you well." Elinora looked at Grayson. "Because the liar's moon is at hand. It will be the end and the beginning tonight."

Grayson felt the chill run down her spine. Corky sat behind his desk. "We haven't figured out the entire prophecy yet."

"How much do we have?" Neala asked.

Megan joined them at the desk. Corky shuffled through his pages. "Let me read the whole thing first."

He put on his glasses and started:

In the shadow of the crescent,
A mark is cloaked unseen.
The traitor's song eclipse the moon,
Blackheart betrays the queen.

One emerges from the night,

At the behest of ancient call
A star falls from a distant realm,
Uniting and revealing all.

Midnight calls upon the light
Uniting moon and stars and trees
To see with eyes no longer veiled
Embrace the path of destiny.

Corky sat back. "We know, or think, that the traitor is Phelan's daughter, who is marked with the rune sign. We know this because Sister Gabriel told us she saw this exact birthmark on her daughter before they took the child away. And whoever this woman is betrays the queen, but we're not sure who the queen is. I suspect it's Grayson, but I'm not totally sold on that idea."

Grayson pointed to the second stanza. "I had a dream, or visitation, from my grandmother last night. She told me that Sebastian is the one from the night, called on by Tatiana. And Elinora is the star called on by Danu, and she would reveal everything. But Elinora said she had told me too much already. If she goes further, it will affect my destiny."

"When did this happen?" Neala asked.

"The other day. We were talking about my new abilities and how I have to respect them and accept them as the gift they are." Grayson noticed Corky had been intently reading. "What is it, Corky?"

"The last stanza," Corky said. "Midnight calls upon the light." He looked up at Grayson. "Midnight is Sebastian. The light is you, Grayson. It's what Tatiana said to Sebastian, that you are both connected. The next line. Uniting moon and stars and trees. The moon is Sebastian, the stars refer to Elinora."

"But what are the trees?" Neala asked.

"If you remember, the druids or ancient ones were often referred to as trees," Corky said. "That's you, Grayson. It will all come together, and 'to see with eyes no longer veiled.' You will see who the traitor is. And embrace your destiny."

"I think you're right," Grayson said.

"Am I the only one who sees we're missing an immortal?" Neala asked.

Grayson and Megan looked around. Elinora was indeed missing.

"Why would she leave?" Neala asked. "If she's part of this and is supposed to reveal all, why not stick around?"

"I agree," Megan said. "It's the first logical thing I've heard. Did you happen to check if this Elinora was marked?"

Grayson shook her head. "It never occurred to me."

Megan gave her an incredulous look. "You thought I was Phelan's daughter, but you just accept this woman, or whatever she is, on face value? You're a detective." Megan headed for the door.

"Where are you going?" Corky asked.

"To find your immortal, if that's what she is," Megan said over her shoulder. "All of you stay put."

Grayson slowly sat down. "She's right. Neala's right. I believed Elinora. I-I didn't check to see. I..." She looked up at Corky, who was frowning.

Neala knelt in front of her. "Grayson, don't blame yourself. My God, she had everyone convinced." She chuckled sadly. "It was Sebastian I didn't trust, for heaven's sake. You've had so much on your mind. Right, Corky?"

Corky looked up from his reading. "Right. No, wrong. Well, right that Grayson has so much on her mind, but wrong in that I don't think Elinora is..." He stopped and scratched his head. "Something's not adding up here."

Grayson was barely listening to him. Suddenly, she felt inept and useless. Megan Gaffney had taken over. Elinora's disappearance was now suspect, and Sebastian was nowhere to be found. "I feel like it's all unraveling, and I have no control over it. What the fuck is the point of these abilities I'm supposed to have?"

"How is Inspector Gaffney supposed to find Elinora?" Corky asked.

Grayson sprang to her feet. "She's not. Maybe Elinora is leading her away from us..." She ran out of the room. "You two stay here if she comes back."

"Gray, where are you goin'?" Corky called after her.

"I don't know, but Megan couldn't have gone far."

Grayson ran through the courtyard, nearly running over Sister Gabriel. "Goodness, where are you going?"

"Did you see Inspector Gaffney, Sister?"

"Yes. She was headed toward Dungarin."

"Thank you, please stay in the monastery," Grayson pleaded.

Sister Gabriel held on to Grayson's sleeve. "What has happened?"

"I can't go into it now, please." Grayson gently pulled her arm away and ran down the path away from the monastery.

She stood in the open green field, turning in all directions. "Where the fuck is she?" Grayson asked.

She must have been searching for at least an hour. She looked to the west; the sun had all but disappeared on the Atlantic horizon. Completely exhausted, Grayson sat on the stone wall. "God, what's happening? Nothing is making sense here."

Suddenly, she heard her grandmother's voice, as she did the night before. *"He has help. He will never do anything alone. You know who it is. Use your logic now. When the time comes, use the knowing."*

"My logic tells me it is not Elinora," Grayson insisted, running her fingers through her hair. In the twilight, she looked skyward. The first of the evening stars had just started to show. Soon the moon would rise. "Logic, logic, MacCarthaigh."

"Grayson!"

She whirled around to see Neala running down the path. She stopped short. "There you are. We've been looking all over. Did ya find her?"

"No, damn it. No sign of Megan or Elinora or fricking Sebastian. Damn it," she yelled into the night. "Where's Corky?"

"I left him at the monastery. He was going over something, and I couldn't wait any longer. I was so worried about you."

As Neala started in Grayson's direction, Megan called out to them. "Stay where you are."

Neala stopped. "There you are. Where have ya been? Did you find Elinora?"

"Yes. Dr. Rourke, please stand still."

Grayson looked at Megan. "What are you doing?"

Megan pulled her revolver and held it at her side. "Everyone stay calm."

"Grayson, it's her. She's the one," Neala said frantically.

"She can't be, Neala," Grayson said, still looking at Megan. "What's going on, Megan?"

"Elinora is not Phelan's daughter. She has no mark on her," Megan said.

"Grayson," Neala said in a worried voice.

"It's okay, Neala," Grayson said. "Okay, so it's not Elinora."

Megan inched her way toward Neala; Grayson still watched her. "Megan, what are you doing?"

"Grayson, please," Neala said, nearly crying.

"Megan," Grayson said. "Talk to me."

"Move away, Dr. Rourke," Megan said, ignoring Grayson. "Just move away."

All three heard Corky calling them as he ran toward them. Grayson never took her gaze off Megan, who watched Neala like a hawk.

Corky held the book in his hand. Grayson tore her gaze from Megan to Corky. "What's up, Corky?" She tried to hold down her own panic. So far, Megan still had the revolver at her side.

Corky looked as though he wanted to cry. His hand shook as he held his book open to a certain page. "I-I hope to God I'm wrong."

"Corky, what's wrong?" Neala asked. "Somebody do something!"

"I am," Corky said in a sad voice. He then started to speak, but Grayson heard Latin when he spoke. He spoke so fast, Grayson could hardly keep up. It sounded like some kind of chanting. She heard the word unlock.

It was then Neala backed up, frantically looking from Grayson to Corky when Corky finished. Grayson watched Corky, who closed the book; he looked so despondent, it confused Grayson.

Neala started to run for Grayson. "Grayson, what's going on?" she cried out.

"Stop!" Corky yelled, putting his hand up.

Megan raised her gun and pointed it at Neala. "Stop now, Dr. Rourke."

Neala flew into Grayson's arms, crying as she clung to her. "Neala, what's...?" Grayson winced in pain as the electric shock flew through her left hand and up her arm. It was nearly paralyzing. Her hand rested on Neala's hip and the small of her back as she held her. Through the intense pain, Grayson held Neala at arm's length. The visions slammed through her brain, causing Grayson's body to jerk and spasm with each one.

Visions of Neala with Phelan at the museum, visions of her in Chicago with Maeve. Visions of Neala reading Corky's book. What was she doing? Grayson thought as the visions bombarded her. Grayson looked into Neala's eyes. With one swift movement, Grayson tore her dress away from her back and whipped Neala around.

In a daze, Grayson stared at the black circle bisected with a line on Neala's lower back.

Neala wrenched her body away from Grayson, pulling her tattered dress around her.

Grayson then saw the bruise on her shoulder and the teeth marks. "Sebastian," Grayson whispered. She remembered the night the vampire fought outside Irene's cottage. *Well, we did scuffle. I believe I got a good bite in.*

"Neala..." Grayson whispered and stumbled backward. The realization ripped through her being as she repeated the prophecy, "Blackheart betrays the queen...My mother." Grayson thought back to all the signs she missed. "My mother trusted you and loved you. All the time you were...you helped him."

Neala shook her head. "Grayson, what are you saying? Of course it's not me! Corky, tell her."

The night they slept together and the morning afterward flashed through Grayson's.

You have wayward hands, Miss MacCarthaigh.

"That night I spent at your flat. We slept together. You stopped me when I touched your back. You didn't want me to see his mark. I-I held you all night." She shook her head as if to purge the tender evening from her mind and continued, "That's why you defended Phelan when he took the stone from the museum. You knew he'd be there and take the stone. How else could you get it out of there without it being in the news?"

Something else now made sense. "You killed Kathleen."

"Grayson, what in the world…?" Neala pleaded.

Grayson didn't even hear her; the scene played like a movie in her mind. She went on in a disbelieving trance, "That's why there was no blood by her car. She recognized you on the side of the road and willingly got out of her car. She had Phelan's personnel file. She came to you, and you butchered that poor girl."

"Listen to what you're saying. It's not true."

"Yes, it is. You're Phelan's daughter." The sadness that swept through her caused a physical pang deep in her heart. "Neala," Grayson whispered, almost awestruck. Tears flooded her eyes and she felt as if she were losing whatever sense she had left as she stared helplessly at Neala. She searched Neala's face, gazed down her body, and when she saw it, her blood ran cold.

Neala held the athame in her hand. The same dagger that Phelan used to initiate the ritual during the residual moon. The very same dagger he drove through her back when he tried to kill her. The evil look on Neala's face sent another staggering jolt through Grayson.

"Destroy her!"

Grayson knew it was Sebastian's voice, but it sounded muffled and far off. Corky was yelling, as well. She looked over to see Elinora easily holding Megan at bay.

Sebastian, with fangs dangerously exposed, snarled again. "Grayson, destroy her!"

They all looked as if they were in slow motion.

"Do not interfere, vampire," Elinora called out in a warning voice.

Grayson looked back at Neala as she raised the athame.

When the time comes, use the knowing.

Grayson raised her left hand toward Neala. The dagger then shot out of Neala's grasp; in an instant, Grayson held it in her left hand.

Clearly stunned, Neala backed up; she kept backing up until she was at least twenty feet away. She then lowered her head and watched—no, stalked—Grayson. She moved a few steps to the right, backing up still. Grayson watched as Neala's appearance began to shift. Her eyes turned blue-green as she angrily swept her long red curls from her face.

It sent a chill down Grayson's spine when Neala let out a deep resonating snarl, "Yes, it's true, and you were supposed to die in that warehouse bombing in Chicago. We're sick to death of you. For a thousand years, my father has waited and hunted down the descendants of those who defied Figol, my grandfather. He was right to rebel against the druid elders. They had no idea what to do with such power. Neither do you. Who are you to deny him his destiny?"

Grayson, still visibly astonished, looked down at the dagger in her hand. "All this time. It was you." She looked at Neala. "You helped us with the prophecy, knowing Phelan would kill my mother. You were at her funeral. You cried with me and Corky, for God's sake," she said, trying to grasp the reality. "You did all this. You fucking bitch."

Neala let out a bloodcurdling howl and ran toward Grayson, morphing into the wolf as she ran. In the last moment, she snarled and leapt at Grayson, who raised the athame and plunged it into the wolf's chest, not before its claws ripped through her upper chest and shoulder.

Grayson cried out as she fell backward, landing on her back. The wolf let out a pathetic whine as Grayson threw it to the side.

It ended that quickly. Off in the distance, she heard a terrifying, tortured howl that echoed through the twilight.

Suddenly, Corky was at her side. "Grayson, are you all right?"

Grayson nodded; she watched the moon in the cloudless sky. The hazy fog that shrouded its light dissipated and allowed the bright moonbeam to gently rest on Grayson as she lay there.

"Get her inside," she heard Megan say in a frantic voice.

Grayson looked into Megan's worried blue eyes while Megan pressed her hand on the oozing wound. "I'm okay."

Megan smiled and bit at her bottom lip. "Shut up."

Suddenly, she was in Sebastian's arms. Grayson chuckled and winced. "Not one word," Sebastian said as she carried her. Grayson thought she saw a ghost of a smile from the brooding vampire.

"You have done well, mortal," Elinora said. "My work is done."

It was the last thing Grayson remembered.

Epilogue

Corky sat at the desk, shaking his head as he closed the book. He was exhausted and frankly very sad. To think that Neala all along was Phelan's daughter was shocking, to say the least. When he saw the despondent look on Grayson's face that night, it broke his heart. He tiredly walked over to the window and looked out at the sunny morning.

Grayson was sitting in the courtyard alone. Her right arm heavily bandaged, she struggled to pull her jacket around her. She looked pale; she looked lonely.

"Grayson was lucky you remembered Neala looking through your book."

Corky looked up to see Sebastian standing in the far corner. She slowly walked up to him.

"I don't know what made me remember. Divine intervention?" He then remembered the dream he had of Maeve. *Liar's moon will be in your hands soon, sweetie.*

"Sheer dumb luck?" Sebastian offered. "So Neala found the same glamour you gave Kendra to guard her lab back in London in the catacombs while she did the same research for the serum."

"Yes. It's why Grayson never got anything when she touched Neala. Why you couldn't read her mind. When I found the spell to reverse and unlock the glamour, Grayson could see. You all could see Neala for what she really was. I'm sure Grayson preferred not knowing. I think she was beginning to fall in love with Neala."

"That was not part of her destiny. Just as it wasn't for me to interfere. Though I desperately wanted to rip her throat out."

Corky agreed and looked out the window again. "I'm sure Inspector Gaffney wanted to unload her revolver, as well. I still can't believe it was Neala all along. She had everyone fooled."

"Everyone but Elinora."

"I wish she would have said something."

"She couldn't. Elinora had to do what they told her to do. At one point, I doubted her. But I remembered her from long ago when she vowed never to allow her emotions to distract her from her duty. They knew she would do what was expected and preserve Grayson's destiny."

"Speaking of destinies, once Grayson heals, we'll need to get on with the translation of Tatiana's book. So we can see what the connection is between your world and Grayson's."

Sebastian nodded. "Tatiana said I would know what our people were like before the dawn. But we have time. Grayson needs to heal her body and soul."

Sebastian looked down at Grayson, sitting alone in the courtyard. Corky looked on, as well. Suddenly, Megan Gaffney appeared. She stood in front of Grayson with her hands on her hips, wagging a finger in her direction. Grayson reached up with her good hand and roughly pulled her on the bench next to her. Megan gently pulled the jacket around Grayson's shoulder. They watched as Grayson held Megan's hand as Megan leaned in and kissed Grayson on the forehead.

"Ah, darlin', our little girl is growing up." Corky let out a wistful sigh as he glanced at Sebastian.

"And we won't have another," Sebastian assured him with a scowl.

Corky laughed as he threw the window open so they could hear the gentle voices of love in bloom.

"Don't play the injured card with me, Grayson MacCarthaigh. I don't care if you're an immortal freak or whatever you are. You're going to tell me everything you know or I'll…"

Corky quickly closed the window. "I think it's the beginning of a beautiful relationship."

About the author

Kate Sweeney, a 2010 Alice B. Medal winner, was the 2007 recipient of the Golden Crown Literary Society award for Debut Author for *She Waits*, the first in the *Kate Ryan Mystery* series. The series also includes *A Nice Clean Murder, The Trouble with Murder,* a 2008 Golden Crown Award Winner for Mystery, *Who'll Be Dead for Christmas?* a 2009 Golden Crown Award winner for Mystery, and *Of Course It's Murder.*

Other novels include *Away from the Dawn, Survive the Dawn, Residual Moon,* a 2008 Golden Crown Award Winner for Speculative Fiction, *The O'Malley Legacy, Winds of Heaven,* and *Sea of Grass.*

Born in Chicago, Kate recently moved to Louisiana and this Yankee doubts she'll ever get used to saying y'all. Humor is deeply embedded in Kate's DNA. She sincerely hopes you will see this when you read her novels, short stories, and other works by visiting her Web site at www.katesweeneyonline.com. E-mail Kate at ksweeney22@aol.com.

You may also enjoy...

Residual Moon
by Kate Sweeney
ISBN: 978-1-933113-94-4

Two young women are found dead on the Chicago lakefront in as many weeks, each murdered in the same fashion. Detective Sergeant Grayson MacCarthaigh is at her wit's end trying to solve the grisly mess before the murderer claims another victim.

Her only common thread is Dr. Neala Rourke, the curator of the famous National Museum in Dublin, Ireland. She is in Chicago with her archaeological exhibit at the Field Museum, which suspiciously coincides with the two murders.

With a strange and eerie turn of events, things start unraveling. Grayson now is compelled to return to her birthplace and follows Dr. Rourke back to Ireland where ancient Celtic beliefs and mythology are thrown into the mix, turning the detective's logical world upside-down.

However, one fact remains for the determined Detective MacCarthaigh: Someone killed those two women and whether real or mythological—he or she will kill again.

Survive the Dawn
by Kate Sweeney
ISBN: 978-1-935216-04-9

With the serum now in her bloodstream, Dr. Alex Taylor must find a suitable laboratory to continue her work to help the woman—well, vampire—she loves, Sebastian. Together they travel to Devon, England, where Sebastian hopes her old, old, friend, the flamboyant vamp Gaylen Prescott will assist them. All the while, they try to keep one step ahead of Nicholae, the elder in the hierarchy, who wants Sebastian destroyed.

They find themselves deep in the catacombs of Guys Hospital in London and to Kendra, a sultry vamp who knew Sebastian quite well a century before, too well for Alex. Kendra is conducting similar experiments of her own.

Alex becomes a reluctant comrade to this sexy vampire, and together they find a way for Sebastian and her world to survive the dawn.

The O'Malley Legacy
by Kate Sweeney
ISBN: 978-1-933113-95-1

Travel through history with the O'Malley women—from the 14th century and Brigid O'Malley, the Irish Barbarian, to the 1820s and sail the Jamaica Winds with Quinlan Stoddard, and finally to Shawn Riordan, fighting for her love and country during the weeks before the invasion of Normandy in Twilight's Own.

Though vastly different in time and generations, the fiercely loyal, independent blood that courses through their veins connects these women. Each a warrior in her own right, three women struggle to find their rightful place in the world in which they live.

Strengthened by the spirit of all the O'Malley women who walked the earth before them, they battle tenaciously for family; they fight passionately for love—they are the O'Malley.

Coming soon from Intaglio Publications.

Jaded
by Jocelyn Powers
ISBN: 978-1-935216-20-9
Release Date: November 2010

Prominent New York acquisitions attorney Courtney Wilhelm had her entire life carefully planned...or so she thought. When Courtney's half sister, Marissa, is found dead from an apparent overdose, Courtney assumes guardianship of Marissa's daughter, Jade.

Courtney knows nothing of children and struggles to find balance as the custodian of a minor, while trying to maintain a high level of expertise expected by her clients and the firm. When she is confronted by Jade's new teacher Lauren McCallum, sparks fly in more ways than one.

Can Courtney let go of the life she has planned so meticulously—and clings to so stubbornly— to have the life with Jade and Lauren that awaits her? Or will the fear of failure keep her from the love and happiness she didn't even know she wanted?

Pitifully Ugly
by Robin Alexander
ISBN: 978-1-935216-21-6
Price: $16.95
Release Date December 2010

Shannon Brycen has decided to enter the dating world again after taking a hiatus from love. There's only one problem—well, many—but her reclusive personality and her sister's disastrous attempts at matchmaking force Shannon to try a different approach.

Hiding behind the online persona of Pitifully Ugly, Shannon finds the confidence she needs to pursue women, and the hunt is on. Many humorous lessons are learned along the way to her perfect match.

Published by
Intaglio Publications
Walker, La.

You can purchase other Intaglio
Publications books online at
www.bellabooks.com or at
your local bookstore.
Intaglio Ebooks are available on our Web
Site

Visit us on the web
www.intagliopub.com